ESPIONAGE AND TRUTH

ESPIONAGE AND TRUTH

INTRIGUE AND ROMANCE DURING THE COLD WA R

Kenneth W. Price

A catalogue record for this book is available
from the British Library

ISBN: 9798264016509

Kindle Direct Publishing, Seattle, USA

This novel is dedicated to the memory of my wife, Brenda.

Contents

Chapter One

Peter, a British Spy.

In spite of his warm blue serge overcoat Peter Smith shivered in the cold wind of a January morning in the year 1956. Although a bright sun was shining, he could still feel the approach of a creeping mist which appeared from the gentle sloping hills in the Peak District.

Peter was standing at ease with about forty other airmen in front of a long wooden table covered in numerous brown envelopes. Seated on a canvas chair on the other side of the table was a young pilot officer who looked somewhat bored. He yawned repeatedly as he picked up the envelopes and read out in Russian the various acquired names of the airmen in front of him. It was noticeable that each individual held the rank of Junior Technician or J/T with the single inverted chevron on the left arm.

The venue for this activity was an RAF base which served as a transit camp for certain extremely gifted airmen trained as Russian linguists to be assessed and then sent around the world on special assignments, usually involving secret operations. It was also an RAF establishment like none other in Great Britain. Indeed, it was almost the replica of a Soviet airbase with names printed in Cyrillic letters throughout: for example *vkhod* for entry, *kazarma* for barracks and *opasno!* for danger! to name but a few. Even the establishment itself was named after Lenin: *Aviabaza imeni Lenina*. The only apparent giveaway that it was not a Soviet airbase was the fact that RAF personnel wore their British uniforms, since the cost of kitting everybody out in Soviet attire was considered too expensive.

Those who worked or lived at *Aviabaza imeni Lenina* were either involved with the military authorities as civilians or members of the RAF. Most were from Eastern Europe-Russians, Lithuanians, Latvians and Poles. The one thing they had in common was that they all spoke Russian. There were a few deserters from the Soviet air force, mainly pilots and ground crew, who taught the J/Ts what life was like in a real Soviet airbase. A few commissioned and non-commissioned officers were conscripted into the RAF to ensure discipline among the airmen and to make sure that they did not lose sight of the rigours of military life.

It was the responsibility of the Russian speaking wing commander of the camp to appraise the strengths and weaknesses of the often volatile J/Ts during their three weeks' intensive training at this 'mock' Soviet airbase. Moreover, he had to ensure that they were posted, first of all to signals intelligence or SIGINT listening stations abroad, and then on to other destinations which often entailed spying. For his part Peter was aware of the fact that in his printed Certificate of Service he was classified as an R/T DF Op1A Linguist, but he did not know what the letters and number meant. Only later was he told that R/T meant voice recognition as opposed to W/T or morse. DF was direction finding, whilst OP 1A referred to the Russian category of operations.

The bored officer behind the wooden table picked up one brown envelope after another and called out the name of a J/T, who in turn responded with the last three of his seven-digit service number, approached the officer, saluted and received his meagre pay.

"Piotr Ivanovich Kuznetsov."

The ringing voice of the pilot officer, who by his accent was Polish, woke Peter up from his dream of being posted to West Germany or at least Hong Kong. Like Pavlov's dog he reacted to his acquired Russian name.

"Trista, sorok, dva," he shouted in a loud voice. Having given the officer his number-342, Peter marched up to the table and received his pay packet. At the same time he saluted, clicked his heels in a mocking fashion and said in a voice full of irony, *"Spasibo, tovarishch."*

At first the Polish officer seemed pleased with Peter's thanks, but grimaced when he used the word comrade and looked furious when he clicked his heels. Nevertheless, he returned Peter's salute and then called out the name of the next J/T.

Only a year before Peter was rejoicing in the fact that he was old enough to vote. A General Election was imminent, and he had to decide which political party would receive his vote. His uncle, Glyn Smith, his late father's brother, who lived close to Peter and his mother in a farmhouse on the outskirts of Rhyl in North Wales, was a die-hard Conservative.

"Well, Uncle Glyn," he asked rather bravely. "What do you think of the Labour Party's promise to continue with its earlier great reforms if elected?" He knew his uncle would react to any political banter. "You must admit that the creation of a first-class National Health Service has been a triumph."

His uncle listened to his nephew's opening debate and retorted with his brows tightly drawn together.

"Not much, Peter. We don't want a return to an austere neo-Soviet state in this country. We need a mobile consumerist free society as advocated by my party. That is why we won the General Election in 1951."

Then he settled down on the leather sofa and reached for his favourite pipe as if to say that the conversation was over.

However, Peter was not put off by his uncle's manoeuvres. He nodded and said,

"It's rather a pompous message the Conservatives are advocating now with their slogan 'Set the People Free.' They seem to think that the Festival of Britain in 1951 and the Coronation of Queen Elizabeth two years later projected a symbol of the nation's good fortune. There is too great an emphasis on their so-called 'feel good' factor."

Nevertheless, Peter's uncle could have argued that, since the Conservatives had come to power, the standard of living had risen, unemployment was down to 2%, more people were buying their homes and dole for those out of work was quite generous. In 1953 the balance of payment deficit was wiped out and food rationing had come to an end in 1954.

Peter watched as his uncle went to the lounge window, looked over the dark fields and knocked ash out of his pipe into an ashtray on the window ledge. He was now angry with his nephew's views, and his words began to tumble out. "More people are able to buy their own homes and business is booming. What else do you expect, Peter?" he said.
Peter looked at him in amazement and would not let the discussion come to an end.

"Surely you have noticed that we have terrible slums in some of the large cities of this country and that people are being pushed into high-rise flats or prefabricated houses?"

Uncle Glyn cleared his throat with some difficulty and began to speak in almost an official manner.

"In my opinion what is needed is better education for the working classes to help them rise above their station in life. Even when I look around Rhyl, I am disgusted by the way some teenagers attempt to express their individuality, or some might say their uniformity, through their dress code: young women in short tight skirts and young men in teddy boy attire."

"We are not all like you, uncle. Can you not see there is a different world out there?" said Peter, almost laughing out loud. "You may want to visit the opera or music hall on occasions, but young people prefer to go to coffee bars and listen to American juke-box jingles. So, they need to dress differently."

Their conversation was brought to an end by Aunt Ethel who brought her husband, Peter and his mother a tray of beef sandwiches and cups of steaming coffee.

"Have this before you go home," she said with a smile, "and Peter, take no notice of your uncle's attempts to persuade you to vote Conservative. And please, do not wind him up."

Uncle Glyn snorted, but an hour later kissed his sister-in-law, Agata, on the cheek and shook Peter by the hand.

"No hard feelings, Peter," he said. "I'll take you both

home by car. It's not safe at night in Rhyl. There are too many drunks roaming the streets and causing mayhem."

Peter Smith and his mother lived together in the centre of Rhyl. After the death of her husband, Ifan, from a stroke in 1952, she missed him tremendously and relied more and more on her son's support. She knew Peter had to complete two years' national service in the armed forces, but she realised that she would dread the long absences this would entail.

The family home consisted of a pebbledash detached bungalow in a quiet cul-de-sac in this dull seaside town. The gardens, both front and back, were well maintained and possessed neat lawns and flowered borders. The décor inside was quite opulent. The living room was tidy and bore the marks of over-zealous cleaning. It had wall to wall carpeting-a luxurious blue patterned Axminster. On the mantelpiece were a number of trophies won by Peter's father when he was a teenager and a framed photograph of the Smith family on holiday somewhere in Devon. In the corner of the room stood a mahogany cupboard full of Royal Doulton figurines and in the centre a matching mahogany dining table and chairs. Behind the living room was a long corridor which led to a small kitchen, a bathroom and a separate toilet as well as two medium-sized bedrooms. There was also a small room which acted as a guest bedroom and contained a large pine bookcase into which were stuffed a variety of books, papers and documents.

Any visitor to the Smith household would have soon realised the reading tastes and activities of the family: the classics, travel catalogues and albums as well as books in Polish, French, German, Russian and Arabic. On the top of this bookcase was a faded black-and white photograph in a frame of Peter's father looking majestic seated on a camel with what seemed to be an Egyptian pyramid in the background.

In January 1955 Peter celebrated his eighteenth birthday and like most young men of his age he had to complete his national service of two years. His mother was worried that, not only would he be away from home, but that he would also be sent to one of the trouble spots in the world such as Malaya, Cyprus or Kenya. Peter tried to defer his military service on compassionate grounds, because his mother might suffer as a result of his absence, but deferment was refused.

1955 was also the year that the Cold War was at its peak. The blockade of Berlin from 1948 to 1949, the takeover of Czechoslovakia and Hungary in the same years and the expulsion of the Chinese Nationalists to Taiwan were the opening shots of Soviet aggression to realise its aim of world-wide communism. There was some hope that, with the death of Stalin in March 1953, there would be a slight lull in the Cold War as the Soviet leaders began to cope with the post-Stalinist period. For a while there was a hiatus, but it did not last long.

To a varying degree the Cold War itself became an important part of winning the hearts and minds of allies or potential allies. On the other hand, the main task of 'fighting' the enemy for the Soviet Union was through the activities of the Committee for State Security, more commonly known as the KGB, and its offspring in the Warsaw Pact countries. For Great Britain it was through the North Atlantic Treaty Organisation or NATO and its two Military Intelligence Sections, the MI5 and MI6.

There were ways of obtaining information from the Soviet Union, but visiting the country often led to entrapment or blackmail. In any case the country was virtually closed to Westerners. Trade and cultural links were also non-existent and 'human' intelligence, such as infiltrating the country was doomed to failure. Therefore, Great Britain's reaction was to acquire immediately a large number of Russian linguists from the armed forces capable of monitoring Soviet intentions, mainly through SIGINT operations.

Into this system 'stepped' Peter as an RAF recruit. After eight weeks of 'square bashing' as an AC2 he was ready to embark on further training which would involve special skills. Undergoing a short test in French, German and Latin and a long interview, he managed to obtain a place on the Russian course at a 'spy' school. Peter confided in his mother one weekend whilst on leave.

"During the interview I mentioned that you were half Polish and half German and that I could speak your native languages quite fluently. Polish was obviously a precursor for learning Russian. As you know, at school I was fascinated by Russian culture and managed to teach myself the Cyrillic alphabet and learn a few phrases in Russian"

Peter's mother was proud of her son. She was the only child of a Polish father and German mother from Gdansk and was able to teach Peter both Polish and German. By the time he was ten Peter could speak both languages quite fluently as well as English.

For Peter the Russian course started in March 1955 at a language school for all the armed forces called Bugle Mountain. He was taught the language by 'quirky' émigrés from Slavonic countries. Many of the students were equally 'quirky', but bright, and sometimes like Peter rebellious. The students wore their uniforms to lessons-army khaki, RAF blue serge and Royal Navy burberries. Peter wrote to his mother and made her aware of the spy school.

"In this former army camp called Bugle Mountain, halfway between Exeter and Land's End, I can imagine the isolation and loneliness felt by Russians during the Tsarist regime who were banished to desolate parts of Siberia or the Caucasus because they questioned autocracy. This isolation is also felt by many of the students here. Even the nearest town seems to remind us that it was created by God because purgatory was full up."

Initially Peter regarded the Russian course as an easy option, even though in reality he was not what the Russians called a *progul'shchik* or skiver. For nine months he lived in an inadequately heated hut with about thirteen other airmen and had to get up at six o'clock each morning. Breakfast was followed by hour long lessons interspersed by physical training or cross-country running throughout the day.

Peter easily coped with the complex Russian grammar which reminded him of his Latin lessons at school. Nor did the intricacies of declining nouns and adjectives and conjugating verbs cause him any trouble. Even though he often complained of the grey weather and the extreme cold of the living accommodation, especially in the winter, Peter was pleased in many ways that he had enrolled on the course. He even became accustomed to the depressing view of the peaks and cliffs of spoiled countryside left over from the derelict china and clay mines.

With the help of certain aids: 'Semyonov's Grammar'

and Pears and Wissolsky's 'Passages for Translation' as well as contrived stories such as the 'Unusual People', Peter excelled in all the tests and the two important examinations. He obtained over 75% in the final examination which meant that he was eligible to become an officer subject to a rigid interview. Imagine his disappointment when he was told that he did not have the right attitude to move from the ranks. Little did he realise that the RAF had already assessed his abilities and were preparing for him to become a British spy.

Throughout his time on the Russian course Peter made friends with only one person, a certain Stefan Bronowski, due to the fact that they both spoke Polish. How to cope with the pressures of the course occupied the minds of the students from the three armed forces. Although Wednesday afternoons and weekends were free, they were expected to take part in the various Russian clubs, societies and drama productions and at the same time find time for revision.

Peter witnessed the suicide of one soldier, whilst a large number failed the unending tests and were sent elsewhere, Peter thought he had an answer. As he explained to his friend, Stefan,

"A safety valve is required. I have found comfort in learning the words and tunes of Russian folksongs and this has added a new dimension to my life. Why not join the Russian choir with me, Stefan?"

However, Stefan had found his solace in drinking the strong West Country cider or 'scrumpy', which on occasions brought him virtually to the brink of oblivion. Soon Peter became disillusioned with the choir, especially after analysing the words of a Russian folksong called *'Stenka Razin'*. Mournfully he told his friend,

"To my dismay the hero of this song throws his wife, a Persian princess, into the River Volga where she drowns. How depressing is that?"

Every Wednesday the two friends would don their civilian clothes and try and visit some of the some of the Cornish towns in the afternoon, making sure they returned for roll call at seven o'clock the following morning. On one occasion after visiting the cathedral town of Truro, they missed the last bus connection to Bugle Mountain language school and had to walk all the way across Goss Moor. Looking bedraggled and forlorn in wet and dishevelled clothing, both Peter and Stefan were picked up by the police at four in the morning. They were suspected of being escaped inmates from a notorious jail in Bodmin. Only after two hours questioning did they manage to persuade the police that they were 'inmates' of the spy school. How could the police confuse them with the criminal classes?

Arriving back at the camp the duty sergeant threatened them with AWOL or being absent without leave. Peter's excuse was quite inspirational,

"We have both been to Truro to see my sick uncle, William Brown, and unfortunately missed the last connection back to camp."

The kind sergeant sympathised with them and withdrew the AWOL charge. He did not know that Brown Willy was one of the highest peaks on Bodmin Moor.

One Sunday Peter and his friend set off on foot to one of the rugged, but in some ways beautiful areas of Bodmin Moor. They chatted amiably about the peculiarities of the Russian course, particularly about the idiosyncratic personalities who taught them. Munching one of the Cornish pasties or 'oggies' which he had brought with him Peter stared at his friend.

"Stefan. You were muttering Russian in your sleep last night in the bed opposite me. I was listening very carefully, and I was pleased to hear you repeat the word *'znachit'* instead of the English 'er' or 'um', to cover a pause or to search for a correct word."

At first Stefan was silent, then he rummaged in his knapsack for an apple and remarked,

"Yes, Petrushka." Stefan always called Peter by this pet name, "I hope I am not going mad. Perhaps it was the strong Merrydown cider I drank before going to bed. It's only 3/6d a bottle. What was I saying in Russian?"

"Well. You were reciting that stupid story about John

and Mary and their baby son called Spitfire," said Peter with a grin on his face. "You know, the family who lived not far from London in a medium-sized house with a small garden."

Peter then noticed that Stefan was delving into his knapsack and extricating a bottle of the cheap cider. He offered some to Peter who refused.

"Oh, that story," snorted Stefan. "We had to learn it off by heart. I am sure it will stay with me to the end of my life."

Peter tried to change the subject.

"I was trying to work out the nationality of each lecturer. Do you realise there is a Pole amongst the teaching staff? He keeps looking at me when I speak Russian because I must use Polish phrases on occasions."

Stefan agreed with Peter.

"Yes I have also met him and informed him that your mother and my father were Poles. He told me that he had fought for the Russians as a *polkovnik* or colonel and later for the Germans as an *Unteroffizier* or non-commissioned officer during the second World War"

Although Peter realised that his friend was getting drunk and that he would have difficulty in slipping him into Bugle Mountain, he tried to end the conversation. Stefan would have none of it. Drinking more of the cider he said,

"What do you think of that old fellow of ninety-two

who falls asleep during the dictation he is giving and wakes up at exactly the same spot where he left off? He ought to be in a home for the aged, not teaching Russian."

Peter was indeed worried about his friend's mental and physical health which had deteriorated over the past six months. Stefan was, in his opinion, sliding into a morbid and debilitating state due mainly to his dependence on alcohol. Shaking him by the collar, Peter tried to remonstrate with him about the perils of drinking too much cider.

"You are becoming an alcoholic, Stefan. Promise me that you will give up the demon that is possessing you. You need to pull yourself together, concentrate on finishing this Russian course and then move on."

Stefan was non-committal at first and ignored Peter but then began to mumble that he had been warned that he would be thrown off the course if he kept drinking. Peter was sure that with encouragement Stefan had the moral strength to conquer his addiction and was more than satisfied with his proposal.

"Tomorrow I shall visit the small psychiatric unit attached to Bugle Mountain camp and, if needs be, seek rehabilitation at a military hospital nearby."

At the end of the language course both Peter and Stefan were able in spite of their problems to assess instinctively the correctness of what they felt in

Russian and could even pass as Russian civilians if dropped behind 'enemy' lines. On the other hand, the British authorities did not realise that for many of the students familiarity with the Russian language was making them rather sympathetic to the Russian common people or *narod* and their culture.

The Russian course in Cornwall for the airmen was followed by a further ten weeks training at an isolated RAF station near Birmingham called Hathwell which was patrolled continuously by vicious Alsatian dogs. This training consisted of wireless intercepts. Peter found out later that it was similar to *radioperekvatki* which were the responsibility of the Soviet Union's KGB's 16th Directorate for SIGINT operations.

Writing in his diary about Hathwell, Peter provided a complete picture of this second spy school to which he had been sent.

"Here, I learnt to tune a B40 to various frequencies, analysed the workings of this radio and listened to military traffic through static. I used a type of shorthand to write down phrases used by aircrews and ground staff. Their often agitated conversations were placed on a reel-to-reel recorder in order to obtain accuracy. This shorthand consisted of letters: for example, KCM? meant 'How do you hear me?' and CBY- 'I hear you satisfactorily.'"

Peter would have been in trouble if the authorities at

Hathwell knew he was making a note of the proceedings at this spy station. One of the most difficult aspects of his training here was for Peter to write down a stream of numbers at a pace which accelerated during each lesson. At the same time, however, he and Stefan were given the opportunity to master morse code, which they accepted with alacrity. They did not realise that this skill was to be of some use later on, well to Peter especially.

So, after the rather quaint and unusual pay parade at *Aviabaza imeni Lenina,* Peter returned to his cold hut which had been his home for the past three weeks. Speaking in Polish to his friend he greeted him with the words,

"*Dzien dobry.* How much did you receive in your pay packet today, Stefan? I have been given two weeks pay, so it looks as though I am going to be transferred abroad. Where? I do not know."

Stefan did not answer at first because he was counting his money, but then turning to Peter, he said,

"Well, Petrushka. It appears that I am also going abroad, because I have also two weeks pay here as well."

It appeared that both had received a small amount, because they had sent money home to their parents to help them with household expenses.

Peter and Stefan rarely talked about their parents. On this occasion, however, Peter opened up to his friend.

"Since the death of my father I have been extremely worried about my mother. As you know, Stefan. I tried to get my National Service deferred for a year, but to no avail."

Then in an almost pitiful voice he began to explain to Stefan how his mother felt rather lonely in Rhyl, almost like an alien in a foreign land.

"The problem is that she always keeps herself to herself and will not call on anybody for help. Yet my uncle and aunt live nearby. She will not mix with members of my late father's family at all, perhaps because they are typically Welsh, even though most of them possess an English surname-Smith."

Forgetting this problem which beset him Peter turned to Stefan.

"I wonder where we will be posted. I do not wish to go to Cyprus where EOKA terrorists under Archbishop Makarios are causing havoc in their attempt to obtain union with Greece. Nor do I like the look of Iraq."

Stefan added to the doom and gloom.

"My cousin, who was on the Russian course a few months back, is living in tented accommodation near Famagusta with no hot water at all. However, I am glad I am going abroad. I do not wish to go to GCHQ in Cheltenham. A friend of mine works there and he tells me that what one has to do is both hard and boring. Like you, Petrushka, I crave adventure."

They then began to reminisce about their Polish heritage. Peter's father, Ifan Smith, had been a minor official in the British Embassy in Baghdad where he met Agata Kopinski who was also working there. He married his Polish 'beauty' just before the outbreak of the second World War. Stefan's father left Poland to live in England in 1933 and trained as a pilot during the war. On a visit to the Lebanon he met and married Stefan's mother, a Maronite or Christian Arab. Although she spoke a form of Aramaic, she taught her son Arabic and often took him on holiday to her native land.

That evening Peter and Stefan went for a drink at an inn not far from the third spy school in the Peak District. After a few drinks, well for Stefan too many drinks, they began talking to some strangers who quizzed them about *Aviabaza imeni Lenina*. Both Peter and his friend were extremely circumspect, even though they had consumed more alcohol than was necessary.

"These strangers are either Soviet spies or else we are being assessed by members of MI5," stated Peter who pushed Stefan outside and then made a hasty retreat.

Indeed these 'strangers' were Soviet agents who were trying to reveal the 'soft underbelly' of British espionage. In fact, even by 1955 spy schools, SIGINT operations and the existence of GCHQ were all known to the KGB. British spies were sometimes offered bribes or blackmailed to entice them to 'spill the beans' or defect. Peter had often wondered what Soviet agents looked like.

"I thought they would be large men in big black overcoats, brimmed hats, black shoes and carrying copies of the Times under their arms." Yet the men they met at the inn looked like ordinary British citizens and spoke perfect English. He was, however, annoyed with himself for drinking too much and with Stefan who had undergone rehabilitation.

The Wing Commander at the 'mock' Soviet airbase kept telling the J/Ts that Soviet agents existed in many forms in Great Britain. He stated that KGB agents often posed as delegates at meetings run by the World Council of Churches and that they accused this country of racism and colonialism. He went on to say that their views were accepted by the Anglican Church which ignored human rights violations in the Soviet Union.

"I know for example that Orthodox priests from the Moscow patriarchate frequently worship in various British parishes and are known to be KGB agents."

Peter and Stefan continued to remain good friends throughout their existence in the three spy schools. Both were swarthy in appearance and to a certain extent handsome. They could have easily been taken as Eastern Europeans or even occupants of countries in the Middle East. Whereas Stefan had dark brown eyes, Peter's were deep blue. Both were of average height, but rather thin. In RAF uniform and in civilian clothes they were to say the least rather untidy in appearance.

They both displayed a casual attitude to life and enjoyed making fun of people and themselves. Above all they resented authority.

"Why do we have to salute officers whom we do not respect?" moaned Peter. "I have been picked up a number of times for not saluting an officer because I was reading a Russian book whilst walking in the camp."

Stefan nodded in response to his friend's venom.

"You are right, Petrushka. Do you remember that last week we had to paint black coal white because we were expecting a visit from an air vice-marshal. It's so ridiculous. Saluting the Queen's commission is one thing, but painting coal white is another."

A few days before the end of their training at *Aviabaza imeni Lenina,* just before the morning parade, both friends talked about their attitude to life. Peter for his part was extremely outgoing-an extrovert, but really a mass of contradictions internally. He was a person, although brought up as a Roman Catholic and who had served as an altar boy, had nevertheless become an agnostic and then an atheist in quick succession.

He produced for Stefan a complete analysis of himself, but it was full of exaggerations.

"I am a person destined to go far-a rolling stone which gathers no moss. I require action, travel and adventure. I need no specific God to refer to or give me support. I will decide my own destiny. In fact, I am ashamed that once I believed in God and annoyed that I did not believe in myself. Like many of my generation I scorn kindness, honesty and pity. Indeed, I have become a victim of cynicism."

Yet, Peter, for all his bravado, could not always face up to the realities of life and would run away from making decisions. His biggest problem, however, was that he despised in spite of himself physical imperfections in a person. He had, for example, a prejudice against blind and dumb people.

"A defect in a person's appearance depicts a defect in a person's soul," he said, looking at Stefan for support, but his friend remained silent.

His attitude to women, apart from his mother, was even worse.

"I compare breeding in a woman to that of a horse. When I see imperfections in a woman's face, such as wrinkles on her brow, I look into her eyes which always appear to be sad-a sign of deep melancholy or even a wicked nature. If I ever find a perfect woman, I know it will be impossible for me to love her for ever."

Although he was often impatient with his friend's wanderings, Stefan was quiet and reserved-an introvert. In spite of this he was full of confidence. He was a man of great spiritual and moral strength and his impulses were basically good. He was a kind person in spite of joining Peter in making fun of others.

"I live, not from my heart, but from my head," he said to Peter with conviction. "I weigh up and control my own passions and actions with a thorough curiosity, but often without involvement."

"It is a pity all this does not apply to his love of alcohol, especially cider." thought Peter to himself, but he was being rather unjust, for Stefan had made great efforts in controlling his 'habit'.

As is often the case with two friends, one is usually the 'slave' of the other, and to a certain extent Stefan was Peter's 'slave' to all intents and purposes. He disagreed with his friend's attitude towards women whom he considered to be pure and precious. This came from the respect his Polish father showed to his Maronite mother. Yet, he never contradicted Peter. To do so, would have been a complete waste of time and energy.

Whilst Peter and Stefan were talking together in Polish and about to go on parade, their conversation was interrupted by the arrival of the burly and often 'sadistic' Lithuanian sergeant. Accompanied by a Polish corporal he came to inspect their bed spaces and their RAF kit. Random inspections like this took place quite frequently. In careful, but accented,

Russian, the sergeant shouted,

"You are breaking camp rules. You know that you must speak only in Russian."

Both J/Ts stood to attention as he tipped over their sheets. blankets and pillows on their beds. He grunted from time to time and then proceeded to complain about their appearance, especially the lack of polish on their boots. Impatiently he said to the corporal,

"Take their names. A few circuits around the parade ground will show them that they need to keep their bedding and their uniforms neat and tidy."

Then in an agitated manner he said,

"By the way you both have to see the commanding officer in his office this afternoon-*Tovarishch* Bronowski at one o'clock and *Tovarishch* Kuznetsov at two."

Only when the sergeant and the corporal left the hut did Peter and his friend sigh with relief and break into Polish,

"*Trzymaj sie, Stefan. Do zobaczenia wkrótce.*"

"*Do widzenia,* Petrushka." replied Stefan, whereupon both left the hut after rearranging their bed spaces and spitting on their boots.

At two o'clock precisely Peter knocked on Wing Commander Cookson's office door. A voice from within seemed to echo right down the corridor. It was gruff, but rather cheerful.

"*Kto tam?*"

Peter gave his name and service number and entered the office, a dark room containing a large desk on which were stacked a pile of documents. Behind the desk was a chair occupied by the tubby wing commander. He was short in height and plump with a smiling face which changed as he stroked his dark moustache.

When Peter stood to attention in front of him and clicked his heels, anger appeared on his face. In fact this airman's lack of respect had been reported to him on a number of occasions. After a short while, however, his anger subsided and his face took on a forced smile, obviously relishing the shattering news he had to impart to Peter,

"Stand at ease, Comrade Kuznetsov," he said in Russian. "I have some important news to convey to you. You are being posted to one of our listening posts in Iraq."

Having said this, the wing commander began to shuffle through the papers on his desk.

Meanwhile Peter looked mortified and his jaw dropped. With his fluent knowledge of Polish and German he expected to be sent to a listening post in West Germany or perhaps West Berlin where the art of spying had almost reached perfection. But Iraq?

His mind started to race as he tried to imagine what this country was like. He could hear his father's voice telling him about this area of the world.

"Iraq lies in the ancient area once called Mesopotamia

and the two great rivers, the Tigris and the Euphrates, run through this land. The Hanging Gardens of Babylon, one of the seven wonders of the ancient world, existed to the south of Baghdad."

From his history lessons at school Peter had learnt that the Kingdom of Iraq was created in 1921 and that it was a constitutional monarchy with King Faisal as head of a pro-western government. He could also recall the words of one of the lecturers at the spy school in Cornwall saying in Russian,

"The Baghdad Pact signed by Iraq, Iran, Turkey and Pakistan was formed to prevent the spread of communism in the Middle East."

Wing Commander Cookson interrupted Peter's thoughts and fixed the poor J/T with a malevolent smile.

"Yes. You will be going next month to Iraq after a further week's training in Kent."

"Not more training." replied Peter, but his words were lost when another person suddenly appeared, emerging from one of the dark recesses of the office. Peter had not noticed this tall man who came and stood next to Cookson. He seemed to remind Peter of a country squire who had fallen on his luck.

He wore a light brown check shirt which was frayed at the cuffs and the collar. Around his neck was a rather dirty yellow cravat, which for all intents and purposes, seemed to have been washed only once. Over his shirt he had a jacket which was brown in colour and quite shabby. On his breast pocket was a crest depicting a sword and a pair of scales. Peter could just about make out the letters ODAT around the sword. This tall man's trousers were made of dark brown tweed. What struck Peter most were his patent leather shoes which squeaked when he walked.

This strange man then approached Peter on the other side of the wing commander's desk, took out a watch from his waist coat pocket and looked at the time. Staring intently at Peter, he said,
"My name is Samuel Jacobson. I am the head of the Organisation for Democracy and Truth or ODAT. Due to your command of a number of languages, which are vital for the security of our country and your father's special knowledge of Baghdad, we have decided to send you on a special mission to Iraq."
As he spoke, he placed a Woodbine in his mouth, lit it with a silver lighter, which he took out of his trouser pocket, and blew a few clouds of smoke in Peter's direction.

After a pause of a few seconds, he continued with what seemed to be a rehearsed speech.
"ODAT is a special intelligence service responsible for collecting, analysing and disseminating information from the Soviet Union's presence in Eastern Europe and the Middle East. Your training at Bugle Mountain, Hathwell and here has been important, but you still need to visit the Middle East

section of our headquarters in London and then to special camps in Kent to prepare you as a British agent."

Jacobson turned to Wing Commander Cookson and asked him to make arrangements for Peter to visit ODAT headquarters and for further training in Kent. With a curt nod Cookson dismissed Peter who saluted and clicked his heels, much to the annoyance of the two men in the office. As he slammed the door behind him Peter wondered what ODAT had in mind for him. He then bumped into Stefan in the corridor and arranged to meet him in the *stolovaya* or canteen later that evening.

Over cups of strong tea and rolls the two friends discussed the afternoon's events.
"Well. At least I know I am going to a signals centre in the Lebanon," declared Stefan with obvious delight showing on his face. "Probably near where my mother lived as a young girl. By the way, Petrushka, I have been given a new name for the Lebanon mission-*Abdul.*"
Peter, however, was perplexed.
"Why have they chosen me to go to Iraq on a special assignment? I know no Arabic, well only a few words, which my father taught me. West Germany or West Berlin would have been a better option."
Stefan laughed at his friend's seemingly persistent desire to go to West Germany or West Berlin. Then in

a consoling voice he said,

"Do not worry, my friend. We shall know all the answers next week. By the way. Do you have to meet that strange fellow, Jacobson, from ODAT in London?"

Peter answered in the affirmative,

"Yes, *Abdul*. By the way the name suits you. Shall I call you *Abdul* or Stefan from now on?"

Stefan began to smile, but did not answer Peter, and changed the subject.

That night Peter fell asleep, dreaming of learning Arabic and imagining what Iraq was like. Over and over in his mind he could see mosques and minarets and himself leading groups of men on camels across the desert like Lawrence of Arabia. Then appeared mysterious looking dancing maidens and Arab men clapping to the sound of oriental music. Peter was in fact enjoying the dream when suddenly the sound of the small bells on the dancers' ankles and wrists started to merge into one monotonous tone. The leader of the dancers approached Peter and tapped him repeatedly on the shoulder.

In fact, it was the sound of the camp bell announcing the six o'clock reveille. The dancing maiden had changed into Stefan who was shaking him by the shoulder.

"Wake up, Petrushka, we have all been given a seven day pass and free travel by rail to anywhere in Great

Britain."

"Thank you for waking me up, *Abdul*. I was having a lovely dream. However, I am still worried about my mission to Iraq," said Peter with some emotion in his voice.

Grinning at his friend's pessimism he began to mock him.

"Well, I can offer you some cyanide pills, if you wish. They will help you overcome extreme forms of torture, because you will die immediately."

At that point Peter pulled a face and seemed to resent his friend's casual and mocking attitude to danger.

Still full of anxiety Peter jumped out of bed, dressed as quickly as possible and ran to join Stefan in the *stolovaya* where they enjoyed a Russian breakfast-*kasha,* oatmeal cakes, jam on toast and tea. Then they both went to the documentation centre to pick up their rail passes, sign further secret service documents and make new wills. Arrangements were also made for their RAF kit to be sent to another spy school in Kent. They put on civilian clothes and left the 'mock' Soviet airbase for the last time.

At first Peter was at a loss as to what he should do over the next seven days. Obviously he had to call on his mother and explain to her what was happening and hopefully relax. He arrived in Rhyl by train at six o'clock on the Friday evening and spent most of the time talking to his mother and listening to the radio.

When at home Peter usually listened to the Light Programme. The Home Service and the Third were to use his own words 'too highbrow and artificial'. He would sometimes tease his mother.

"Do you still listen to Mrs Dale's Diary, mother?" he asked, and when she declared that she did, he began to imitate some of the characters, especially the cultured tones of Mr and Mrs Dale as well as their son, Bob.

Later in the evening Peter spoke to his mother about the events of the previous four years since the death of his father. These years had been really traumatic at a time when Peter was involved in revising for examinations at school. His mother was proud of her son's achievements, especially with his success at the local grammar school. With six good passes at GCE 'O' level which was a step on the way to matriculation and eventual entry into university, the headmaster persuaded him to continue with French and Latin at 'A' level.

It was here that Peter questioned the school's policy that he should also learn Welsh in the sixth form.

"Why do I need to learn this ancient Celtic language? What use will it be for me in life? It is only spoken in Wales and in some remote areas such as Patagonia. In any case people here in Wales speak English fluently."

Eventually, however, it was his Latin teacher who made out a good case for Peter to study Welsh to a certain standard.

"You will be learning more about the culture of the country in which you live, Peter. Besides, a knowledge of Welsh will perhaps be of use to you one day. Latin is a dead language, but it helps you understand the grammar of many European languages."

Peter agreed. In fact, this Celtic language was to be of some benefit to him in Iraq and Iran of all places.

Peter's mother was terribly proud when he received high marks in both his 'A' level subjects and she made it her business to thank all the teachers in the grammar school for their efforts. Then she took her son to one side and said,

"Before he died your father made me promise that I should persuade you to gain entry into either Oxford or Cambridge. Ifan often said that those who graduated from one of these universities possessed self-confidence and considered that they could rule the world."

In order to heed his father's wishes, Peter had applied for a place at his father's alma mater, Oxford, but he had been unsuccessful.

That evening his head was spinning because his mother continued to press him about applying for a place at Cambridge University before he completed his military service.

"*Mamo pzrestan, daj mi spokój-* leave me in peace,

mother", he said, "My chances of going to Oxford were spoilt by a farcical interview conducted by a professor who smoked throughout and who sat casually on the edge of his desk. I am not depressed by the refusal. It was just one of those things. I promise you that I shall apply for Cambridge."

This seemed to placate his mother for the time being at least.

The following day Peter went to visit his uncle and aunt in their farmhouse and spent his time there making final arrangements for them to look after his mother when he was away in Iraq.

"Please call on my mother at least once a week, because I shall probably be away for one year or perhaps two," he explained. "Even though food rationing came to an end two years ago, the cost of food is still quite high. She appreciates the extra produce from your farm and that keeps her going. We are both extremely grateful."

This time Peter did not tease his uncle about politics, But he did ask to stay for the evening and watch one of the programmes on the small black-and-white television set which his uncle possessed. He was disappointed, however, due to the fact that it was being repaired.

Only five days left and Peter needed to use his free rail pass. So for the next two days he went to Birmingham to stay with one of his father's cousins who lived there. As a young boy Peter was an enthusiastic filmgoer and Birmingham possessed a continental cinema as well as other cinemas. When he was a child Peter was fed a diet of thrilling cowboy and exciting Walt Disney films as well as supporting features such as 'Flash Gordon' and the 'Three Stooges'. As he grew older his tastes began to mature and he started to enjoy the classics such as 'Oliver Twist' as well as foreign films in French and German. When he could get to the big cities, odd Luddite films such as 'Whiskey Galore' provided him with more entertainment.

This time in Birmingham he was able to see the silent film by the Soviet producer, Eisenstein, called 'Battleship Potemkin'. Later he confided to his friend, Stefan.

"I had always wanted to see this magnificent film so much, but travelling to a large city to view it when I was at the spy schools was impossible."

As he watched the film Peter was transported back to the events of 1905 when the Bolshevik sailors on this battleship mutinied against their oppressive Tsarist officers.

Viewing all types of films, listening to the radio and reading were for Peter a form of escapism. He remembered as a young boy how frightened he was when Rider Haggard's 'King Solomon's Mines' was dramatised on the radio. In the 1950s Ealing Studios were beginning to produce gentle nostalgic comedies at the expense of traditional British ones. They were half-mocking and half-congratulatory films associated with the gradual collapse of class divisions.

Perhaps without recognising it, Peter was gaining an unusual all-round education outside the confines of academia. The poetry of 'Under Milk Wood' by Dylan Thomas was written for the radio and Peter digested chunks of it. He also read the novel by Kingsley Amis called 'Lucky Jim' about the absurdities of university life.

"Only three days left," said Peter to himself. "What shall I do before going to London. I notice that my rail pass will take me to Scotland, a country I have never visited."

So, he used his free pass to view the sights of Edinburgh and stayed at a YMCA hostel for one night.

On Thursday he was due to report to ODAT headquarters in London. Nursing a headache on the account of bagpipes being played continuously on the streets of Scotland's capital, Peter tried to sleep on the various trains on Wednesday and early Thursday before he arrived at King's Cross Station just in time to take a short snack at the station buffet before joining the late rush hour traffic on the underground. Time was running out and he had promised to meet

Stefan at two o'clock outside ODAT headquarters. People were crowding on the underground trains and with all the pushing and shoving he missed the first connection to Oval Station. When he eventually boarded the next train, he was annoyed that there were so many stops even between the stations and delays in the tunnels. There were so many people getting on and off at various stations. Eventually the train moved slowly into Oval station and Peter was able to breathe a sigh of relief,

It was eleven o'clock when he emerged in front of Oval Underground Station, clutching his black briefcase in his right hand and his suitcase in the other. From time to time, he felt like turning back and giving up this part of the spy adventure. He tried to think of what he was letting himself in for and this caused his hands to become quite clammy. Sweat appeared on his briefcase and occasionally he made an attempt to wipe it off with his handkerchief. There were quite a few vehicles on the roads-lorries, taxis and private cars carrying people and goods to their destinations Peter often had to keep to one side of the road and use the subway where possible. He passed a few individuals exercising their excited dogs, nannies pushing luxury prams and healthy types going for a late morning jog.

Grabbing a sandwich and a coffee a few streets away from the underground station, Peter eventually arrived in front of a tall concrete building at exactly two o'clock where he was pleased to see his friend, Stefan, already there and looking anxiously at his watch.

"*Salam alêkum, Abdul*," said Peter, pleased to display his extremely limited knowledge of Arabic to his friend.

A smile appeared on Stefan's face and he replied, "*Wa alêkum es salam. Kêf halek?*"

This time Peter was completely lost and had to resort to Polish.

Both friends then entered ODAT headquarters to be met by a slim, but not unattractive, blond female who asked them for their names. She consulted her list and gave both of them security tags which they clipped to the lapels of their jackets.

"Please report to room 101 on the fourth floor," she said in an official manner and then turned to greet a number of other men who appeared at the reception desk.

"That's a good omen. Room 101," thought Peter, as he and Stefan moved towards the lift.

However, the lift to the right of the reception desk was quite full, so they decided to use the staircase to the left. The steps were rather slippery and there was a definite musty smell everywhere. The staircase spiralled quite steeply upwards and both men found it difficult to climb to the fourth floor. They arrived out of breath just as the lift stopped opposite room 101. Gulping for air, Peter and Stefan then followed the contents of the lift into the designated room.

Room 101 itself was well lit, but rather unusual. Virtually devoid of furniture, apart from a few wooden chairs, it contained seven doors which included the main one from the corridor. As they entered, they were struck by the swarthy appearance of the men in the room, most of whom, according to Stefan, were speaking Arabic. At the same time, they were trying to locate the few chairs scattered around, so as to avoid standing.

"There's that fellow, Jacobson," exclaimed Stefan. "I think he looks like an Oxford don."

"More like a country squire who neglects hygiene and does not change his clothes very often," whispered Peter. Indeed, the man they were talking about, Samuel Jacobson, was standing on a small, raised platform behind which was a large painting.

"It's the same as the motif on his breast pocket when he met us last week," declared Peter looking carefully at the painting.

In fact, the painting was a large photograph which showed a massive sword with the letters ODAT around it and a pair of scales. Peter was transfixed by the photograph and strained his eyes to discover some Latin words underneath- *'Vitam impendere vero'*

"That means 'Devote your life to that which is true,'" said Peter, always ready to show off his knowledge of this ancient language.

Suddenly the opening notes of the British National Anthem resounded from loudspeakers in the room. All the occupants were so surprised that they all stood to attention, some singing at least the first verse. Others like Peter and Stefan just stared into space. Jacobson then motioned with both hands for all to be seated. Some reclined on the small number of chairs, whilst the majority had to be content with sitting on the floor.

Jacobson looked tired and drawn, but, when everybody in the room was quiet, he announced the following, choosing his word very carefully,

"You have all been selected or volunteered for a special ODAT assignment in the Middle East in order to infiltrate Soviet intelligence and discover the activities of Soviet agents there."

At this juncture he had a fit of coughing which unfortunately resulted in the next few sentences losing their usual co-ordination.

"We know that Soviet agents have been planted in Iraq, the Lebanon, Syria, Palestine and Egypt. Although not an Arabic country, Iran has also been targeted. At this very moment these agents are trying to find out what Great Britain and the United States of America are intending to do in these areas."

Jacobson stopped at this point and referred to his notes. Peter began to look again at the photograph on the wall behind him. What did the sword and the scales signify? What type of organisation was ODAT? Was it part of MI5 and MI6? Whilst he was asking these questions, Jacobson cleared his throat and recommenced his speech.

"You will be flown to the countries I have mentioned before in the Middle East, but before you go you will need to undergo more specialist training at two camps in Kent."

After a further pause Jacobson read out the names of the British agents allocated to the six countries,

"The following are destined for Iraq: Peter Smith, Jalal Iqbal, Ahmed Hussein and Mustafa Islam."

Peter knew that he was going to Iraq and the announcement came as no surprise, but who were the others? He looked around him as three other men stood up.

"The four of you must now follow your ODAT commander, Tariq Siddiqi, into the room marked Iraq to my left," declared Jacobson, "and then return to me after you have been briefed."

Unable to read the Arabic script on the door Peter was forced to follow the other three British spies and Tariq Siddiqi into a small room. There, Tariq politely asked them to relax on the leather armchairs and introduced himself.

"As you can ascertain, I am in charge of ODAT's Iraqi assignment called Operation *Babylon*. I will be your commander in Great Britain to whom all information will be sent in the final analysis. Although I am a British citizen, my native country was Iraq, and I was born and lived there until I was thirty years old."

Occasionally he broke into Arabic, which of course confused Peter, who once again began to wonder why he had been chosen for Operation *Babylon*.

"Perhaps it was because my father was an embassy official and knew Baghdad quite intimately and the fact that I am dark skinned. But I know virtually no Arabic. Why choose me? What use will I be?"

Tariq interrupted Peter's thoughts.

"Operation *Babylon* is only one small part of Operation *Sandstorm* which covers the whole of the Middle East, including Iran. Let me inform you of the procedure from this point onwards. First of all, you will be attached as R/T DF Op 1A operators to a listening post near Baghdad called Camp Ddibben. Later you will be moved as civilians to Baghdad, Kirkuk, Basra and Mosul. There you will become ODAT agents in different roles in order to 'smoke out' Soviet agents or at least find out what is happening in those areas."

Peter was mystified. Why was he going to Iraq? Time and time again he kept asking this question. How could his knowledge of German, Russian and Polish help the British authorities in Iraq? As if reading his thoughts Tariq began to speak again,

"Peter. You will be sent to Baghdad after you have spent some time in Camp Ddibben and your code name will be '*Abyadh*'. Jalal you will be transferred to Kirkuk-code name '*Aswad*' and Ahmed to Basra-code name '*Akhdhar*'. This leaves Mustafa who will settle in Mosul-code name '*Azraq*.'"

Peter was still not satisfied with the information he was obtaining from Tariq and was about to ask him why he was the only non-Arabic speaking agent going to Iraq when he knew only a few phrases in the language and could not read the script. But he was then comforted by some good news from his commander.

"By the way. All of you will be automatically promoted as commissioned officers as from today, but you will need to retain your present rank as an immediate cover for security reasons. Peter. You will become a flying officer, whereas Jalal, Ahmed, and Mustafa will become pilot officers."

These words gave Peter great satisfaction and his desire to be sent elsewhere in the world began to evaporate. However, he wondered why his rank was superior to the others.

The answer came with Tariq's next announcement.

"You, Peter, will be the lynch pin of Operation *Babylon*. The others will report to you each week once spying operations begin. I can see from your face that you are wondering why you have been chosen for Operation *Babylon*. Well. Your mother has been persuaded to hand over your father's diaries and notes which he wrote when he was working in the British Embassy in Baghdad. You will be allowed to study them in more detail when you take part in the final training sessions in Kent. You have been primarily chosen as an ideal student to learn Arabic at a language school in the capital of Iraq, which we know attracts Soviet agents."

Now Peter felt more at ease. Not only was he told the reason why he was selected as a British spy for Operation *Babylon*, but also that he was now becoming a commissioned officer, which had been his dream when he was at the language school in Cornwall. Furthermore, there would be more money to send home to his mother. More at ease, he said to himself,

"All this is what I want and crave for- the excitement of a new adventure which will dissipate my disappointment of not being posted to West Germany or West Berlin."

As Peter was basking in a warm self-contented glow, Tariq continued with more instructions.

"All of you have been given two passports; a legal one and counterfeit, both of which you will pick up later on. You will then be transferred to isolated camps on the Romney Marshes in Kent where all the agents connected to 'Operation *Sandstorm*' will be stationed. There you will undergo further training in survival and espionage techniques before you fly off to Iraq. Good luck! Remember. Great Britain depends on the success of these enterprises for its safety and security. Remember the motto of ODAT- 'Devote your life to that which is true'. Our Sword of Truth and the Scales of Justice will be responsible for spreading democracy, British democracy, to the whole world."

Having said this, Tariq gave each Iraqi operative a metal badge with the sword and the scales on it around which were the letters ODAT. He then dismissed them.

Peter, Jamal, Ahmed and Mustafa returned to the main room as previously requested. Peter wanted to find out more about ODAT, so he approached Jacobson and asked him for an explanation of the significance of the sword and the scales. Jacobson was only too pleased to give him an explanation.

"Both the sword and the scales are symbols of ODAT. The sword of truth has its origin in Medieval Britain because its strength was meant to protect the rights of the down-trodden and to help damsels in distress."

"Like the knights in the court of King Arthur," said Peter rather sarcastically. "They used the sword to protect the righteous and the just."

Jacobson ignored Peter's sarcasm, and he began to speak with pride about ODAT's symbols.

"Yes. The sword was used as a personification of truth, whereby its very sight would cause criminals to fear for their lives. Literally, it was also used to spread

Christianity and British justice throughout the world."

"The British up to their usual imperialistic tricks and using religion and democracy as an excuse to invade other countries," murmured Peter, but he allowed Jacobson to continue with his interesting explanation. "Some of the swords were engraved with Christian prayers asking mercy for both the executioner and the accused. A motto on one sword read 'I wish the sinner everlasting life.'"

"What about the scales?" asked Peter, now becoming rather tired with Jacobson's explanation. "They reinforce truth with justice," replied Jacobson, as if reading from a script. "ODAT believes that the sword of truth and the scales of justice will remove the evils of despotic and communist regimes and bring democracy and fair play to the Middle East and Eastern Europe, which is our sphere of influence."

Indeed, in Great Britain, truth and justice had since antiquity been closely linked. Lady Iustitia was the Roman goddess of justice and since the Renaissance was depicted as a bare breasted woman carrying the sword and the scales. This icon often adorned court houses or rooms. Iustitia was often depicted with a set of weighing scales suspended from her left hand upon which she measured the strength of a court case's support and opposition. Sometimes a double-edged sword in her right hand symbolised the power of truth, reason and justice to be wielded for or against any party in dispute.

By now the whole room had filled up with the spies involved in Operation *Sandstorm*. Jacobson then ignored Peter and turned to the men in the room and wished them good luck. He also remarked that he would meet them all in the first camp in Kent the following day. Thus, all the operatives left, using both the lift and the stairway, in order to vacate the building.

Once outside ODAT headquarters Peter met up with Stefan and mentioned that he was now a flying officer and in charge of the Iraqi mission called Operation *Babylon*. Cheerful and apparently self-confident for a change Stefan looked at his friend and retorted, "I have also been promoted to the same rank and I am in charge of the Lebanese mission called Operation *Shenlan*. Let us celebrate our good fortune. We have to return to this building at four o'clock to collect our passports. Not only are we going on a new and exciting journey into the unknown, but we shall soon have more money in our pockets. I was also told we could now sign on for a further three years and increase our pay even more."

"Let us talk about this in the café opposite and the cost will be on me," said Peter full of largesse as they headed towards a drab looking building which looked as though it served food of some description.

Over cakes and coffee Peter pestered Stefan.

"What does my code name *Abyadh* mean?

"*Abyadh* is the Arabic for white," explained Stefan and carefully poured coffee into Peter's cup.

"Why white? thought Peter as he sipped the contents of his cup and ate part of his Victorian sponge. "So, the other code names must be colours, I assume?"

Stefan was patient and explained that *Aswad* meant black, *Akhdhar*-green and *Azraq*-blue.

Peter's first reaction was that it was strange that all these colours in Arabic began with the letter 'a'.

Towards four o'clock both Peter and Stefan went to pick up their passports from the documentation room in ODAT headquarters. Peter was issued with an official and a bogus passport. In the official one there were two photographs of himself, one as a young boy of fourteen in 1951 and the other of a young man of nineteen in1956. On two of the pages were stamps issued by the British Embassy in Baghdad which read as follows:

'These stamps allow the holder of this passport to travel to all foreign countries and that he is a member of the British forces in Iraq.'

The bogus passport was issued in the name of Peter White, a citizen of the United Kingdom and Colonies. The two photographs of Peter White showed that he had been a schoolboy and was now a student. As he read through the bogus passport Peter was struck by the fact that there were two visas which allowed him to travel to Iraq and Iran as a student.

"Ah. Now I know why my code name is white or *Abyadh*, He said to himself. "But why Iran? Am I going to that country as well?"

However. Peter soon forgot to worry about this and spent a while back in ODAT headquarters writing a short note to his mother saying that he was being posted to an RAF station somewhere in Kent. So, that same evening a fleet of trucks arrived to take Peter and the others involved in Operation *Sandstorm* to a former disused military establishment near Hythe on the Romney Marshes nicknamed 'The Farm'. On arrival they were met by Samuel Jacobson and later by Tariq Saddiqi, both of whom had decided to come that evening in order to start preparing the spies for the following day.

"Welcome to the first of your two intensive training camps in Kent," announced Jacobson. "We shall see you tomorrow for the first part of your training, but after that we shall probably not meet again until you have completed your part of Operation *Sandstorm*. Remember ODAT's Sword of Truth and its Scales of Justice as well as its motto. Good luck!"

Thereupon all the British commanders of the countries making up Operation *Sandstorm* left to allow the spies to enjoy a substantial meal in a large canteen attached to a hanger. At ten o'clock in the evening they were given instructions for the following day by a fit-looking member of the Special

Activities Staff or SAS.

"You have before you four days of hard training which will include techniques relating to survival and torture. Most of the training will be in 'The Farm', but you will be moved to another camp near Lydd to complement your training here and to understand the different methods of torture which I hope you will not have to practise or endure."

Peter nudged Stefan who was also listening to the SAS instructor and said,

"More training, *Abdul* my friend. Are you capable of the physical aspects of spying?"

"Of course I am, *Abyadh*," replied Stefan, pleased that Peter had used his code name. "Remember. I used to always beat you on the cross-country runs in Bugle Mountain."

Their conversation was interrupted by the SAS officer.

"The going will be tough, but your chances of survival and accomplishing that which you have been chosen to do abroad will perhaps be enhanced by what you learn over the next four days."

Peter's shoulders dropped. He could scarcely believe what the SAS officer was saying. Surely spying did not involve all this?

However, he concentrated on the list of instructions issued for the following day and retired to the sleeping quarters allocated to the spies of Operations *Babylon* and *Shenlan*.

That night Peter slumped on his bunk bed in the hut provided and fell asleep still wondering whether he had done the right thing by 'volunteering' for or accepting the Iraqi mission as it stood. Nevertheless, the adrenaline seemed to be still flowing through his veins and he then became more and more excited by the thought of becoming a real British spy. He was also extremely pleased that Stefan had apparently recovered from his alcohol addiction and was still with him as an important member of Operation *Sandstorm.*

Peter was awake by seven o'clock, ready for action. In the briefing room they were all met by yesterday's SAS officer and six other similar healthy-looking types. The airmen were then placed into groups; for example, Peter in Group Babylon and Stefan in Group Shenlan. Jalal, or to give him his code name, *Aswad,* came up to Peter and said cordially,
"Salam alêkum, Abyadh.
Not to be outdone Peter replied,
"Wa alêkum es salam, Azraq."
Jalal informed him that he was *Aswad*- black and then proceeded to give him the code names of the other Babylonian operatives, both in English and Arabic. Indeed, Peter had forgotten already the colours in Arabic.
"How am I going to cope with my lack of Arabic?"complained Peter. "I am at a complete loss."
Jalal comforted him and then broke into Russian,

"Relax. You do not need to worry. In a few months you will be able to converse quite fluently in our beautiful language."

Peter, however, was not so sure.

At ten o'clock the first part of the intensive programme began. At 'The Farm' the operatives were subject to SAS type training, working in teams of five, an instructor and four operatives. This first day was devoted to paramilitary operations such as sabotage, personnel and material snatches, raids and hostage taking as well as rescue and weapon handling. The second day's programme was more specific; unarmed combat, team training and leadership as well as becoming acquainted with the use of explosives and survival in a hostile environment. The third day was spent learning how to steal and photograph documents and equipment and gather 'extreme' intelligence, all of which demanded risk taking. By the end of this day Peter realised that the SAS officer they had met when they arrived at the 'Farm' was right. He was exhausted and was not looking forward to day four.

Yet, on the fourth day Peter was presented with his father's diaries, notes and photographs relating to his time as an official in the British Embassy in Baghdad. He spent the whole day reading and consolidating what his father had accumulated. Later he said to Stefan,

"I did not realise that my father was so methodical in collecting and collating material about Iraq and that he had a vast knowledge about Arab life and customs."

His father had also written that he was concerned about the Kurds and their desire to form a Kurdistan from areas in Turkey, Iraq, Syria and Iran. Although roughly 80% Sunni and 15% Shia Moslems, they were united in their desire to form a new nation. His father also made a note that their leader, Mustafa Bazani, had founded the Kurdistan Democratic Party or KDP in 1946, but had been exiled to the Soviet Union when the organisation was declared illegal.

On the evening of the fourth day the British spies engaged in Operation *Sandstorm* were moved to another isolated RAF camp near Lydd and here the emphasis of training was centred around surviving methods of torture and combating them in the first place. In the morning they watched films and listened to accounts of torture inflicted on those who fell into the hands of a Soviet organisation called KPOK. Ahmed, an SAS officer,who had accompanied the operatives to the new camp from 'The Farm', explained,

"We do not know what KPOK stands for, nor do we know what their intentions are, but I have been a victim of the KGB's methods of torture when I was in Iran. All we know is that KPOK is like the KGB, a state-run organisation which sends Soviet agents to countries in the Middle East which support Western imperialism. If you happen to be captured by the extreme elements of KPOK you will certainly be beaten and suffer physical pain. I was.....”

At this juncture Peter looked gloomily at the floor and began to feel sick. Ahmed continued with his speech. “..... fed hallucinogenic drugs which tended to scramble my brain. However, agents of KPOK have now realised that these methods are rather counter-productive, if used on a large scale, and resulted in the acquisition of unreliable information. Therefore, new methods of torture are being introduced as you will see later on.”

During the morning of the fifth day, all the operatives were shown a film of an individual being placed in a dark room, blindfolded and kept standing for hours on end. This type of torture increased his fears and phobias and he was only released from his ordeal when he confessed to his crimes. Other films followed showing the ’new’ torture techniques of both the KGB and KPOK.

In the afternoon of the final day of training in Kent the spies were shown a detailed torture manual which had been smuggled out of the Soviet Union, but was reputed to be a copy from a source in the USA. In a slow and precise manner the SAS instructor said,

“You will understand that I do not wish any of you to encounter this form of torture. The manual contains instructions and pictures showing what is done to spies from the West if they do not co-operate after undergoing the so-called 'warm-up treatment'."

He then beamed pictures and information in English and Russian from the manual onto a screen. Peter and the rest watched with horror as they saw pictures of a man standing in the dark until fluids in his legs caused them to swell. The operatives could read the captions under the pictures which showed that the man was tortured, suffered kidney failure and died. Once again Peter felt ill watching this and hoped with all his heart that it would not detract him from the romanticism which he still associated with spying.

Later that evening Peter began to ponder on the events surrounding his training in the two camps in Kent. What mystified him most was that no mention was made of the precise operational tactics needed when the four spies involved in Operation *Babylon* arrived in Iraq. Where and how would they be able to locate Soviet agents and what to do once located? All was revealed when he was handed at about nine o'clock a large buff coloured envelope marked TOP SECRET. He opened the envelope and read the following: 'For the Attention of Flying Officer Smith'.

This Guide gave Peter strict instructions regarding his role in Operation *Babylon*. For three months he was to remain as an R/T DF Op 1A Corporal at Ddibben camp near Baghdad, although his real rank would be that of a Flying Officer. It also pointed out that the geographical position of Ddibben was a natural collection point for long-wave traffic from Soviet airbases and missile testing sites in the southern republics of the Soviet Union. Collecting a considerable amount of material on different frequencies, such as brief conversations from pilots and their controllers during and after the end of each flight, was of paramount importance.

The Guide went on to inform Peter that his role would change after three months and that he would assume the name of Peter White and use his bogus passport. He would then be transferred to Baghdad as a student of Arabic at a school which seemed to be a focal point in the past for Soviet agents. At this juncture information gleaned by Peter and instructions from ODAT commanders in Britain and from the British Embassy were to be limited to land lines, unless otherwise stated. Also contact with his mother could only be made through Ddibben camp and would be censored.

There then followed a long list of telephone numbers and a description of what to do once Soviet agents had been located. Peter read that these numbers were really important and that he had to write them down in English and Arabic as well as committing them to memory. Finally, he was advised to destroy the Guide before he left Great Britain. Peter's reaction was to feel at least relieved that the Guide would help to a certain degree his actions abroad. However, a vague sense of danger began to engulf him as he continued to read the Guide, but fear soon passed when he thought that he was now a real British spy.

That final evening Peter and Stefan spent the time talking about ODAT and the way they had both been 'hijacked' as spies.

"I wonder if ODAT is an offshoot of MI5, the United Kingdom's Security Intelligence Agency, responsible for protecting its citizens at home and overseas?" asked Peter. "Or, is it connected to MI6 which gathers secret intelligence outside the country in support of the government's security, defence, foreign and economic policies-or both? What do you think, *Abdul?*

Stefan, who had also been trying to analyse the existence of ODAT, replied,

"Well, Petrushka. I mean *Abyadh.* Jacobson informed me that ODAT is unique and separate from both MI5 and MI6 and is only responsible to the Foreign Secretary. In my opinion it seems to be closer to MI6 than MI5.

In reality ODAT was a semi-independent organisation which was responsible for spying activities in Eastern Europe and the Middle East. It liaised closely with the chiefs of staff of the armed forces as well as with MI5 and MI6. Its recruits were trained to find out information about the designs of the Soviet Union in these areas of the world and to locate Soviet agents there. Peter and Stefan had been recruited from the RAF because, not only were they proficient in SIGINT work, but they possessed a command of a number of languages necessary for obtaining information and both seemed able to cope with the intricacies of spying through a medium of 'black' propaganda, bluff and counter-bluff.

Surveying their kitbags stacked by their bunk beds in the hut provided as sleeping quarters, both friends slumped wearily on their mattresses. A pile of clothing and material had to be transferred to Iraq, and in Stefan's case later to the Lebanon,-RAF uniforms, civilian clothes, passports, legal and bogus, as well as other equipment and documents necessary for their stay in the Middle East.

Peter and Stefan talked excitedly about their flight to Iraq, which was to due to take place the following day, and also about the start of a new adventure as spies. Operation *Sandstorm* was about to begin. Peter's last words to his friend sleeping opposite him were important to him because he knew that Stefan would only be in camp Ddibben for a short while.

"Abdul. To jest mój numer telefonu w Bagdadzie. Please do not telephone me on this number until I am installed in Baghdad, probably sometime after July."
He then handed him a piece of paper with a number on it. Stefan accepted it, thanked him and said goodnight,

"OK, Petrushka. i dobranoc."

Peter kept turning in his sleep, dreaming first of all of exciting adventures in a country in the mysterious Middle East. However, later questions began to pile up in his dream and he found it difficult to answer them.

"Can I find glamour and glory in espionage? Am I able to become a pathological liar who will be able to tell fibs to my advantage? Have I the ability to play dirty and win the jackpot? How can I avoid being seduced by a delectable female Soviet agent? How will I cope with blackmail and torture?"

By the time he had attempted to answer these questions a new dawn had broken for Peter, a British Spy.

Chapter Two

Asya, a Soviet Agent

"Pay attention, comrade. You need to consider more carefully the position of your arms and feet. The plié and the battement are important because they give strength and flexibility to the entire body and allow you to perfect posture and placement."

This admonition by Elena Goncharova, one of the main instructresses at a Moscow ballet school, made her pupil, Asya Alievna Amampourov, blush.

"You must practise these positions until they are perfect," she continued and shook what seemed to be a warning finger in Asya's direction.

Having completed what she had to say, Elena Goncharova turned to the next ballerina. Asya remained silent, grimaced and bit her lips, but she obeyed the instructions given.

Asya was a beautiful Asiatic-looking teenager who possessed an unusual elasticity of waist, with slender arms and legs and a delicate way of balancing her arms. She had short black hair tied in a bun at the back of her head and this contrasted delightfully with the golden colour of her neck. It was, however, her facial features which enhanced her overwhelming beauty, especially her high oriental cheekbones, her limped, yet deep-set and reflexive brown eyes as well as the rich curves of her mouth. When she smiled or laughed her large eyes lit up, whereas her pouting lips seemed as if they had been caressed by a lingering kiss.

When she was in her early teens Asya received dance training in the classes of the Young Pioneers' Palace in Moscow and then continued her studies later at one of Bolshoi Ballet's feeder schools. This slight dancer with large eyes showed, even at an early age, an innate lyricism in her dancing. Elena Goncharova had to admit that this pupil had definite qualities.

"In a few years time I am sure she will be able to perform in productions such as Giselle. Already she is beginning to show the fragility of a bird and to display an innocence which often borders on a sense of doom."

However, at first Asya was able to perform ballet scenes without having to bare her arms, legs or shoulders, thus retaining her modesty. As she began to take on more demanding roles she was forced to reveal those areas of her anatomy which were 'forbidden' for a female Muslim.

Asya dreamt that one day she would become famous and fit any role. After seeing a production of 'Swan Lake' at the Bolshoi Theatre she remarked to her mother,

"I can imagine myself in a few years time able to fit

the role of Odette, the innocent maiden, transformed into a swan or even Odile, the wicked enchantress."

Full of confidence, Asya was sure that now she was ready to step on to any stage and establish her sense of style and authority. On occasions she would say to her mother,

"Would it not be wonderful if I could obtain top Soviet honours in dancing and win the Lenin prize?"

Little did Elena Gorcharova, and for that matter the rest of the ballet school, realise that this delightful and demure eighteen-year-old, the daughter of an engineer from Tajikistan, also had a sense of freedom and justice. In fact, she had absorbed many feminist ideas, even though she had to struggle with the dichotomy which existed between her atheist education at school in Moscow and her Shia Muslim upbringing at home. For example, she would rarely drop her eyes to the ground as was expected in her religion.

Asya pestered her mother.

"When the Bolsheviks came to power in 1917 women were in theory given the right to vote and enjoy equal opportunities with men in all spheres of life, yet now in the 1950s they are still demeaned and required to produce a large number of children for the sake of the Soviet Union."

Asya's mother, who before her conversion to Islam had been an adherent of the Russian Orthodox Church, sighed.

"Asya. We are witnessing under communism the continuation of the Byzantine belief that females are impure. I know that the status of women is diminished."

Asya was silent for the moment, but she was in a determined mood.

"Do you remember, *matushka,* when I was a young girl I was bewitched by the series of fictitious females in Russian folklore, such as the strength of the *Rusalki,* the virgin mermaids or water spirits with powers of witchcraft. And I was obsessed and frightened by *Baba Yaga,* the witch with the wooden leg, who was always scaring young children."

Acknowledging her active mind and innate qualities at an early age, some of Asya's teachers nicknamed her *Vassilisa,* the mythical woman, who was cleverer and wiser than all men. It was indeed in practice quite unusual for a female, especially a Muslim, to question the superiority of men in Soviet society.

As she became older Asya was classified as one of those females who spoke up for the equality of the sexes like the *Ravnopravki* in Russian history, yet she was quiet about all of this whilst she was in the ballet school. She was inspired by famous women in history: Catherine the Great, the eighteenth-century monarch who introduced liberal laws into the country, Catherine Dashkov who headed the Academy of Sciences and Sofia Kavaleskaya, the respected mathematician, astronomer, physicist and writer. It was, however, in Russian literature that Asya read about the fate of women in society. She felt strongly about the difficulties encountered by the 'heroines' thrown up by the great Russian writers of the eighteenth and nineteenth centuries.

She would in her mind often compare herself to some of these 'heroines', for example Lermontov's Princess Tamara. Referring to this tragic person she considered that the devil in her case was the communist society in which she lived, whereas the protecting angel was her Islamic religion, even though she could not fully understand why. Having read this author's 'Demon' she said to her mother, "After reading about the fate of Princess Tamara, I have decided that I will never allow myself to be seduced, kissed and die like her." Then to please her mother she added, "because my saviour will be Allah who will never forsake me."

Nevertheless, Asya, like her father and the rest of the family, knew that in order to survive she would have to embrace elements of communism and pretend that she was an upright and true Soviet citizen in spite of the fact that her religion clashed in many ways with Soviet ideas. Asya's perception of the role and position of women in society was influenced by her father's interest in Islamic law which stated that women could inherit property, choose their husbands, work and initiate divorce. Her father, however, held a different interpretation of women's rights under Islamic law.

"Whatever the law says about women's rights is alright in theory, but in practice it does not work. I support the teachings of the Shia *Ulama* or wise men who state that women should be domesticated, bring up children and follow the behaviour of the Holy Family. Mohammed as the grandfather figure, his daughter, Fatima and son-in-law as mother and father and his children represent the model family for all Shia Muslims to follow."Asya pulled a face and could not believe that her father was serious. Jokingly she said.

"If you had your way, father. I would be forced to wear the veil and not put on any lipstick or cosmetics."

But her father was serious and to a certain extent right. Muslim writers attacked Soviet and western societies over the influence they brought to bear on Muslim women who lived there and in some cases resulted in promiscuity, adultery, divorce and the breakdown of the family unit. Ali was not going to let this happen to his daughter, Asya, but he could see that he had a fight on his hands.

During the rest break at the ballet school Asya slumped into a chair, kicked off her ballet shoes and began to think carefully about what she had achieved and whether she had chosen the correct career. In

January 1956 at the age of eighteen and, in spite of her father's objections, she wanted to prove to her mother at least that she could succeed in her chosen profession. Both Asya and her brother, Parviz, who was a year older than her, had successfully completed the highly centralised Soviet government-run education system, the worst features of which were inflexibility and suppression of the truth as well as its emphasis on Marxist-Leninist doctrine.

Their father was pleased with his offspring and their achievements at school. Proudly he said to his wife, "Without too much difficulty our son and daughter have found that they are able to work within a system which the Bolsheviks called 'a complete dedication of the people to the state through psychological training which includes specialist subjects'. Throughout their school life they have achieved a *pyatiorka* or grade five in every subject. Parviz gravitated towards engineering, whereas Asya was prominent in the life and social sciences."
Anastasia, his wife, agreed with him, but she always agreed with her husband.

Parviz would occasionally remind his father that both he and Asya had to suffer the boredom of lessons in Marxist-Leninist ideology.
"We condemned in silence the lay-out of text books which were often full of propaganda," he declared.
Asya nodded in agreement with her brother Both had

been taught more or less together in an elementary school, but Parviz later attended a *technikum,* whereas Asya studied at a secondary specialist school. Parviz promised his father that he would look after his sister. "We are still on the same campus, so I can keep an eye on my determined, but often wayward, sister."

In the final analysis both brother and sister passed their *attestat zrelosti* or maturity certificate which meant they could attend a *VUZ* or higher educational institute, which for Parviz was Moscow University, and for Asya, a Bolshoi Ballet feeder school.

Ali was not happy with his daughter's choice of a career and he remonstrated with his wife who secretly gave her daughter some encouragement.

"I toiled and laboured to become a student at the prestigious Lomonosov University in 1918. I was one of the few citizens from the Soviet Republic of Tajikistan to gain a place in the Engineering Department even though I belonged to the minority Shia sect. I am very pleased that Parviz and I have become important cogs in the machine to help the USSR surpass other countries in the western world in science and technology."

Then a grim smile transformed his usual complacent face.

"But what about Asya? She is following a decadent career."

That evening Asya was late coming home because the January snow on the ground supplemented by sleet and rain had turned Moscow into a quagmire. She was very tired after a full day at the ballet school and a long walk to her parents' flat. She knew that there was going to be another confrontation with her father over the ballet lessons. Indeed, there were often furious rows in the Amampourov household as she became more and more independent and stubborn over insisting that she should make her own way in life. In her father's eyes she was becoming idolatrous. Ali attacked his daughter the moment she entered the flat. "Asya, Up to now I have been quite pragmatic in allowing you to follow your inclinations and realise that we have to relent on certain Islamic principles and compromise our faith in an atheistic society. But enough is enough. You must abandon your chosen career now."

Anastasia tried to intervene and give some support to her daughter, but she was frightened by the anger on her husband's face.
"Please leave Asya alone, Ali. You can see she is worn out."
Then turning to her daughter, she suggested what might defuse the situation.
"Oh, Asya, Try and meet your father halfway. He is only thinking of your welfare as a Shia Muslim. I respect your choice of a career but explain to him that you will cover parts of your body when performing certain ballet scenes, He becomes rather distressed when you reveal parts of your anatomy to the general

public."

Ali Amampourov was a Shia Muslim. There were both Sunni and Shia Muslims in the southern republics of the Soviet Union, for example in Turkmenistan, Uzbekistan Azerbaijan and Kirgizstan as well as in Transcaucasia and Georgia. In Tajikistan, for example, where Ali was born the Sunnis completely outnumbered the Shi'ites. However, both these main Muslim groups were united in their faith-Islam, but with a difference of interpretation of the Holy *Qur'an* and also the *Hadith* or sayings of their prophet, Mohammed.

By a decree promulgated by the Council of People's Commissars on the 22nd January 1918 the Soviets separated the state from the Russian Orthodox Church. Although this did not affect Muslims directly, it meant that Russia, and later the Soviet Union, was officially atheist, that is to say it supported an anti-God ideology and tended to suppress religion and all religious groups including Muslims.

Ali was born in Dushanbe, the capital of Tajikistan in 1900. Both Russia and the USSR were aware of the hydro-electric power potential of this landlocked country and scientists and engineers were needed to work on projects for the internal use of its electrical energy. By the 1950s this southern republic also had aluminium deposits and large cotton enterprises which were owned and controlled by the state. Yet, much to the disgust of Ali and other educated Tajiks it was also a transit for Afghan narcotics bound for the USSR and other parts of Europe

After the overthrow of Imperial Russia, Ali's father, also called Ali, became one of the *Basmachi* who waged war against the Bolshevik armies. Only in 1925, when guerrilla fighting ended in Tajikistan, did his father, the son of an Iranian man and Tajik woman, lay down his arms for the Islamic cause and independence of his country. His son remembered with some bitterness these events.

"I was only a teenager when the Bolsheviks came to Tajikistan and burned down villages and mosques. It was never my father's desire for me to study at Moscow University, but the Soviets had made an effort to appease all Muslims with their 'Appeal to all Muslims of Russia and the East' and to hand back the Qur'an of Osman to the Muslims of Petrograd in 1918. This was the main reason why I accepted communism. In 1929 Tajikistan became a constituent republic. Even *sharia* law was allowed to prevail in certain areas, controlled, however, by the Soviets. My father never accepted the reality of things and died a broken man."

Ali's respect for the Soviet Union was further enhanced by the government's policy of *korenizatsia* or indigenization, which on the surface put an end to the conflict between the nationalists and the Soviets.

It was at university that Ali became a member of the Muslim Socialist Party and later the Communist Party. In the same year, in 1922, he was witness to the renaming of Russia to that of the Soviet Union. As he said,

"At first I was worried by the attacks by the Soviet government on the traditions and practices of Islam, but I was aware of the fact that many of the Mullahs in Tajikistan sided with the bourgeoisie."

Parviz asked on one occasion,

"Were you not concerned father by Stalin's statement that the Communist Party could not be neutral towards religious groups and needed to conduct an anti-religious struggle against any and all such religious prejudices?"

Ali answered his son's question quite frankly,

"You are right, Parviz. I was worried by his announcement, but I was torn between respect for the Imams and Mullahs, who were the judges, lawyers, teachers and intellectuals, and respect for Soviet laws and edicts. I had to accept the principles of communism without hopefully prejudicing my faith. This is called *taqiyya* or religious dissimulation, a system practised by Shia Muslims when danger threatens."

Realising that her father was in a more conciliatory mood as the evening progressed and, obviously forgetting his quarrel with her and reflecting on the past, she brought him round to his favourite topic.

"Tell me, father, once again. How did you meet my mother?"

Ali's face began to light up whenever he talked about the first encounter with his beloved Anastasia.

"It was in 1935 and I was suffering back pains as a result of my work as a practising engineer. So, I decided to visit the spa town of Pyatigorsk in the Caucuses. On the southern slopes of Mount Mashuk I tasted the healing waters of the mineral springs there in the hope of relief from my pain. At one of the research centres dedicated to the development of new cures I met my future beautiful wife."

Then in his usual unctuous way he prudently said,

"I was always susceptible to a woman's charms, but my lovely Anastasia was something else."

Anastasia laughed, stroked her husband's face and said, virtually 'purring like a cat who had tasted the cream',

"I could not resist you either, Ali. You were so handsome and polite. I fell immediately in love with you. Even though I was a firm believer in Russian Orthodoxy at the time, I converted to Islam and now my new faith is important to me. I never want to look back."

When Anastasia's parents realised that she was going to marry a Muslim they were horrified. Her parents had brought her up in the strict beliefs of the Russian Orthodox Church. The village near Pyatigorsk where they lived and the church in which they worshipped as a family were of paramount importance to them. They hoped that Anastasia, her future children and their future grandchildren, would be baptised and spend their lives in accordance with the Ten Commandments. They wanted Anastasia and her offspring to find peace and consolation as well as understanding and salvation in God the Father, God the Son and God the Holy Ghost. Anastasia remembered her mother's last words after she had married Ali in a Muslim ceremony.

"Oh, Anastasia. Why did you not marry a believer of our church- a Christian, so that on your wedding day both your father and I could listen to the vibrant hymn of the incarnate God 'sung' by the boisterous *zvon* or peal of bells?"

That was Anastasia's last contact with her parents and relatives. She could only explain that she had found peace and contentment with her husband and her new faith-Islam. However, she would sometimes confide in Asya, when her husband was not present, that at first she missed her parents' love and devotion as well as the sight of long-bearded priests in gold clothing swinging sweet smelling incense around and passing jewelled Bibles to one another during services.

"But don't mention any of this to your father. I beg of you. Now the sight of icons painted on cheap wood of the Virgin Mary and Child in gold and being kissed by parishioners makes me realise how idolatrous the

Russian Orthodox Church is. My Islamic faith is now strong, but I need your father's help and Allah's assistance to guide me through life."

The following evening Asya hoped that her father was in a good mood and even offered to prepare the evening meal. Yet, Ali was not finished with his admonitions and returned to criticising his daughter.
"Asya," he said. "You know that since you were born your mother and I have had only two major quarrels and both were about you. The first was when you came into the world. I wanted to call you Khadija after our prophet's first wife, or perhaps Fatima after his daughter, because you were a perfectly formed and beautiful baby girl."

At this point Anastasia glance sharply at her husband and interrupted him and said,
"I pointed out that both of these names would sound ridiculous in the eyes of the Russians. So, I persuaded your father to call you Asya after the wife of the Egyptian pharaoh who saved Moses from drowning in the River Nile. To this day she is regarded as a Muslim. Also, Asya is the heroine of one of Turgenev's short novels. Therefore, you have a Muslim and Russian connection to your name."

Slightly upset by his wife's intervention and the look his daughter gave him, he nevertheless continued with his complaint,

"Before we were married your mother was an admirer of great people associated with the Russian ballet. I was forever bombarded with tales about Diaghilev, Bronislava and Nijhinski as well as how she had hoped to become a ballet dancer. She was delighted when you took up ballet lessons, but I was unhappy. By displaying the female form you are being disrespectful to me and Allah."

By now Asya was only half listening to her father's protestations. She now knew what he was going to say. She had heard it all before. She lowered her head and became quite tearful, but she was determined to follow her life's ambition to become a successful ballerina. Her father could moan all he wished, but she was not going to change her mind. She went to the window and looked over the Lenin Hills. She could see the colossal construction which was her father's alma mater-Moscow's Lomonosov University. There it stood, a majestic building, symbolizing Soviet learning. Asya wiped tears from her cheeks and said quietly, but irreverently,
"I know my father would like me to study at this university and at the same time remain a good Muslim, but my life is not controlled by him or by Allah. My wish is to become a famous ballerina and travel the world."

To go to different countries was also Asya's ambition,

so the acquisition of a number of languages was equally important to her. She could speak Russian and Tajik fluently and at school she was quick to learn English. Once a week she attended with her brother a Qur'an school in a neighbour's flat and, although she picked up the complexities of Arabic mainly by rote learning of the Qur'an, she only did it for her father's sake. Asya sometimes confided in her mother and said,

"I cannot help it, but my heart rules my head and I consider ballet and its attractions, learning languages and travelling the world more important to me than a dull obeisance to Islam."

Yet, her mind was not at rest Even though she was fully integrated into Soviet society, she could not completely neglect her Muslim environment at home. Each week after studying the Qur'an, her teacher reminded her that she was neglecting her devotion to Islam by becoming a ballet student. As he pointed out, "The Holy Qur'an states that you as a female must not display ornaments or show your figure. At the same time you must always guard your modesty."
He above all was aware that Asya was the type of female Muslim teenager who, because of her dazzling beauty, would attract the attention of both male believers and unbelievers for the wrong reason.

Over the days which followed, Asya's father became more direct in his attempts to persuade his daughter to give up her career intentions.

"One of these days, Asya. I shall take the whole family to an orthodox Muslim country where I can force you to wear the *hijab* as prescribed by the Holy Qur'an. Even here in Moscow you should cover your head and shoulders with a scarf and wear a loosely fitted dark garment to cover both your arms and your legs."

Asya gave her father a disparaging look and did not respond to his threat. However, he kept on with his complaints.

"Every time you go to that accursed ballet school you display yourself and it is an abomination to Allah."

On hearing this Asya did respond.

"I would rather leave home than to go with you to one of those places mentioned by you where I would not be seen, heard or noticed, bending my head to the ground and wearing a veil for protection."

The Amampourovs appeared to be keen observers of what was going on in the Soviet Union in the 1950s. Although they lived in an apartment in an uninspiring and drab uniform tower block, which some people referred to as a *trushchoby* or slum, they had a telephone, a radio and a bicycle. The possession of a telephone was virtually unheard of for ordinary citizens, let alone non-ethnic Russians, but Ali and Parviz were important to the Soviet economy and needed to be contacted quickly. They were not rootless cosmopolitans, like for example the Jews, but important and necessary engineers. So they enjoyed certain 'perks'. Ali warned his family on a number of occasions,

"Be careful when you receive or make a telephone call. The concierge listens in and he is a dedicated KGB snoop. The line is tapped and you need to know that a KGB member of the Ninth Directorate is monitoring your conversations."

The Amampourovs' apartment consisted of three rooms. The largest was the living room which contained a sofa covered in drapes and two cane chairs. On a small table covered with a white linen cloth were cups, saucers, plates and a *samovar* which seemed to be used continuously. A tall open cupboard housed books, newspapers and various documents relating to the men's work as well as a copy of the Qur'an which rested on the very top. On the walls were a few pictures, mainly of the family, and even one of Asya completely covered in a decorous ballet costume. Only one window in this room let in the light, but it provided an excellent view of Moscow's hills. The living room led into a sort of alcove which housed a small sink and a stove to provide heating There were only two medium-sized bedrooms. The smaller one was for Ali and Anastasia and the larger one for Parviz and his sister. This second bedroom contained two separate beds and was divided into two sections by a curtain to accommodate the modesty of the two teenagers.

After 1953 the Stalinist focus on heavy industry was partly relaxed and ordinary people were allowed to voice their concerns over the lack of consumer goods. The Amampourovs were nevertheless quite satisfied with their life on the whole. As Ali put it,

"The cost of renting this flat is low and domestic power, water, medical care and transport are virtually free. If we are in trouble, the state will provide."

Whenever people in the Soviet Union in the 1950s mentioned the state, it was spoken with awe. "The fifth Five Year Plan is coming to an end, and more consumer goods are appearing in the shops," declared Ali with obvious delight.

However, there were complaints. In February 1955 Ali announced to his family,

"Comrade Malenkov has resigned as Chairman of the Council of Ministers. He was about to advocate a greater emphasis on consumer goods, and I was in line for a television set and a washing machine. What will happen now?"

Only a week later the family received a washing machine, but it did not spin too well and had no rinsing facilities, yet there was no television. Underproduction and overproduction of goods had resulted in barter and a serious black market began to emerge. In fact on a number of occasions Ali and his son were unable to purchase razor blades, but there was at the same time a surplus of razors.

January 1956 was a terrible month for Asya on the whole. Not only was she spending too long at the ballet school and arriving home late in the evening, but young men were ringing her up at home. Her father became more annoyed and started to think of ways of curbing his daughter's independence. Taking her to one side he said.

"Asya. I know that your beauty is on the one hand a blessing, but on the other hand it is also a curse. Your attraction is a gift from Allah and you should treat it with respect."

He explained to her that her good looks were due to his grandparents on his mother's side who were Pamirs from Gorno-Badakhstan where the people lived 'close to heaven'.

Whenever he referred to his maternal grandparents he let slip that probably Mongolian blood was flowing through his daughter's veins. He would then break out in a language unknown to the rest of the family. He would even sing in a local dialect which he had learnt at his mother's knees. This singing was then followed by a translation, first of all in Tajik and, for the benefit of Anastasia, in Russian. The song was about Pamir which lay 'at the feet of the sun'.

"People who live there are proud of the mountains and rivers and celebrate Allah's gift of nature. It is a region comparable to the Garden of Eden, where one's soul can find comfort in the peace and quiet of

Allah's creation."

Then, turning to his family he said,

"One day I hope to return with you all to Tajikistan and perhaps, when I die, to be buried with my maternal grandparents in Gorno-Badakhstan."

Asya was confused and frightened. What was her father thinking of? At first he was threatening to take the whole family to a strict Muslim country and now to Tajikistan or even Gorno-Badakhstan. She wondered whether he was becoming senile at the age of fifty-six. She tried to persuade her mother to reason with her father, but Anastasia always insisted that Ali was the master of the household and they must do what he said. This, however, was not Asya's way of thinking and she thought long and hard to avoid such a development of events outlined by her father.

As the days rolled by Asya saw less of her father and brother who were away on projects in Tajikistan. Necessary engineering work was demanded in Khujand, Kulob, Panjaket and Istarasha, the urban centres, as well as in Dushanbe. This Soviet Republic was becoming more and more important, not only to the Soviet economy, but because it was a land locked mountainous country with Afghanistan to the south, Kyrgyzstan to the north, Uzbekistan to the west and the Peoples' Republic of China to the east. No wonder Ali and Parviz were in demand to explore further its potential electric power and to ensure that the area remained stable.

During the month of February a catastrophe took place in the Amampourov household. Asya's father found out that his daughter had lied in order to become a member of the Communist League of Youth, the *Komsomol*. She had stated that she was an active 'atheist' in order to become a member of this organisation. Her excuse for lying in her opinion was of necessity.

"I had to join this organisation at the age of fourteen because then I had access to healthy activities, sport and education as well as the choice to take part in voluntary and industrial ventures. Moreover, it allowed me to seek help in training as a ballerina," she declared to her father, but he was not amused. He had approved of her being a member of the junior organisations-the Young Octobrists and the Pioneers. Nor did he mind her being one of the *Komsomoltsy,* but he was annoyed that she had declared herself to be an atheist.

Lenin called the *Komsomoltsy* the 'shock troops of the Revolution'. They were drawn from schools, factories and farms as an active creative force in society and as Communist Party helpers they acted as 'a school of communism for youth'. The Pioneers were organised into brigades and attached to local *Komsomol* cells. Asya was right. Belonging to these organisations helped her gain a scholarship to study ballet. Why was her father so angry? She could not understand why he was so upset over this atheist declaration which she had made but did not intend to keep. As she said to him, she was only following the right of Shia Muslims to practise *taqiyya* at an early age. She pointed out to her father that he had on many occasions declared that the family had to practise this right in order to survive persecution and even death, especially in an atheist society.

"Remember, father, that the *Qur'an* states that 'whoever disbelieves in Allah after believing is damned, except for those who are compelled to do so, whilst their hearts are firm in the faith'. This applied to me when I signed the declaration to join the *Komsomoltsy* when I was fourteen."

"You did not have to swear such an oath, Asya. You did not even have to become a member of this organisation," retorted Ali. "You have already shown that you can become an accomplished ballerina without resorting to falsehood."

Asya felt like giving up. She was never going to convince her 'senile' father that she intended to remain true to her calling in life. Really, he wanted her to abandon her career. She opened her mouth, in order to say that she would leave home and find her own way in life, but the words would not come out, so she went to help her mother clear the table and wash the dishes. Before going to bed, she made up her mind that some action was needed before things got out of hand.

Fed up with the rows at home Asya decided to meet her *Komsomol* group leader, Larissa Semyonova, at the local House of Culture where she explained, like many other *Komsomoltsy,* that she wanted to leave home.

"My father is threatening to take me to a strict Muslim country abroad or to Tajikistan, But I want to remain here in Moscow and further my career," she said tearfully to Larissa. "After much reflection I have come to the conclusion that I must act now. Can you help me?"

"We *Komsomoltsy* are active in society and part of the Communist Party's creative force for young people to progress in life. I will set up a meeting with somebody who will be able to help you in your time of need," declared Larissa, putting her arm around Asya to comfort her.

For her part Asya was excited by her leader's reply and this gave her great satisfaction. At least something was going to be done to end the everlasting rows between herself and her father. So, it transpired that two days later she received a telephone call from Larissa stating that a member of an organisation called KPOK would help her solve her problem on condition that she did one small favour for her country- the Soviet Union. She was given an address off Lubyanka Square and asked to report there in three days time. This was opportune because her father and brother had once again left for Dushanbe and would be absent for a few weeks.

The evening before she had to report to KPOK headquarters she wished her mother goodnight and retired to bed The window of her bedroom was slightly open and she could hear the soft sounds of a three-stringed balalaika playing the 'Volga Boat Song'. Every evening one of her neighbours played one of the traditional folk melodies on this instrument. However, she needed her sleep, so she closed the bedroom window, determined to get a good night's rest.

Asya awoke at five o'clock to the sound of the chimes of the clock on her bedroom wall. She counted them- *raz, dva .... pyat'*. Reaching five she jumped out of bed, ate a bowl of *kasha* and a few cucumber rolls and started to dress. She put on a long black skirt and a jumper over which she placed a dark quilted jacket called a *vatnik*. She fetched her black boots from a cupboard by the side of her bed and also put them on because she could hear the rain pounding against the window in the living room. Finally, she placed a kerchief over her head tied at the neck, attached her red *Komsomol* armband to her right sleeve and left the apartment without waking her mother.

Not far from her block of flats she passed a number

of similar square concrete buildings which looked like huge layers of yellow cakes which in turn housed hundreds of tenants. Building workers were still active at this early hour and they greeted Asya with shouts of 'Hello, Comrade. How are you?' Everywhere there seemed to be a fever of activity, especially in the construction industry. Indeed, the Soviet Union was in the 1950s in a frenzy of building apartments, factories and railway stations. Along the banks of the slow Moskva river, new streets, tunnels and bridges were beginning to appear.

Moscow was also starting to absorb neighbouring villages like Cheremushki. Within months city districts of five-storey houses arose, containing sub-houses with one or several numbers. Moscovites, born and bred in the city, only knew it within the limits of the *Sadovoye Kol'tso* or Garden Ring. They could not imagine that such transformation would take place in their lifetime. Because she usually walked to work and back during the week Asya knew every *tupik* or dead-end, every *val* or bank and every *proseka* or cutting in the forest.

"Only last week at this spot the building had two storeys, now there are five," Asya said to herself and then added, "I wonder what has happened to the people dislodged from their wooden houses as a result of this building?"

Yet, she already knew that the state would look after them by giving them apartments there or, if they worked on the land, they would be sent to collective or state farms elsewhere.

As she continued on her way she met groups of young people also wearing red armbands like herself, pioneers and *Komsomoltsy* who patrolled the streets of Moscow, making sure that *styliagy* or hooligans did not cause trouble.

"*Dobroye ootro*," they shouted when they recognised her armband and she replied cheerfully,

"Yes. It is indeed a good morning because today my life is going to change for the better." or so she hoped.

Then groups of peasants from collective or state farms appeared, pushing carts laden with vegetables and fruit destined for the centre of Moscow.

On approaching one of the last remaining block of flats on her way to KPOK headquarters Asya saw a young man disfiguring a wall with graffiti. She went up to him and said sternly, "Comrade. This is not a cultured thing to do."

He looked embarrassed and immediately apologised when he saw her red armband.

"Sorry, comrade. I forgot what I was doing. I am bored with nothing to do. I will clean it up at once," he said and began to scrub the wall vigorously with his torn jacket.

The numerous flats then gave way to more ordinary looking buildings as well as churches and monasteries, their spires, turrets and pinnacles glowing in the early morning sun

"No wonder Moscow is called the 'City of Forty-by-Forty Churches' and the 'City of Gold'", whispered Asya to herself as she walked steadfastly along the now broad pavements. As she approached the centre of the capital of the Soviet Union the Kremlin bells in the Spasskoye Tower chimed eight o'clock. It had taken her almost three hours to get this far.

She was now conscious of groups of women in grey and black shawls sweeping the streets They were replaced by crowds of people- men in badly cut suits and grey caps and women in drab costumes with pink or blue kerchiefs over their heads, most of whom were on their way to work. Here and there Asya could pick out Uzbeks wearing their embroidered skull caps and other ethnic groups. The traffic also began to build up-cars, buses and trucks, all uniform in design and moving along the straight roads.

Occasionally a fire engine or ambulance drove swiftly in the middle of the three lanes which was reserved for emergency traffic as well as cars carrying the political elite. Asya remembered her father's advice.
"Always avoid accepting a lift in a private black *zhiguli* car."
Twice such a car screeched to a halt near the kerb with its engine running. Asya, however, was firm and ignored the request by the driver to jump in.

At nine o'clock precisely Asya, both tired and exhausted, stood in front of a long imposing building with a shabby orange façade off Lubyanka Square. By counting the rows of windows, she guessed that it contained five storeys. Before going through the main entrance, she paused and said to herself,

"Am I doing the right thing? What does this organisation called KPOK intend to do with me and what proposition am I going to be offered?"

Yet, an inward voice seemed to be encouraging her to continue with her intention to leave the family home at all costs, so she stepped cautiously into the building through the main door.

She gave her name to the female receptionist sitting behind a huge desk who rummaged through several piles of papers and then said,

"Oh yes. Asya Alievna Amampourov. Please report to Room 104 on the third floor. Here is your security pass. Keep it safe and, if challenged, produce it at once. Here is also a *znachok* to pin on your *vatnik.*"

Asya looked at the *znachok* or badge and realised it was virtually the same as those worn by members of the KGB whom she had met when they visited the ballet school on various occasions. The main difference was that under the sword and the shield were the capital letters KPOK in black Cyrillic script. Asya thanked the receptionist and moved towards the lift on the right. A young man, who had been sitting in an alcove nearby, stood up and followed her. When they were both in the lift, she took a good look at him and noticed straight away that he was not an ethnic Slav. He casually lit a *Troika* cigarette in front of her and thrust a copy of *Izvestia* into the briefcase he was carrying.

"Which floor do you require?" she asked impatiently. "The third," he exclaimed. "I overheard what the receptionist said to you. I am also going to Room 104."

Asya glanced at the five buttons by the door of the lift and pressed the one which displayed *Etage 3*. She then took a further look at the young man as the lift ascended. He also had a *znachok* attached to the lapel of his jacket. She noticed he was of average height and appeared to be extremely healthy. His eyes were dark and his black hair was closely cropped. He wore a short beard, a trimmed moustache and sideburns. His smart brown suit gave him an air of distinction. Her attention, however, was distracted by the noise of the lift which moved upwards, squeaking, creaking and groaning, only to stop with an ear-shattering, bone-shaking thud on the third floor.

Room 104 was directly opposite the lift and, when Asya and her 'companion' entered, it was already occupied by about fifty individuals. Some were obviously Slavs, but the majority seemed to be of Asiatic origin. Asya noticed that there was only one other woman in the room apart from herself. A tall serious looking man stood on a dais in front of everybody. Suddenly, indicating with his hands that there should be silence, he pressed the play button of a tape recorder, and the crackling notes of the 'Soviet Hymn' filled the room, the words which Asya knew off by heart. All stood to attention and most of them sang this patriotic song which glorified the Soviet Union.

When the singing had finished this tall man then addressed the assembled audience and gave his name, which Asya missed because she was too busy surveying the people around her.

"Comrades," he said in rather a high-pitched voice. "I am the head of the Committee for the Defence of Communism or KPOK which has been since the 1930s one of the official political intelligence services of the Soviet Union dedicated to operations in the Middle East. You have been brought here today because we need volunteers to find out more about those countries who do not support our socialist cause. Our intended operation is called *Svoboda.*"

Asya felt uncomfortable at first and wondered why the operation referred to by the head of KPOK was called freedom. Perhaps freedom from capitalism? Then her gaze wandered to a large picture behind the speaker which consisted of a sword over a shield with the letters KPOK underneath, almost the same as the design on the *znachok* she was wearing.

"I have not volunteered to be a member of KPOK," she gasped. "It looks as though I have been conscripted."

She then decided to concentrate on what the tall thin head of KPOK was saying, even though annoyance was beginning to envelope her because she considered that she had been deceived by her *Komsomol* group leader, Larissa.

"We need you all as agents-provocateur to infiltrate and target groups in certain countries in the Middle East. You will be required to pose as sympathisers for a cause or a group and then relay back any information you have to us. One of your tasks will be to locate British or American agents there and you may be called upon to influence policies and even arrange kidnapping."

Having finished this part of his speech the head of KPOK paused and looked intently at his audience.

"Arrange kidnapping," said Asya to herself. "Not if I have anything to do with it. What have I let myself in for?"

At that point the speaker noticed that Asya and many of the others were looking at the picture behind him.

"Comrades. I notice that you are intrigued by the symbol of KPOK. Let me tell you that the sword represents truth and the shield defence, that is to say the truth of communism and defence against injustice. The sword is an attacking weapon which metaphorically spreads the truth of communism throughout the world. The shield represents strong defence against the enemies of our country."

Asya was becoming interested in the explanation of the symbol, but she then became annoyed when the young man she had met in the lift began to whisper in her ear. Disdainfully she ignored him in order to concentrate on what the head of KPOK was saying, yet he grabbed her arm and said,

"If you look more closely at the picture, you will see underneath the words 'Proletariat of all Countries Unite'. The sword and the shield are also symbols of the KGB."

"I know," exclaimed Asya exasperated and moved away from her tormentor who followed her and continued to pester her as she went to look more closely at the picture.

"My name is Behrooz," declared the persistent young man. "Do you know this motto 'Proletariat of all Countries Unite' is on the front page of Pravda with a picture of Lenin and the KGB's symbol?"

Now Asya tried to recall what she had learnt during those boring political science lessons at school. She remembered that truth and justice were closely linked in the Soviet Union. Complete emphasis was on egalitarian justice, whereby goods could be distributed equally. People demanded equality of opportunity and equality of outcome. Ideally a Soviet citizen should be a person in just the right place doing his or her best and giving the precise equivalent of what had been received. This was based on Karl Marx's detailed and popular concept of social justice which had become a kind of new and improved substitute for socialism and collectivism. The ideal was for the monstrous injustices of the capitalist system to be replaced by social justice. This meant concentrating the production and division of wealth, the cultivation of land, the development of factories, the organisation of commerce and the application of capital to production to the one and only banker-the State.

The head of KPOK took a drink from the table to the side of him and started to read out the names of various people in the room. Flash cards were also displayed to reveal their names as well. There was a pause after four names had been read out and four individuals were then sent to a briefing room related to a specific country in the Middle East. Asya wondered when her name would be read out. After sixteen names and four countries- Egypt, Syria, Jordan and the Lebanon were mentioned, Iran appeared and she then heard her name followed by the names of three men, including Behrooz, her previous tormentor.

"You four operatives will be going to Iran, and you need to follow your commander, Tahereh, to Room 83 on the second floor," said Dimitry whose name Asya managed for the first time to pick out above the movement of the people in the room.

Once inside Room 83 Asya and her fellow Iranian operatives were surprised to find two tables on which were spread typical Iranian food- *jujeh, hendevaneh* and *dugh* as well as non-alcoholic drinks.

"Help yourselves. Comrades," exclaimed Tahereh. "You must be hungry and thirsty after your long journey to KPOK headquarters."

After partaking of this delightful meal, Tahereh began to speak to all of them, first of all in Russian and then in Farsi, the language of Iran. Asya found some of the words rather strange, because she only knew Tajik, an archaic form of Farsi. After a while, however, she was beginning to understand what was being said and in any case her commander spoke slowly when she directed the conversation towards Asya.

There then followed a briefing given by Tahereh which allowed Asya to understand why she had been chosen as a Russian agent to operate in Iran.

"After a careful analysis of all your backgrounds we have chosen you as ideal KPOK agents for the Iranian enterprise. We know that all of you have relatives in Iran and are able to speak Farsi. First of all, let me say thank you for volunteering for the task in front of you. The next procedure will be to send you on a course to familiarise you with present conditions in Iran, how to infiltrate mainly the British and American intelligence services and what you need to survive there."

Asya was about to say,

"I have not volunteered for this so-called Iranian enterprise. I have been brought here under false pretences. All I want to do is to leave home and follow my career as a ballet dancer. KPOK was going to help me achieve this, but I have been deceived." However, she kept quiet and listened to what Tahereh had to say next.

As if reading from a script Asya's commander said,

"Asya. You will be transferred to Tehran, Behrooz to Tabriz, Koorosh to Isfahan and Amir to Mashad. In Tehran there will be a need to have at least two working agents. Therefore, Asya, you will be joined by a person who cannot be with us today. His code name is *Rumi*. In fact, all of you have been given code names based on great Persian poets. For example, Asya will be *Ferdowsi*, Behrooz-*Saddi*, Koorosh-*Khayyam* and Amir-*Hafiz*."

Asya asked why they had been given the names of Persian poets. Tahereh gave her the following answer, "Well. The poets were chosen by me at random. You will find many wonderful words of wisdom if you read their works. Your code-name, *Ferdowsi*, was a tenth-eleventh century Persian poet who wrote *Shahnameh* or Book of Kings which was all about Ancient Persia. Read his poetry and you will learn a lot."

After informing the agents about their code names

and giving them information about each poet, Tahereh then dropped a bombshell which took Asya completely by surprise.

"In charge of this operation in Iran called *Azady or Freedom* will be a colonel called Ali Alievich Amampourov."

Asya's face turned white, and she gasped several times with surprise. Tahereh noticed her discomfort and said,

"Yes, Asya. Your father has been a KPOK operator for many years, even when the organisation was a section of the NKVD. This time his code name is *Rudaki* after another Persian poet. He has agreed to take you and the rest of your family to Tehran and pretend to seek political asylum there. We had to persuade you to become a member of KPOK by offering you the chance to become a distinguished ballet dancer later. By the way, your father is very experienced. He trained as an intelligence officer at the KGB's Red Banner Institute."

By now Asya was bewildered and her head was beginning to spin, but she was intelligent enough to agree with everything her commander in the Soviet Union was telling her. Anything to become a famous ballerina, even though at first she had to become a Soviet agent. "Furthermore," added Tahereh, "Your father wishes to settle in Tajikistan after this enterprise and in any case, he is ready for retirement. Then you and your brother can return to Moscow and follow your careers."

Tahereh realised that she had more important information to divulge to the four agents and said in a solemn voice,

"I wish to remind you all that you are now Soviet agents. Remember you are carrying out Operation *Azady* for the sake of the Soviet Union and the Communist Party. We shall meet again in a few weeks' time in Camp Badkube in Azerbaijan so that you may become acquainted with espionage and survival techniques. Always keep in mind the Sword of Truth and the Shield of Defence, KPOK's weapons against untruth and injustice. Travel arrangements will be made by *Rudaki* to get you to Camp Badkube. Any questions?"

Then Asya and her fellow agents left the building together and this time she was relieved to strike up a conversation with her previous tormentor, Behrooz, or to give him his code name, *Saddi*. As they both left KPOK headquarters she was surprised to learn from him that he lived in the same block of flats as herself. Instead of walking to their *trushchoby*, Behrooz suggested that they might travel on the metro for the first part of the journey. What an experience for Asya because she always walked to work and back. Escalators took them swiftly deep below the city of Moscow. The train then transported them past beautifully decorated shops which shone like golden balls on the platforms.

"It would be wonderful if I could dance along the

platforms which appear to be lit in the fashion of the theatres of a by-gone age," said Asya clapping her hands.

At last, they reached their destination and emerged from the subway just as the heavens began to open and sleet poured onto the two travellers. Now there was just half an hour's walk to their block of flats.
"Did you notice that it was a female's voice which announced each station we stopped at?" enquired Behrooz.
Asya nodded and Behrooz then said with authority,
"For most of the time we were travelling on the Sokolnicheskaya Line started in 1935. However, on all the lines travellers can determine the direction of the train by the gender of the announcer."

Asya looked somewhat sceptical and grinned as her companion continued with his knowledge of the city's metro system.
"On each of the lines travellers going towards the centre of Moscow will hear a man's voice announcing the stops, whilst those leaving the capital will hear a female's voice."
Asya was about to say,
"A lot of female Russians have masculine voices and vice-versa. This would confuse the issue." but she stopped in time and said admiringly,
"You seem to know a lot about the metro system Be..., sorry *Saddi*. It is a pity I am not a man You

seem to have the freedom to do what you like."

Behrooz looked at Asya longingly and said,

"Perhaps we can spend a whole day exploring the underground system one day."

He then produced a map, but, seeing that Asya was losing interest, he put it away.

At one of the kiosks Behrooz bought a copy of *Pravda* for his parents and a copy of a satirical magazine called *Krokodil* for himself. This magazine criticised westerners and sometimes Soviet politicians when they fell out of favour. Together the two agents sat on a bench in what the locals called Little Gorki Park, both laughing and giggling over the contents of *Krokodil,* especially the cartoons. On reaching their block of flats Behrooz turned to Asya, stroked her across the face and said gratefully, "I have enjoyed meeting you. It is a pity that we have to say goodbye."

"I've had a good time as well," declared Asya and smiled at him. "But you know my parents would be annoyed if they found out that we had been seeing each other. Maybe our paths will cross someday."

"Well, comrade. That is true. I shall see you in Camp Badkube in a few weeks time," said Behrooz as he waved goodbye.

Asya was silent and blushed. She had grown quite fond of Behrooz after initial embarrassment. He was an interesting medical student at Moscow University and extremely intelligent with a sort of wicked sense of humour.

Two weeks later Asya confronted her father on his return from Tajikistan. At first she was livid with anger over his duplicity.

"Why have we had so many rows when all the time you were going to agree to my request to become a ballerina?" she enquired, her face distorted with rage over her father's lack of respect towards her. "Why did you not tell me about Operation *Azady* before?"

"I am truly sorry, Asya," replied her father looking upset. "You will soon realise that what I have done is for the sake of the family and for the Soviet Union, not to mention that it is also for the will of Allah. It is true that I have been a member of KPOK for a long time and I have to carry out this last mission. I wanted to do it alone, but I was forced to involve the whole family. I was unsure what you would have said if I had told you about Operation *Azady* before. One more task for the Soviet Union and I shall be able to retire and you and Parviz will be able to resume your careers here in Moscow."

At this point Anastasia, who had been listening to the conversation between her husband and her daughter, cried out in anguish and left the room in tears. It was obvious that Ali had not told his wife anything about going to Iran. Nevertheless, he was not going to be diverted by his daughter's anger or his wife's objections and was determined to explain to his daughter at least the reason why his mind was made up to carry out this final command by KPOK.

"You know I hate the Shah of Iran and the support he receives from western imperialists. So, I have volunteered, or perhaps been recruited like you, to pretend as a family that we are seeking political asylum in Iran and then hopefully infiltrate various groups to overthrow this puppet regime. For me it will also be a sort of *jihad* or holy war."

After talking throughout the night the family, apart from Parviz who was still in Dushanbe, eventually came to an agreement that would suit them all, even though the venture had its risks.

"Although I had doubts about going to Iran, we do have relatives there who will help us in our mission," declared Ali with some relief when he saw that Anastasia and Asya were beginning to warm a little to this new adventure. He realised that his wife was the biggest problem. She could only speak Russian and a few words of Tajik and she above all would have difficulty in coping with a new environment and a new language-Farsi. Asya also had her doubts, although in some ways she welcomed becoming a Soviet agent, but felt she had been trapped by KPOK and this annoyed her.

Two days later Parviz returned from Tajikistan and seemed quite composed by his father's news. Asya was surprised that her brother did not raise any objections to the Iranian enterprise and wondered why. Ali stated that the whole family had been granted a few days holiday in Moscow before setting out for Camp Badkube in Azerbaijan and all paid for by KPOK. He had also arranged for Asya to take leave of absence from the ballet school and for Parviz to obtain a sabbatical from his studies at the university. Asya was concerned, however, for her mother's sake and Ali had to somehow placate his determined daughter who could at any time cause the operation to be aborted.

In a rather unctuous manner he said,
"Asya. What would you like to do over the next few days? You above all have suffered greatly from my deception and therefore I am giving you first choice to decide what we should do as a family before embarking on Operation *Azady.*"
Asya was delighted. This was probably the first time her father had been courteous towards her. So, in a determined voice she said,
"I have always wanted to visit Lenin's tomb and to explore the Old Arbat. Although I have lived my whole life in the capital, I have never been to these two places. I also want to spend a day on the metro. Only two weeks ago I returned home on the *Sokolicheskaya* Line with a friend." But she did not dare mention it was with a male friend-Behrooz.

The very next day Ali kept his word and took the

whole family by tube to Red Square. As they sat comfortably in their seats Asya noticed, as Behrooz had confirmed, that a man's voice announced each station as the train rushed towards the centre of Moscow. Or, was it a woman's voice? Or, more likely had Behrooz been fantasising about the gender of the announcers on Moscow's underground system? The family joined the queue at the mausoleum which contained the embalmed bodies of Lenin and Stalin lying in state. Most frustrating was that the line of people seemed on occasions to almost move backwards. because some jumped the queue and foreigners were escorted to the front.

"Make sure you have your identity cards with you, or you will be fined," announced one of the visitors to the tomb, so Ali checked that everything was in order. Two hours later they were in the mausoleum itself, a building that was made of red basalt, yet appeared black in colour and formed a sort of cube. Groups of fifteen people were allowed inside at any one time and, much to his annoyance, Parviz had to leave his expensive camera behind. Inside it was appropriately dark and cool and guards were posted in all four corners of the dimly lit room. The visitors went round the two recumbent figures so they could be seen from all angles. Parviz and his sister were rather disappointed. Both Lenin and Stalin did not look real, but more like wax-cut replicas. Only their hands seemed life-like and blue.

Asya especially was glad to get out into the fresh air and then on the spur of the moment insisted on visiting the sixteenth century St. Basil's Cathedral, also on Red Square. This building maize was constructed on the orders of Ivan the Terrible who ordered that the eyes of the architect who designed it be put out to prevent him creating a similar labyrinth. The whole construction lacked symmetry, which was part of its attraction. The domes, spires and doors were all of different shapes and the style of architecture ranged from Greek to Gothic. Both Asya and her brother got lost for over two hours in the cathedral's maize much to the amusement of their parents who had been to visit the large departmental store-GUM. That evening Asya fell asleep, dreaming of the two figures in the mausoleum. Suddenly they seemed to come alive and like the pharaohs of old began to drive people in lines to build a bigger and better tomb to house other communist leaders.

Asya awoke on the Thursday morning and, although it was raining heavily, she made her father keep his promise to go to the Old Arbat which was in the process of being given a 'face lift' after the austerity of Stalin's regime. The whole family took the underground railway as far as *Park Kultury* and then walked to *Ploshchad' Arbatskaya*. Ambling along one of the oldest streets in Moscow Asya gasped in amazement.

"What beautiful street lamps and flower boxes. There

are even attractive coloured benches to sit on."
Parviz added to the picture.
"These sixteenth century streets are named after tradesmen who worked there: *plotniki* and *serebrany.*"
Asya closed her eyes and tried to imagine what the scene would have been like with carpenters and silversmiths sawing and hammering away in these streets.

The Arbat was originally a suburb of Moscow where traders from the east arrived with their caravans. By the eighteenth century it had become popular with the intelligentsia and the artistic community. As the Amampourovs strolled along the one and a quarter kilometre span as far as *Ploshchad' Smolenskaya* they gazed avidly at the picturesque pastel facades of the houses, the artisans at work, the activities of the soap-box poets and of course the souvenir shops. Anastasia turned to her husband and said,
"I would like to visit the blue and white house, number 53, which was the home of my favourite poet, Pushkin, and later to Tolstoi's house in adjoining Kolishin Lane."
Ali looked at his daughter for approval, but she was so happy that her father was showing her deference that she agreed with her mother and went willingly to view the two houses.

As a treat Ali took the whole family to what he said

was a grand hotel, but in reality was a small restaurant with old fashioned décor. It had lace curtains on rings. Black leather or plastic chairs were grouped around six or seven tables and the crockery and cutlery were covered in muslin cloth and oil paintings in gilt frames hung on the walls. Nevertheless, the family enjoyed the Russian black bread with the taste of corn in it, hot *borsch*, black caviar, smoked salmon and sardines followed by several glasses of *sok*-lemon, orange and apple.

The following day-Friday the members of the family rested because it was a Holy Day and Saturday was spent packing large trunks and preparing for the long journey to Camp Badkube. Asya, however, was in a petulant mood.

"Why are we going on this accursed Operation *Azady*? "

she asked her father after witnessing the permanent frustration and dismay on her mother's face.

"The whole enterprise will kill my mother. I do not wish to take part in a venture which will cause her harm."

"Do not worry, Asya," said her father, trying to comfort her. "I have talked things over with your mother. Today I received some good news from KPOK headquarters in Baku. We have been granted four days holiday in this lovely city by the Caspian Sea. Your mother always wanted to visit this resort town favoured by people of all ages."

Asya was not completely consoled by her father's explanation and retired to fuss around her mother.

Before leaving Moscow Asya speculated on the situation of being a Soviet agent. She also questioned once again the relevance of spying for the Soviet Union and the dangers of Operation *Azady*.

"Father. This *jihad* against the Shah of Iran, which you are so keen to carry out, is surely not obligatory for Shia Muslims like us?"

Her father rose to his feet and answered his daughter with an element of rebuke,

"Yes it is, Asya. It is obligatory at least for all able bodied male Muslims to take part in a *jihad*. Imams in Iran are calling on us to make an offensive against the non-Muslim world, that is to say against British and American interference in this country. Surely you and your mother will help us?"

Anastasia, who had been listening to the encounter between her husband and her daughter, sighed again. She always did this when she was exasperated.

"I'm glad that I'm a woman," she said rather sarcastically. "My *jihad* is a continuous battle against bad desires and inclinations in my life. But I will follow Ali through thick and thin until I die. We are in this enterprise together, Asya, whether we like it or not."

Asya shrugged her shoulders and was annoyed that her mother always gave in to her father and did not stick up for herself at all. It appeared that Operation *Azady* for the whole family was going to go ahead as arranged in spite of everything.

Within three days the family was ready to set off for Baku by coach- a long and arduous journey lasting about a week. Their flat was re-let for a year and their furniture was put in store Their necessary belongings for travelling and remaining in Iran were placed in large trunks on top of the coach which wound its circuitous way from Moscow to Baku, stopping at various towns en route. Throughout the journey the travellers seemed to exist on a diet of sliced cucumbers, boiled eggs and salted fish. The landscape changed. Left behind were the white birches of the north with their yellow, red and golden leaves to be replaced by more barren and wild terrain. Entering Azerbaijan the coach headed towards Baku. Parviz explained to his sister,
  "As we travel south you will feel the weather becoming somewhat different."
However, in Baku the weather was reasonable in this 'wind -pounded city'. The family was lucky because there could have been fierce storms and harsh winds, even at the beginning of March. Tired and exhausted after the long journey everybody slept virtually for two solid days in a large hotel just across from Neftchilar Avenue. Then Asya and Parviz were ready to explore both the inner city and the promenade with its neat gardens. At the waterside they enjoyed the

view over the Caspian Sea which was 'full of contradictions and whims like a woman' declared many of the locals. During the afternoon they played outdoor chess and billiards and towards the evening visited a Muslim restaurant which consisted of one dimly lit room at the bottom of a flight of stairs. It had a low wooden ceiling and the floor was covered in multi-coloured carpets. They ate *golubtsy*-meat balls, *halal* of course, and *dovta*-a soup of sour milk and rice.

The following day Asya dragged her brother to Fountain Square.

"Parviz. We must buy something at one of the shops in this up-market area," she shouted, full of delight.

Parviz was not amused but followed his sister to Baku's area of sophisticated shops and restaurants.. In the afternoon they were joined by their parents who wanted to see the House of Soviets created by Rudnev and Muntz and built by German prisoners of war in 1955. They also admired the twelve metre high statue of Lenin which was sculptured by the famous Kariagdy.

During the evening even Ali was beginning to have doubts about the Iranian enterprise his family was committed to.

"I have sinned considerably over the past years, but I hoped to make amends by going on Operation *Azady* which I have called my *hajj* or pilgrimage. I shall never be able to wear a simple garment of unsown cloth in two pieces called a *ihram* and go to the Holy City of Mecca, but at least I can combine a pilgrimage and a Holy War in Iran. As you know there are holy Shia Muslim places in Iran as well."

Asya was unable to follow her father's wanderings. What was he talking about?

Ali looked as though he was in a trance and holding the Holy Qur'an up high above his head he said,

"I hope to look for divine justice and will submit to the legitimate authority of our Imams on earth until the judgement day."

"What on earth is he talking about, Parviz?" asked Asya, wondering whether her father was losing his mind again.

Her brother explained. He was always explaining religious things for his sister.

"As a devout Shia Muslim he is waiting for the messianic Imam called the Mahdi or 'Well Directed One' to appear on earth."

"Well. I am not," retorted Asya. "I want to return to Moscow as soon as this mission to Iran is completed. I have set my heart on becoming a famous ballerina. Nothing and nobody will deflect me from this aim, neither the Mahdi or Allah himself."

With complete resignation the other members of the family looked at one another and hoped that the following day would allow Asya to calm down and concentrate on what lay ahead.

KPOK's Camp Badkube lay ten kilometres south of Baku and the Amampourovs were transported there from their hotel in a Soviet army truck. It was a lonely desolate place- a squat grey building in the middle of a large swampy field. Previously, KPOK's training camp for Soviet agents being sent to Iran had been on one of the many islands in the Bay of Baku, but it had been requisitioned by a state oil company for the past five years. As Asya stepped out of the army truck she could see that the earth around was bare, wrinkled and worn out. Everywhere there were pumps extricating oil from the depths of the earth. However, once inside the building the family was relieved to be met by the other Soviet agents involved in Operation *Azady-Saddi, Khayyam* and *Hafiz*. Asya avoided looking at *Saddi* alias Behrooz who occasionally tried to attract her attention. She was frightened that he would reveal to her father that he had been out with his precious daughter.

The interior of the building itself was surprisingly bright and it was obvious that it possessed high-tech equipment because the agents noticed there were a number of men and women in white coats. Towards the back of this establishment were quite delightful living quarters, in fact a whole suite of rooms for the Amampourovs. Before retiring for the night Ali, Parviz and Asya were summoned to report to the administrative centre where they were told, along with the other agents, that from this time onwards conversation would be conducted in Farsi. Asya asked about her mother who could really only speak Russian, but she was told that an exception would be made in her case and that she would not be involved in the operations at the camp or in Iran.

The first day at Badkube Camp was spent touring the Operation and Technology Department which included all the laboratories and scientific research useful to Soviet agents such as bugging, taping and shooting devices. Laboratory 10 was interesting in that it developed poisons and manufactured psychotropic substances.

"I hope we do not have to use or be subject to any of these things," declared Asya, shivering slightly. Ali took his daughter to one side and said with firm conviction,

"No my dear, but they may be of use to us as a last resort. I made it quite clear to KPOK that, if my family was involved in Operation *Azady*, it would be simply to infiltrate pro-government forces in Iran without resorting to bloodshed or killing. However, somehow, we must seek a way to weaken the militaristic, economic and psychological climate of western imperialism in a subtle way, but not by using instruments of death."

During the three days of their stay in Camp Badkube the Amampourovs and the other Soviet agents were told how communist fifth columnists had so far operated in Iran in subverting the Shah's government from within. They were also joined by Tahereh who was able to provide them with a further incentive for success in Operation *Azady*. Mentioning each member of the Iranian venture by name she said,

"Thank you *Rudaki, Rumi, Ferdowsi, Saddi, Khayyam* and *Hafiz* for agreeing to find out for the Soviet Union any impending military build-up in Iran, to locate western spies and infiltrate various groups."

Asya looked around here. Who was *Rumi*? The only other person in the room who had not been given a code name was her brother, Parviz.

It was obvious from what Tahereh said that the Soviet Union was becoming almost paranoid regarding a possible attack from Iran and that Soviet agents seemed to be the only means whereby the regime could be destabilised and a wedge driven between this country and the west. Tahereh also gave the agents written instructions about their role in Iran and emphasised that Ali alias *Rudaki* was their final transit of information to her and the Kremlin. She then followed the agents through the training camp, offering advice at various points.

The Amampourovs were rather embarrassed and concerned over certain aspects of what they heard and saw at camp Badkube. Disinformation techniques they could cope with, but kidnapping and assassination was something which they could not stomach. All of them categorically refused to take to Iran exotic devices of assassination such as poison pens that fired hydrocyanic gas or undetectable poisons which could be 'slipped' into food and drink. Asya particularly shuddered at the thought of disposing of a person at all.

"How can I be persuaded to take with me a lipstick pistol called 'the kiss of death' or a 4.5mm simple shot revolver encased in rubber and disguised as a tube of lipstick?"

Ali was aware of course that the camp contained an assassination team called SMERSH- short for 'death to spies' in Russian, but he disapproved vehemently of their methods of disposing of traitors and defectors.

On the very evening of their departure for Iran Tahereh called on the Amampourovs in order to persuade them that they were ideal agents who could in turn persuade certain elements in that country to try and assassinate the Shah, a request which was once again turned down by Ali as head of this 'ideal' family. He summed up the feelings of himself, his wife, his son and his daughter.

"We do not mind causing discord and havoc in Iran, but assassination is out of the question. If KPOK wishes to assassinate the Shah, then the organisation should ask the head of the KGB, Ivan Aleksandrovich Serov to do it himself."

Having made this bold statement, the whole family went back to the sleeping quarters in preparation for the long journey across the border between the Soviet Union and Iran to Tehran. Asya began to pack both western and Middle Eastern clothes befitting a woman. She also took with her a few gadgets important for spying in an alien country including a miniature camera and some false documents. On top of her belongings, however, was a copy of the Holy Qur'an which she was attempting to re-read on a number of occasions. She found that the contents of this Holy Book gave her confidence to relate her activities as a Soviet agent with that of a true and devout Shia Muslim, but she was troubled nevertheless. The two large trunks the Amampourovs had brought with them were left at the camp to be retrieved by them on their return.

Before retiring to bed a new and more co-operative Asya approached her family and thanked them for all the help they had given her in her time of distress. She was of course still annoyed with her brother.
"Why did you not tell me that you were *Rudi*, the other Soviet agent? You could have trusted me."
Parviz looked embarrassed and distressed and did not say a word. Then speaking in commendable Farsi, Asya said,
"*Madar va pedar, va Parviz jan. Merci keili mamnoon az komakhaye shama. Shab bekhair.*"
She then kissed everybody and repeated in Russian

for the benefit of her mother her appreciation of the help the whole family had given her.

Hugging her father, Asya then surprised everybody by saying,

"So far I have enjoyed being a Russian agent and, if this Iranian mission is part of Allah's will, I will be supportive. The first part of Operation *Azady* has been exciting and makes me think that there is more to life than dancing around the world."

Ali returned his daughter's embrace and gave thanks to Allah, read a short piece from the Qur'an and prayed that that they would be successful in their *jihad* in Iran. By the time they went to bed there was not a dry tear anywhere. Before wishing his wife goodnight and God bless, Ali whispered, "Has Asya settled all disputes with us? I hope she decides to relinquish her idea of a future career as a ballerina. I am sure she is at last seeing sense. *In shâ Allâh.*"

Asya, however, could not catch her sleep at first. Tossing and turning in her comfortable, but primitive bed, questions began to flood her mind. Was she still upset by being duped by KPOK into spying for the Soviet Union? Would she ever be able to return to Moscow after Operation *Azady* was completed? Was there even more excitement to come in a foreign land? By becoming a Soviet agent was she carrying out Allah's will? By the time she had attempted to answer these questions and many others Asya, a Soviet agent, had fallen into a deep sleep.

Chapter Three

Infiltration and Intrigue

It was the beginning of July 1956 when a group of students met in the coolness of the morning to study Arabic in one of the well-known language schools which existed in Baghdad. Although the electric fan was working perfectly, conditions in the small classroom were stifling and rather clammy. Peter White from England and Georg Schulz from West Germany were attempting to carry out a simple conversation in Arabic. Seven other students were listening intently as well as their teacher, Ibrahim al Baghdadi. Both Peter and Georg had been given Arabic names. Georg began the conversation.

"Salàm alêkum, Mohammed."

"Wa alêkum es sàlam, Hassan."

"Kêf hâlek?"

"El hamdu lillah
  Istarîh, min fàdhlek."

"Muteshekker."

This short contrived conversation was a role play exercise which possessed elements of politeness and built-in etiquette.

Ibrahim, an inspirational teacher, looked pleased and only interrupted when he considered that his students' pronunciation was poor.

"Well done. Just a few minor mistakes, but only after three lessons you are able to carry out a simple conversation in Arabic," he declared in perfect English. Whenever he praised his students, he would always look for ways of improving their Arabic even more. Encouragingly he said,

"Now, I am sure that all of you will be able to write out what Peter and Georg have said in the Arabic script."

At this point Peter White alias Peter Smith started to take notice of the other members of the group which contained five nationalities-two from Pakistan, two from West Germany, two from France and two late arrivals from Iran who introduced themselves as brother and sister. Peter was the only student from the United Kingdom.

Parviz Amampour from Iran was a quiet, handsome and dark haired man with a clean shaven face and Asya Amampour, his sister, the only female in the group, sat next to him and seemed intent on avoiding the devouring eyes of the men. Peter could not keep his eyes off Asya. Her face was without blemish and makeup, yet it exuded beauty, rather oriental he thought. She held her head erect and occasionally threw back her hair in what seemed to be a tantalizing manner. She wore an old sweater with à la mode patches on the elbows and a pair of jeans torn at the knees- quite a modern outfit really. From time to time she covered her head with a scarf. Peter also noticed that her eyes were extraordinarily brown and dazzling. On a number of occasions he would whisper in Polish that her eyes were beautiful.

Peter hoped that she would at least look at him, but she did not. Yet, a crimson flush appeared on her face when he spoke. He also noticed by her conversations in Arabic a definite determination combined with innate intelligence. Obviously she had great energy, was always in control and completely disciplined. His heart kept missing a beat whenever he looked at her, yet she always lowered her gaze and seemed to avoid him. He was stung by jealousy when on the odd occasion she paid attention to one or other of the students in the group. This annoyed him because, in spite of everything, he was outwardly sure of himself with regards to the opposite sex. However, he began to lose patience when she started to cling to her brother for protection whenever he made a gesture in her direction.

Peter had other problems to contend with in his attempts to learn Arabic. The first lesson had been spent coming to grips with the twenty-eight consonants and the three main vowels as well as their combinations within words and sentences. Moreover, the students were given numerous words to learn. The second lesson centred around diphthongs, stress and learning short instructions such as '*Wên kitàbek? Where is your book?* and of course the necessary answers. The two students from Pakistan, and now the Amampours from Iran, showed that they could master Arabic more swiftly, mainly because of the script and partly because of certain similar abstract and religious words in their languages. The students from Europe began to lag behind and this made Peter especially more determined to catch up with those students from the Middle East. He had to improve rapidly at all costs, since this was part of his nature.

During lesson three Parviz noticed Peter's determination and difficulties associated with learning Arabic and, choosing his words carefully, he said,

"Peter. Our language, Farsi, contains Arabic words. If you wish, you can sit next to me and I will help you as much as I can. When we were very young my sister and I used to sit on mats reciting from the Qur'an from memory, sometimes in unison and occasionally individually."

Peter wondered why the Iranian students were so good, and now he knew. Nevertheless, this gesture by Parviz gave him some hope, but most of all it gave him the opportunity to sit closer to Asya and enjoy her company.

Ibrahim was satisfied that the four students from the Middle East were beginning to offer help to the

European contingent. He realised that it would be impossible for the class to continue if a gap opened too widely between certain students. Meanwhile, Peter felt that, when Parviz spoke to him in English, he somehow recognised that he had met this handsome Iranian somewhere before. Turning to face Asya he said,

"I am sure that I have seen your brother before, but I cannot remember where."

Asya did not answer, but her brother stared straight ahead and quietly replied,

"I have never seen you before today, Peter. Perhaps I have a double somewhere."

That evening in Hotel Kadimiya where he was lodging Peter reflected on what events had taken place since he flew from RAF Lyneham bound for Iraq at the end of February. He was part of a group of about twenty airmen who were destined to fly to a SIGINT centre as part of Operation *Sand Storm* before moving on to other areas in the Middle East. The aircraft which transported them to Iraq, a Hercules, stood on the runway, its engines ticking over ready for the departure. Although capable of taking troops and freight, its size and shape worried Peter.

"How can such a monster get off the ground packed with RAF personnel, vehicles and boxes of rifles and ammunition?" he asked himself.

The doors closed and a few minutes later the engines began to roar, louder and louder, as the Hercules taxied along the tarmac. Then it moved faster and faster along the runway until it rose effortlessly, somewhat like an elegant bird, into the air It was Peter's first flight by air and, even though he was excited, he was also rather apprehensive. He spoke to Stefan who was sitting on the seat next to him,

"I hope it lands as safely as it took off."

Stefan, who had flown to the Lebanon many times by air, replied,

"Do not worry, Petrushka. All will be fine. Just remember that this is the beginning of our new adventure into the unknown. Take heart!"

Once in the air the spies of Operation *Sand Storm* unfastened their seatbelts and began to relax. For most of the time they could only look out of the window and see endless clouds floating above, below and to the side of them. However, on occasions they could pick out the outlines of France and Spain as well as other countries bordering the Mediterranean. Apart from some frightening experiences, when the plane hit a number of air pockets and descended rapidly, the flight to the capital of Malta, Valetta, proceeded quite normally. The evening was spent in a hotel near the airport and Peter especially was conscious of the heat building up.

The following morning a short stop was made in

Amman, the capital of Jordan. Stepping out of the plane Peter felt a rush of hot air as if from a furnace. He panicked and wanted to return to the coolness of the Hercules.

"Oh dear," he said to Stefan. "I shall never be able to cope with this heat and it is only late February."

Stefan just laughed at Peter's predicament and said, "Don't worry about it. You will soon become accustomed to all sorts of peculiarities in the Middle East. In any case we must keep thinking about our exciting future as spies."

Whereupon, both he and Peter rushed after the other airmen into the airport lounge where they partook of refreshing drinks served by Arab waiters.

Destination was Camp Ddibben near Lake Habbaniya, about fifty miles from Baghdad. The plane landed in a sand storm and, as it taxied to one of the hangers, Peter could not even see out of the window. As he stepped out of the Hercules he realised why. A wind laden with sand whistled and whined around him, sending with it flurries of what looked like birds' feathers and chips of wood. A heavy haze obscured everything. Trees on this airbase swayed and crackled and there was dust everywhere, even between Peter's teeth and in his eyes.

"With the extreme heat in Amman and now this sandstorm in Iraq I wonder what type of world I am coming to?" he said to himself.

Camp Ddibben was classified as a flying station and was situated between the towns of Ramad and Falluja, virtually on the east bank of the river Euphrates. During World War II it had been a large training school for pilots and had been besieged by the Iraqi army during the Rashid Rebellion of 1941, the siege being lifted after a short struggle. Towards the end of the war it became an important airbase on the southern route between Great Britain and the Soviet Union. By 1956, however, it was a strategic staging post, mainly for military aircraft bound for Iran, India and the Far East. It was also a vital SIGINT post due to its close proximity to the southern republics of the Soviet Union.

For almost three months Peter worked as an R/T DF Op 1A corporal at Camp Ddibben. The work was an extension of his training he had received at Hathwell, namely listening to transmissions in Russian between pilots and ground staff. When the frequency was inactive Peter often tuned another radio set to Radio Luxembourg, only to be brought back to reality when a Russian ground controller started to count-*raz, dva, tri…….. desyat'* -*KCM*? When he had reached ten, Peter logged the numbers and the KCM or 'How do you hear me?' in Russian and then scribbled CBY or 'I hear you satisfactorily', which was the response of the pilot being contacted. Then Peter concentrated on the message which often produced a series of numbers and some vital information.

In his first letter home to his mother Peter wrote mainly about his leisure activities.

"I am now in Iraq and working hard at an RAF camp. There are many distractions here- an open-air cinema and an excellent swimming pool. I have also played football for one of the section teams called the Sparklers, winning the station cup in the process. I have also been learning to sail on Lake Habbaniya nearby and I have met King Faisal at the Rest and Leave Centre."

Peter often wondered, whilst he was enjoying his carefree life in Camp Ddibben, whether SIGINT operators in the Soviet Union were having such a wonderful life as himself. However, little was known about the organisation called GRU which intercepted and deciphered communications from the western powers.

In a second letter to his mother Peter gave her more information about the foreigners who worked on the camp.

"I have had only slight contact with the local population who work here- mostly Arabs, Assyrians and a few Jews. The Arabs, mostly Sunnis, wear either traditional robes or old western style suits. A few don discarded RAF jackets. Our cleaner, Abdul, an Arab of about fifty, is working in order to afford a second and younger wife and he is helped by his son, Rashid, who is able to speak quite good English. The civilian café here employs a number of Assyrian waiters and a group of Jewish merchants also come to the camp once a week in order to sell watches and all sorts of jewellery."

Nevertheless, he did not tell his mother that there was an existence of suspicion between the Jews and the Arabs since the early 1950s after a series of pogroms which resulted in an exodus of many Jews from Iraq.

Peter was doing his best to learn Arabic, mainly colloquial Iraqi, such as 'la taq'ad fish shêms-don't sit in the sun' or 'la tishrab hel mai-don't drink this water'. Also RAF personnel destined to do guard duty had to learn sufficient Arabic to stop and detain Arabs wandering about in the camp at night. Peter's attempts to prevent Arabs coming into the camp in the early hours of the morning was often met with responses in English and disbelief that a British airman should try and learn any Arabic at all. In fact he felt so foolish approaching Arabs on their way to work and telling them to stop or he would use his rifle. Apart from the occasional visits to Lake Habbaniya and a short trip to Falluja to enrol on an Arabic course Peter was allowed only one excursion to Ctesiphon which contained the remains of the largest unsupported arch of the ancient world. Experts believed that it was the widest and highest single-spanned vault of baked bricks built in the third century A.D. It was here that a cheeky Arab boy sold Peter a brick from the arch for one dinar, even though later he saw hundreds of such bricks lying scattered around.

June arrived and Peter was beginning to wonder when the important part of Operation *Babylon* would materialise. After a night spent in a hut in the cool desert quite a way from the signals unit and, trying to cope with the demands of direction finding, Peter hoped to spend the morning by the swimming pool and to sleep in the shade until midday. However, he was woken at ten o'clock and summoned to command headquarters. A young-looking squadron leader informed him that on the following day he would have to proceed to Baghdad and assume a new identity as a student of languages. At last the important part of Peter's mission to Iraq was going to take place.

The squadron leader, who was a member of ODAT as well, had the following information to impart to Peter, "From this point onwards you are no longer Peter Smith, but Peter White. Your code name will still be *Abyadh*. Actually, the four of you involved in Operation *Babylon* will be leaving Camp Ddibben separately tomorrow to take up positions in and around Kirkuk, Mosul, Basra, and of course for you, Baghdad.
Your hotel in the capital is called Kadimiya, the telephone number of which you have already in your possession. You have been enrolled on a beginner's

course to study Arabic. I am giving you an emergency number in case there are any problems. Furthermore, if you write to your mother, you must send the letters to me where they will be censored."

The squadron leader paused and then continued with his instructions to Peter.

"You will need to pack all your RAF belongings together with your 1250 and put them in store this afternoon. Civilian clothing has been issued to you as well as two hundred dinars extra allowance. You will leave the camp at nine o'clock tomorrow. By the way a two-way radio is already in your hotel room, but only use it in an emergency. Otherwise use the normal telephone service to contact the other operatives involved in Operation *Babylon* You must meet them at six o'clock this evening in my office to make final arrangements."

So, at six o'clock Peter, that is to say *Abyadh,* met *Aswad, Akhdhar* and *Azraq* in the squadron leader's office in order to make plans for contacting one another. *Aswad* suggested that a colloquial Iraqi phrase *'raml el chôr hârr'* or 'the sand of the desert is hot' would be a good introductory sentence to begin any conversation by telephone or at any meeting in Iraq. Peter said he needed to think about this, but after a short while agreed with *Aswad.* Then followed a long conversation in English and Russian and a decision was made that telephone conversations would be in Russian because so many educated people in Iraq spoke English and in any case Peter's knowledge of Arabic was extremely limited. Finally with a *'fi amàn Illàh'* the operatives said goodbye and left the office.

Tired, but elated, Peter decided that he had one more job to do before leaving Camp Ddibben and that was to contact Stefan, whom he had seen from time to time. In this respect he failed because his friend had left for a destination unknown that very morning.

"Well at least I have given him my telephone number in Baghdad if he wishes to contact me," said Peter to himself.

At eight o'clock Peter retired to bed after completing all that he had to do, eagerly waiting for the morning which would be the start of a new adventure, or so he hoped.

As arranged he was picked up by a cheerful looking Arab taxi driver in a brand new Dodge and was transported via Falluja to the capital of Iraq. His first impression of Baghdad was not favourable since he arrived at the height of what seemed like a sand storm, but was rather different to the one he had experienced when he first arrived in Iraq. When he stepped out of the taxi in front of Hotel Kadimiya and paid the driver, he had to contend with the choking yellow and brown dust which clogged his hair and caused his eyes to smart. This was the second time he had to contend with these conditions and he was not pleased.

Hotel Kadimiya, situated near the River Tigris, was not disappointing. In spite of the weather Peter managed to look up at its quite imposing façade and noticed that all the windows had white shutters with elaborate overhanging balconies called *shenashily*. He found out later that similar balconies existed to the rear of the hotel as well. The Arab receptionist gave him the key to room eight and shouted for a furtive looking porter to help him carry his belongings to his room on the second floor. He handed this porter a tip of one dinar and stepped into the bedroom which was situated at the back of the hotel.

Opposite the door into the room was an open window with faded curtains drawn back either side. At one time they had been blue in colour but were now almost white with age. On the left was an ornate iron bed to the side of which stood a small cupboard made of pine which acted as a dressing table as well. Under the bed Peter found the two-way radio which the squadron leader at Camp Ddibben had mentioned the day before. On the wall to the right were wooden pegs on which the occupant could hang clothes or other objects. There was also a side door which led into a sort of en-suite bathroom and a primitive shower. The wooden floor was covered in different coloured rugs and in the centre was a large pine table onto which Peter placed his briefcase containing his diary and important papers.

Peter looked out of the window and could see the River Tigris glistening in the sun. Everywhere there seemed to be men leading donkeys along paths down towards the river. These donkeys looked weak and pathetic and seemed reluctant to move on occasions. The paths were slippery and from time to time these poor creatures slid from side to side, throwing up stones all around them. He could hear in the distance the barking and howling of wild dogs and the sound of the capital's noisy traffic. He went onto the balcony, took a deep breath of warm air, ignored the smells which hovered around his mouth and then shut the window. He needed sleep, so within a minute or two he was dreaming of anticipating the unexpected.

For the next few days Peter tried to explore Baghdad. His usual pastime was to visit the various *sûqs* or markets. In this bustling city there were either permanent or ambulatory *sûqs*. The larger ones included goldsmiths, dyers, tailors and other workmen employing their trade. Peter was often fascinated by his favourite market's arched world of alleyways inhabited mainly by tailors and metal workers sitting cross-legged, whilst they stitched cloth and hammered metal goods to sell.

On one occasion Peter had the opportunity to visit a large *sûq* in the centre of Baghdad which contained in the middle of it a mosque, so that both sellers and buyers could carry out their activities in a clean and honourable manner. A visit to an Arab restaurant in the market was a delight. Not only did it have a roof to keep the temperature low, but it also served wonderful *kelouh* kebabs and chicken with rice. The rest of the capital for Peter appeared to be a city of public steam baths, roadside butchers selling *halal* meat and children playing in the streets.

Whilst Peter White alias Peter Smith, code name *Abyadh,* was settling in the signals unit at Camp Ddibben and then proceeding to a language school in Baghdad, Asya Amampourov, code name *Ferdowsi,* and her family had managed to reach Tehran as the first part of their KPOK mission-Operation *Azady.* After suffering a journey of almost 1,300 kilometres from Moscow to Baku, the family checked out of the hotel in the capital of Azerbaijan and travelled, escorted by a Red Army patrol, along the western shore of the Caspian Sea through Ali Bayramli and Astara to the Iranian border. It was then quite easy for the Amampourovs, with the help of Soviet border guards and communist sympathisers, to slip over to Ardebil.

As soon as they crossed the border Ali explained to the rest of the family that from now on all of them had to be extremely careful to insist that they were genuine refugees. Noticing the anxious looks on the faces of his wife and daughter, he sought to warn them again of the dangers which might confront them.

"If the Shah's State Security Service, the SAVAK, finds out that we are not political refugees, we may be subject to the torture methods mentioned in Camp Badkube."

"Why bring this up now?" thought Asya. "What a pessimistic attitude. It spoils the romanticism of being a Soviet agent."

The Amampourov's first sighting of Tehran was when they descended from the Elbruz Mountains followed by the slopes of Shemiran. At the foot of Mount Damavand the capital was experiencing its brief spring weather. The *jubes* or open air canals lined with plane trees running alongside the main roads had become raging torrents. All the members of the family breathed a sigh of relief when they saw the large boulevards of the capital based on a French design.

"It gets very hot here in the summer-forty-two degrees centigrade, and very cold in the winter-eight degrees," declared their communist guide who took them to a cheap, but respectable, hotel near Ferdowsi Square. "You will not see me again," he added. "Remember your surname is now Amampour, not Amampourov."

Ali was pleased with the first few days in Tehran, although he was rather disturbed by the shouts of '*to quashangi'*-'you are so pretty', remarks made by a number of uncouth men and directed towards his daughter whenever the family went out together. Yes, he knew she was beautiful, but the attention she received from certain elements of the male population was very disconcerting.

"Why did Allah create my daughter so that men cannot help but comment on her beauty? There must be a reason," he said mournfully.

Indeed, there was a reason, especially for the Kremlin and its servant, KPOK. They had already considered that Asya would be able to infiltrate a male dominated western organisation and become excellent bait to trap male spies.

At the beginning of May Ali received notification from KPOK that his son and daughter might be needed for missions in Iraq which was a breeding ground for communism and nationalism. Whereas the Sunni Muslims were happy to support Pan-Arab nationalism, some Shia Muslims were attracted to communism along with other minorities. The Soviet Union realised that Shia Muslims and Kurds could play an active role in changing the political order in Iraq. Locating, infiltrating and even eradicating British agents in this country would be helpful in some ways in destabilising the regime and remove obstacles to possible revolution.

Ali broke the news to his son, Parviz, first of all.

"KPOK has informed me that a British spy has been located at an air force base near Lake Habbaniya in Iraq. We know that his code name is *Abyadh* and that his full name is Peter Smith. Next week you will need to proceed to Iraq with the help of Iraqi communists and they will find work for you in this air force base. Try and find out all you can about this person and report back to me. Be careful, however, because some airmen there know Russian and, if you speak this language, they will be suspicious."

Ali had a special reason for wanting his son to become a special agent in Iraq. In 1948 he had the opportunity to meet the leader of the Iraqi Communist Party in person and fully sympathised with his aims and objectives.

A month later Ali approached his daughter.

"Asya. Your brother has found the British agent, formerly called Peter Smith, but he has changed his name to Peter White. He is now posing as a student at a language school in Baghdad. I am rather unhappy for you to join Parviz there, but the decision is up to you."

Asya's eyes lit up and her father could see that she was ready for further excitement in another country and would agree to serve the Soviet Union.

"In that case, Asya," he said. "Parviz will enrol you both on the same course as this Peter White. I shall make arrangements for you to accompany your Uncle Daryouse who has agreed to go with you to

Baghdad."

The journey to Baghdad with a group of pilgrims from Tehran lasted three days, travelling via Saveh, Asad, Kormanshah and Qasr-e-Shirm before reaching the Iraqi border. Both Asya and her uncle as well as the other travellers on the coach noticed the devastation of earthquakes in the mountainous areas and all of them had to be vaccinated before they could enter Iraq due to a severe outbreak of smallpox. A number of stops were made on the way to allow the pilgrims to pray and for everybody to sleep at the various ramshackle hotels. Asya's concern was that she might catch malaria, so she insisted on covering herself with a mosquito net at night.

After her first encounter with Peter in the language school Asya wrote in her diary,
"Peter White or *Abyadh* is about nineteen years old, good looking with dark hair and blue eyes and definitely not over- nourished."
Asya had been told that most western men were imperial, pompous, ate too much and drank alcohol all the time. She continued to write down her own impressions of Peter and she was delighted that he did not display any negative qualities.

"He has a firm and determined look and likes talking and deliberating," she wrote. "His vivid blue eyes flash when he examines people in detail and his face displays his emotions. If he dislikes somebody, for example, one of the French students who is arrogant, his features change and become distorted, probably in anger. But, if he takes a liking to somebody, like my brother, his features light up and he shows true affection He also has boundless energy. I am not sure of his feelings towards me. I must try and gain his confidence, but on the other hand I must reject his advances."

Asya had to remember that Peter was a British spy and she was a Soviet agent. She and her brother had been told to infiltrate the language school and to find out from Peter what the intentions of his country were in Iraq.

Ibrahim's favourite technique as a teacher was to use the phrase '*Kêf taqûl hàdha fi arabi?*' or 'How do you say this in Arabic?' During Peter's fourth lesson and the Amampours' second the whole group was faced with a translation into English of the Arabic phrase '*indi sundûk fîl bêt*'. Ibrahim asked the students to think carefully. "Who can give me the meaning of this sentence in English?" he said.

Everybody appeared to look blank apart from Peter who put up his hand and said triumphantly that it meant 'I have a big trunk in the house'. All the students were amazed by Peter's knowledge of the Arabic word *sundûk*.

Peter accepted their praise with a gratified smile.

Parviz and his sister also smiled because they knew the answer as well, but kept quiet. "How did you know this word, Peter?" asked Asya.

"Because I know Russian and the Arabic word is the same in Russian-*sundûk*".

Without realising what they were saying and almost in unison both Asya and Parviz could not hold back what their father had advised them not to reveal.

"We know Russian as well because we were both born in Moscow and lived there for many years before moving to Tehran. We are Tajiks." Peter was flabbergasted by this news, but secretly pleased. His reaction was predictable, and he said to himself

"Perhaps I have found two Soviet agents in Iraq. They seem to be friendly and understanding, but you can never tell. I must cultivate their friendship before I inform ODAT of their existence."

So, Peter decided to become more acquainted with the two students from Iran, or maybe the Soviet Union, and invited them back to his hotel to find out whether his new 'friends' were actively involved in espionage here in Baghdad. Thus, the three students' evenings were spent in Hotel Kadimiya discussing the Arabic course and then politics and foreign affairs. All of them were delighted because they could converse in Russian and occasionally in Arabic.

"This is much better than the endless quarrels and disagreements I had with my father," said Asya quite naively to her brother, who on the other hand had to keep reminding her that their main task in Baghdad was to infiltrate British intelligence.

It was Asya who tended to monopolise the conversation at first. Ibrahim had invited his nine students to an evening meal at his grand house in one of the residential areas of the capital. Peter thought that what had taken place was a great success and that he had learnt more about Arab customs and etiquette than in a classroom situation. Asya, however, was critical of certain aspects of Peter's behaviour and the choice of words used. In a gentle manner she complained of his lack of knowledge of what to do when invited to an evening meal by a Sunni Arab.

"Peter. You made a terrible mistake right at the beginning of the visit," she declared. "You asked after Ibrahim's family but did not use correct Arabic words."

Peter's face seemed to show some remorse, but he was not offended.

"I promise to remember this in future, Asya, "he replied. "I noticed that you did not seem too happy when I started to explain in Arabic about the antics of my neighbour's pet dog back home in Wales."

"No," said Asya. "You do not mention a dog, or for that matter any animal or unclean thing, unless you prefix it with the Arabic word *'hàshàkum'*".

Although Peter thought that Asya was being rather

curt and to a certain extent rather bossy, he nevertheless thanked her for this important explanation. Then, he tried to exonerate himself and said,

"But I shook hands with Ibrahim on entering his house, removed my hat and received the coffee offered to me with my right hand and accepted only three glasses. Moreover, in reply to our host's *'sharraftum'* at the end of the meal, I said *'sharraf Allâh qadrek'* and everybody seemed quite pleased."

If only Peter could read Asya's thoughts, he would have realised that she was proud of him and the progress he had made in learning Arabic. She was also happy with the evenings which she and her brother spent at Hotel Kadimiya with Peter. As she said to him on a number of occasions,

"Peter. You are what we call in Russian a true *'drug'* or friend and we can talk quite openly and intimately- *'po dusham'*". Peter was also excited by the chain of events and this strange development in the field of espionage and intrigue, particularly since he was convinced that his new 'friends' were Soviet agents. He felt that he had infiltrated the enemy camp, so to speak, without too much difficulty. In any case he considered he had the upper hand because he could monitor the situation and report back to ODAT that he had made contact with Soviet agents and would be able to feed them, that is to say the Amampours, with disinformation.

The main topic of conversation at the evening gatherings soon switched to the crisis that was building up over the Suez Canal. Most Arabs were aware that Gamal Abdul Nasser of Egypt had attempted to nationalise the Canal in July. Parviz asked directly what Peter thought the British would do. "Well," explained Peter, "my country is still involved in operations called 'in aid of civil powers' in Malaysia, Cyprus and Kenya, so I do not think that anything will be done immediately. It is a crisis that might blow over with a touch of diplomacy."

Feeding false information to Soviet agents was the name of the game for British spies and Peter was enjoying this role.

"But the Suez Canal is an important waterway for British trade and security, is it not?" said Parviz emphatically.

Peter's answer was carefully thought out.

"Yes, that is true. We are aware that Nasser is the head of a movement which appeals to Arabs in the Middle East and that he is dedicated to ending imperialism, the monarchies and feudalism in the Arab world. Even though British forces are being attacked in the area of the Suez Canal by guerrillas connected to the Moslem Brotherhood and the communists, I do not think that Great Britain will send more troops to that region. We are committed to other parts of the world. Besides the French have a part to play in this debacle as well."

At this point Peter noticed that Asya was writing something down in Tajik in a jotter. He asked her what she was doing and he was told that she was making notes about their wonderful evenings together.

"For posterity," she said with a forced smile. Parviz, however, was persistent with his questioning.

"Can you guess what you prime minister, Anthony Eden, intends to do?" he asked.

Peter replied dryly,

"All I know is that Nuri es Said, the prime minister of Iraq, has told Eden to stand up to Nasser over the nationalisation of the Suez Canal and has promised to send an Iraqi brigade to Jordan to reinforce the Arab Legion there in the event of an attack by guerrillas."

Asya continued to write down more of the Tajik script in her jotter. Peter looked over her shoulder and murmured,

"Oh. It is a pity I do not know this language. Perhaps you can teach me some day, if possible."

Asya agreed, but she was interrupted by Parviz who wished to impart some important information to his friend.

"I will give you some interesting news, Peter. The Soviet Union has decided to supply Egypt with tanks, MIG fighters and Ilyushin bombers as well as destroyers, minesweepers and radar equipment."

He said all of this as if he were planning this supply of equipment to Egypt himself.

Then, without realising it Peter advanced the conversation and gave away certain secret information.

"I am sure that, if Nasser continues with nationalization, he will anger not only Great Britain, but also the French. I know for certain that the French have landed troops in Cyprus and that the Israelis are concerned over Nasser's support for the Fedayeen raids into their territory. So, I expect three countries will invade Egypt if things are not settled."

Thus, the conversations about the Suez Crisis continued late into the night, which was a worry for Asya who had to be back in a woman's hostel by ten o'clock. For a female to be out in Baghdad after this time could lead to catastrophe.

Meanwhile Peter became bolder in his approach to Asya. She bewitched him with her intelligence and beauty and he felt that gradually and quietly he was falling in love with her. All this was happening in spite of the fact that in the past he tended to despise women generally. Yet, in Asya he could find so far no physical or mental flaw. She was perhaps opinionated and bossy, but Peter considered this to be a strength in a woman's character.

One evening both Parviz and Asya told Peter the

reason why they were in Baghdad, but they twisted some of the truth. They described in detail their life in Moscow and that they had been forced to become Soviet agents, which was not strictly true in Parviz's case.

"So, they are Soviet agents," thought Peter and at the same time he became more perplexed and confused about their identities.

Asya looked Peter straight in the eyes and said,

"The Soviet authorities sent us to Iran to destabilise the Shah's regime, but then we were sent to Iraq to foster discontent in this country as well because we speak both Arabic and Farsi."

By now Peter was becoming completely confused, especially when Asya added to her story.

"All I wanted to do was to become a famous ballerina, but I was recruited, well persuaded, by an organisation to complete one mission for my country before continuing with my training in Moscow. Now we have both become disillusioned with the whole enterprise and are looking for a way out. Even my desire to continue with my life's dream is waning day by day."

Peter wondered whether they were telling him the whole truth. Why were they at a language school in Baghdad to learn Arabic when they could speak the language so well? Were they hoping to become double agents after revealing everything to him? He did not know what to think. All he could do at this juncture was to keep an open mind on what they said and what they did.

On one occasion, however, Peter was extremely upset when he noticed that the box which contained his diary had been tampered with. Had Asya or Parviz, or perhaps both, been looking through the pages when he was out of the room? The contents of his diary did not reveal anything incriminating or worthwhile and in any case he had written everything down in Welsh. The cover of the diary was emblazoned with the red Dragon of Wales rampant and the words '*y ddraig goch ddyry gychwyn*'. Surely no foreigner would understand this ancient language? He was more concerned, however, about Asya. What was she writing about in Tajik, a language which he could not decipher?

As tension over the Suez Crisis increased between July and October, so did the thought in Peter's mind revolve around perhaps more espionage and intrigue to come.

"Do you think that your country, together with France and Israel, will invade Egypt now? "asked Parviz again.

"No. We have been over this before," retorted Peter. "Great Britain has a lot to lose if a force is sent to the Suez Canal. In any case America is against an invasion. What will the Soviet Union's response be if an invasion does take place?"

"Well. I am sure it will try and speak out against aggression and hope to restore peace given the opportunity. Military help for Egypt will be out of the question due to the fact that there are geographical obstacles and there are no Soviet ships in the Mediterranean," said Parviz.

As the meetings in Hotel Kadimiya continued Peter, in spite of everything, still felt that he was falling madly in love with Asya, perhaps even against his will. In his usual exaggerated manner he began to philosophise.

"I have up to now enjoyed doing mischief in the world. Deceit is not new to me and my heart is still full of poison. I have like the devil wandered proud and carefree- a stranger to heaven and earth. I have been lonely, an isolate, torn by inner conflict as a person who has bowed to fate and pathological tendencies."

Then, every time he looked at Asya he knew that he was beginning to change. He spoke to her in Polish so that she would not understand him.

"I have been reborn by your presence to enjoy innocent delights, hope and freedom. I, who have scorned kindness, love and pity, am no longer a victim of cynicism. I am sad. However, because I love you, Asya. I never thought it would be possible to love anybody, but you are so different."

Every weekend, usually on a Saturday, it was

Ibrahim's custom to take two or three of his students on a sight-seeing tour of Baghdad, explaining in Arabic the function and sometimes the history of certain buildings. On the last Saturday in September he picked Peter and the two Pakistani students, Sahil and Rehman, to accompany him on what he called 'a romantic journey'. As they passed a large mosque they were jostled by a large group of radical Islamists who were carrying placards and banners and complaining about Iraq's lack of support for President Nasser and demanding that ties with Great Britain should be broken. These mainly Sunni Muslims virtually pushed and carried the three students and their tutor as far as a square near Shorza Market where they were met by another group demanding the withdrawal of British troops from Iraq.

Two Arabs were holding a green and white flag on which were written in Arabic 'There is no god, but Allah and Mohammed is his Prophet'. Underneath these words were two crossed swords. Ibrahim pointed to the flag and explained,

"The swords represent truth and justice. They are symbols in support of the freedom of conscience and represent a magnetic force to pull all people to the true faith-Islam."

"But the sword has been used by Muslims in the past to physically attack the enemies of Islam," interjected Peter.

"No," said Ibrahim. "This is a misconception by the

west. The Islamic Swords of Truth and Justice are symbolic only and are used to eliminate all falsehood as light wipes away darkness. The spread of Islam can only be achieved by the force of truth, reason and logic. The Islamic Sword of Truth especially is also the sword of intellectual and convincing argument that will conquer the minds of….."

His words were cut short by a rifle shot which echoed across the square when the bullet struck a bollard. A second shot grazed Peter's right arm and he yelled in pain. As a small amount of blood trickled out of his arm, he noticed that the same bullet had struck Ibrahim who was lying on the ground in agony and screaming. Peter noticed that his tutor was holding his left leg from which was flowing a vast amount of blood from a wound just below the knee. Within seconds the square was empty apart from Peter, Ibrahim, Sahil, Rehman and a couple of Arabs who anxiously rushed to help the two victims. Peter indicated that it was only his tutor who needed assistance. Who had fired the two shots and why? Were they aimed at him or Ibrahim? From the corner of his eye Peter also noticed that the green and white flag about which they were discussing lay abandoned on the ground nearby.

Soon the square was filled with uniformed policemen and an ambulance was called to take Ibrahim to hospital. It was obvious that he had lost a lot of blood and needed an operation to remove the bullet from his leg. Peter on the other hand was treated by a doctor on the spot who happened to be one of the two Arabs who had remained to give assistance. As he was being examined more people began to appear and with them a few witnesses who confirmed that they had seen the glint of a rifle in the window of one of the hotels overlooking the square. After interviewing them four policemen rushed into a shabby looking hotel and emerged to ask Peter was he well enough to accompany them to a room on the hotel's second floor.

On entering the bedroom Peter saw the figure of a man lying on his back near an open window with a revolver in his right hand and a discarded rifle by his side. A bullet hole in his chest seemed to suggest that he had taken his own life with the revolver after firing with the rifle on the people in the square. Peter went over to the lifeless body and looked at a short clumsily built man with powerful shoulders, dark rumpled hair and a pleasant face in spite of the distortion of death. Suddenly Peter felt suffocated in this clammy bedroom. The room whirled round and round and everywhere seemed to become dark, for Peter had recognised immediately that the dead person was none other than the British agent from Mosul, or to give him his code name, *Azraq*.

He looked again at the corpse of the British spy and

let out a suppressed cry. At the same time he was conscious that one of the policemen was questioning the proprietor of the hotel.

"He booked in yesterday for a few days," answered the owner of the hotel. "My opinion was that he seemed normal, but rather mournful. He asked for his evening meal to be brought up to his room. He had one visitor this morning, a Kurd, I think, but on reflection I did not see this stranger depart at all. I heard voices raised in anger on occasions This visitor must have slipped away when there was a commotion going on outside."

He then went on to describe the Kurd.

Meanwhile Peter's mind was in a turmoil and said to himself, .

"*Azraq* did not know Ibrahim. So, he must have been shooting at me. But why has he committed suicide?"

Sitting down on a wicker chair Peter gazed once more at the British agent's body and at the doctor who was examining him. He then turned to an inspector of the police who had just entered the room and said,

"I notice that the revolver is a World War I United States army issue- a colt 45 automatic and the rifle is probably a Winchester. I know the dead person, but I cannot understand why he was trying to kill me and how he got hold of these firearms."

The inspector ignored Peter because he wanted to question the doctor who was still bending over

Azraq's body. He then faced Peter and said,
"The answer is quite simple. It looks as if these weapons were brought in by another person, probably the Kurd mentioned by the owner of this hotel. And, by the way, your acquaintance did not commit suicide because he has been dead since this morning. It appears that he was garrotted and then shot in the chest and then the revolver was placed in his right hand after death. You need to accompany me to the main police station here in Baghdad and make a statement."

Peter realised he could not do this because it would compromise Operation *Babylon*, so he gave the inspector a telephone number in order to contact an important Arab official who was a member of ODAT and that was the end of the matter. At the same time Peter began to ponder over the chain of events and the fate of *Azraq*. Only two days before this incident the operator from Mosul had contacted him about unrest which was building up there. Due to the ethnic mix of Arabs, Syriacs, Armenians, Turkmens, Jews and Christians *Azraq* was worried that communist sympathisers had been able to stir up trouble. This was further exacerbated by the Kurds who at the same time were demanding an independent Kurdistan and were being supported by the Soviet Union in order to foment further discord.

Was *Azraq* killed by a Kurd because he knew too

much about the situation in Mosul? How did the killer and the deceased know he was going to be in a crowd on that very Saturday? Also, did the crowd virtually carry Peter, Ibrahim and the two Pakistani by chance or on purpose to the square near Shorza Market? Peter was suspicious of his friends, Parviz and Asya. They knew about Ibrahim's 'romantic journey' on that fateful day. Surely they were not implicated because they had assured him that their activities as Soviet agents were over, but were they telling him the truth?

Once outside the hotel Peter hobbled to the tattered and torn flag which lay abandoned on the ground and looked more closely at the two swords below the Arabic writing. What had Ibrahim told him about the swords of truth and justice which were intertwined? He remembered somewhere that for Muslims truth and justice went together. Peter had always considered that Islamists believed in the theory of retributive justice-a life for a life, a wound for a wound and a stripe for a stripe. Perhaps in strict Muslim countries this was the norm, but generally justice was an expression of the truth of Allah's teachings-Allah the Merciful.

That same evening Peter met Parviz and Asya in Hotel Kadimiya and both seemed to be concerned when they saw his bandaged arm.
"Did they catch the Kurd who tried to kill you?" asked Parviz in all innocence.

Peter's head began to spin. How did Parviz know about the events which had taken place and how did he know a Kurd was involved? Had he arranged for *Azraq* to be garrotted? Clearing his head, Peter just said that he was alright and changed the subject. Instead, he mentioned the flag which he had seen and wondered about the swords of truth and justice.

"Peter. You know that truth is not telling lies or falsehoods," explained Parviz. "In Farsi we call the sword of truth *'shamsir haghiga'*. Only our prophet, Mohammed, brought us truth, but unbelievers only believe in that which is not true. Those who reject the truth of his word are victims to the vices of sin and corruption which will prepare them for damnation."

Peter was intrigued and decided to explore the themes of truth and justice further.

"Islam's Sword of Truth must be a powerful weapon. What will damnation be like for those who tell lies?" asked Peter.

Asya then broke into the conversation.

"My father says that for those who do not tell the truth there will be no shade, only a blazing fire and shadows of smoke and sinners will be subjected to sparks which look like yellow camels." Of course Peter did not understand her reference to 'yellow camels'.

It was then that Asya suddenly put both her arms around Peter's neck and innocently hugged him.

Realising that she had acted in rather a coquettish and inappropriate manner, she moved away from him, staring directly into his eyes, and said,

"I can tell you, Peter, that, if you were to become a Muslim, your fate after death on earth will be that you will enjoy in heaven cool shades and spring water as well as eating fruits from the Garden of Eternity. This is the final bliss of salvation."

As Parviz and Asya spoke Peter thought of his mother's description of heaven and hell as propounded by the Roman Catholic Church. What similarities!

Before dispersing Asya asked Peter whether he would ever consider converting to Islam. Peter shrugged his shoulders and did not answer. What were his friends up to? First of all, they were trying to kill him, although he had no definite proof of this, and now they wanted to convert him to what seemed to him to be an alien faith. He needed to know whether his friends were still Soviet agents or whether they had decided to abandon espionage activities. After they had left he was on the phone to ODAT, relaying what had transpired that day. He was, however, mortified when he was told that Parviz and Asya were still enemy agents and he needed to be careful. He was also told that there were bugging devices in his hotel bedroom, but that ODAT would remove them as soon as possible. Furthermore, he was informed that he should continue to infiltrate the enemy camp by pretending to remain their friends.

By the end of October British, French and Israeli forces had attacked Egypt which meant that SIGINT and the agents of Operation *Desert Sand* and Operation *Babylon* were on full alert. The operatives in Basra and Kirkuk made several contacts with Peter who was also told that a replacement was due to be installed to replace *Azraq* in Mosul. In early November he received two important phone messages, one from *Akhdhar* in Basra and the other from *Aswad* in Kirkuk. Both had important information for Peter and requested an urgent meeting in the Iraqi capital.

Akhdhar's call was persuasive and, speaking the first five words in Arabic, he explained in Russian about the situation in Basra,
"*Raml el chôl hârr, Abyadh.* I have reason to suspect that the Shia Muslims in this city on the Shatt al Arab are preparing to destabilise, not only Basra, but the whole of Iraq. Both Iranian nationals and Iraqi communists are involved. Can I see you soon in Baghdad?"
Aswad's call was less specific, but equally important.
"*Raml el chôl hârr, Abyadh.* Both the Kurds and Arab communists here in Kirkuk are up to something. I need to meet you soon to explain everything in detail."
Peter gave both operatives the name of a café in the

Ath Thaura district of Baghdad and arranged to meet them there in the evening in three days time.

At first Peter intended to meet the two operatives alone but realised that he did not have the confidence or sufficient knowledge of Arabic to visit a café in a poor and dangerous part of Baghdad. In spite of the progress he had made in the language, he was aware of his limitations. He, therefore, sought the advice of Parviz who suggested that they should both go there dressed in conventional Arab clothing. A new tutor had replaced Ibrahim, who was still in hospital, and he was delighted to give them information about typical clothing worn by male Arabs and at the same time teach them important words relating to each item.

Aziz, the new tutor, as was his custom, knew about the garments to be worn and arranged after Arabic lessons to show Peter and Parviz a collection of these clothes which was kept in lockers in the language school.

"First of all," he explained. "a Sunni Arab wears a *zebun,* a long dress which is slipped on like an overcoat and strapped to the waist by a belt."

Peter and Parviz each chose a *zebun* and put it on without any problem.

"Over the *zebun* you need to wear a loose overcoat without sleeves woven in light brown homespun woollen yarn," continued Aziz.

With the minimum amount of fuss both men tried on the overcoats. Parviz chose the correct fit, but Peter was rather slight and had some difficulty in adjusting the garment to his body.

All the time Aziz was increasing the two students' vocabulary by including Arabic words connected, not only to the clothing, but also to measurement, colour and of course to various parts of the body.

"You need to put on a *kufiyah* or type of oversized handkerchief to cover your head, neck and shoulders as well as a black *azal* or rope to tie around the *kufiyah* to keep it in place," said Aziz, showing infinite patience.

Peter and Parviz went to the mirror to adjust their headgear, whilst Aziz brought them sandals for their feet.

"This is the exciting part of espionage," said Peter to himself as he saw his reflection in the mirror and admired Parviz's efforts as well.

The day arrived when Peter was to meet *Akhdhar* and *Aswad*. Dressed in Arab garb he and Parviz proceeded on foot to the café where they were due to meet the two operatives. They pushed their way through crowded streets and tried to avoid bicycles, donkeys, horses and carts and other forms of transport. The noise was deafening. Even though it was early evening vendors were still trying to sell fruit and vegetables from makeshift stalls, whereas others were trying to get rid of cheap merchandise. Peter and his friend often had to jump out of the way when taxi drivers wound their way down streets, sounding their horns and shouting '*bàlek, bàlek!*' to all and sundry.

Akhdhar and *Aswad* were already in the café when both men arrived. They were also dressed in Arab clothes, each smoking a multi-stemmed glass-based water pipe called a *shisha*.

Both welcomed Peter with a '*Raml el chôl hârr*', forgetting that Parviz was there. Peter replied with the same words and said,

"I've tried this before, but it took me a long time before I became accustomed to it."

He had indeed experienced smoking the hookah on his trips to the *sûqs* of Baghdad and was often surprised when many Arabs declared they would rather be deprived of food than give up their *shishas*.

So, Peter and Parviz joined the other two and sucked at the stems operated by water filtration and indirect heat.

"What a pleasant surprise," said Peter to Parviz in Arabic. "This hubble bubble smoke of herbal fruits is definitely not disagreeable at all."

He took a deep breath and sucked even more violently at the pipe. The sweet aroma caused him to splutter at first, but after a while he became pleasantly light-headed.

An hour later *Akhdhar* informed Peter that a separate

room had been allocated for them to introduce their reports on events in Kirkuk and Basra. Parviz understood that Peter wished to converse with his friends alone and indicated that he would remain in the hookah room and then join them later. Partly in English and Russian Peter started his report which he found difficult to deliver due to the effects of smoking the *shisha*.

"We must take stock of what we have found out in Iraq so far. I must admit that part of my mission in Baghdad has been rather disappointing. All I can ascertain here is that communism is attracting a small number of Arabs, especially the young. In fact, communism and nationalism appear to be potent anti-government forces. However, I have located two Soviet agents, one of whom is in the room next door. They insist that they are giving up the process of spying, but I cannot be sure."

Akhdhar and *Aswad* seemed to agree with Peter's analysis of the situation. *Akhdhar* spoke first, referring to his notes and reported on what in his opinion was happening in Basra.

"I have not located any Soviet agents. Here in Basra the greatest threat is from Iran. I have mingled with porters, ferrymen and taxi drivers who ply their trade from the city's waterfront across the Shatt al Arab and along the Iraq/Iran border. There are some communist sympathisers there, but I am certain that war between the two countries will break out sometime in the near future."

Peter made a mental note of what *Akhdhar* had found out and said that he would report back to ODAT as soon as possible.

Peter then turned to *Aswad* and asked him to make his report. This operator from Kirkuk also looked at his notes and said,

"Here in this city of stone and alabaster there is a sense of rebellion. As you know, Kirkuk straddles the trade route between Turkey and Iran and I am sure Soviet agents are up to something there. However, it is the Kurds, helped by the Soviet Union, who are waiting to overthrow the legitimate government in Iraq and to create a Kurdistan."

"That is what *Azraq* in Mosul was probably going to tell me before he died, that is to say murdered, in Baghdad by a Kurd who was also trying to kill me," shouted Peter, remembering the events of September. It was obvious by the look on the faces of the two operators that they did not realise that *Azraq* had been murdered.

After explaining to the two operatives about the events surrounding *Azraq*'s death Peter then tried to sum up.

"Well, we have a situation here in Iraq whereby King Faisal and his prime minister, Nuri es Said, are confronted by communists, nationalists, the Kurds and even the Iranians."

"Correct." said *Akhdhar,* "Moreover, I have heard that there could be conflict between the communists and members of an organisation called *Da'awra,* which is especially strong in Najaf and Karbala. There have also been minor uprisings against Faisal's regime by the armed forces. All this will spill over into the general chaos."

Peter agreed with *Akhdhar's* observations and promised to put them in his report to ODAT. He also sensed the worry both operatives had, not only over the confusion which was enveloping Iraq, but also over the assassination of the operative from Mosul. Finally, Peter remembered that he had one more piece of information to impart to them.

"You have probably heard that the *Ba'ath* Party founded by Aflak and Bitar is growing stronger, especially in Baghdad. It is just waiting for a 'rebirth of freedom and unity' for all Iraqis in order to get rid of the pro-western government."

At that moment Parviz popped his head round the door and said in Arabic and English to Peter,

"*Ta'al bil âjel*-come quickly. It is time to leave." And then in Russian when he saw the three men were reluctant to move, "*davai, davai.*"

After paying the bill the four men stepped out into the darkness of the late evening. Suddenly a beggar, who was loitering near the café asking for alms, lunged at *Aswad* with his crutch. *Aswad* leapt into the air, dropped his briefcase and let out an almighty yell. He then fell to the ground, holding his left leg.

"What's up?" asked Peter anxiously and rushed to help him to his feet.

"Something has bitten or stung me. It feels like a sharp needle," said *Aswad* and leaned against Peter, but then fell to the ground.

Meanwhile Parviz raced after the beggar, who had dropped his begging bowl and the coins in it, and was hurtling down the street. He caught up with the miscreant, grabbed his crutch and stuck it into his side, whereupon he collapsed to the ground.

"Quick," said Peter to the operative from Kirkuk. "Let me have a look at your leg."

He rolled back *Aswad*'s *zebun* as far as his knee and said, pointing to a tiny spot from which trickled a small amount of blood,

"There it is. There is a small hole in your skin about two centimetres below your left knee."

Parviz returned, holding the limp beggar in his right hand and what seemed to be a crutch in his left. Then, turning to Peter and dropping both the beggar and the crutch, he said,

"Here is the would-be assassin and also the weapon which was used on your friend. As you can see there is a sort of needle at the end of it."

The beggar meanwhile moaned and groaned pitifully for a while and then let out a blood curdling shriek and passed away before their very eyes. The wound which Parviz had inflicted on him was large and red gore gushed from several parts of his body.

Peter, however, turned his attention to *Aswad* who had rallied to his feet.

"Well. It's not one of those awful insects so common round here which has bitten you, but a cut from the thin blade of a knife. I'd better put some ointment on the wound."

Peter always carried a pack on his back containing iodine or soothing cream. He took out the iodine and applied it to *Aswad*'s wound.

"You'd better take him to a hospital," remarked Parviz. "I am sure there is some form of poison in your friend's system right now."

Peter looked more closely at the dead beggar's crutch. Indeed, there was what looked like a needle jutting out the end of it.

It was Parviz who then began to take control of the situation. Turning to Peter, he said,

"Go with your two friends to hospital. I will sort things out here and will report back to you if I find out why this beggar tried to kill.....What's his name?"

"*As....,* replied Peter, then after some hesitation, said, "Jalal."

Peter and *Akhdhar* telephoned for an ambulance at the café and accompanied *Aswad* to Baghdad's main hospital. Fortunately, although the poison had entered *Aswad*'s blood stream, it had only produced a sedative effect on him and he recovered fully, returning to Kirkuk the following day.

The following evening as Asya and Parviz visited Peter at his hotel the conversation was all about the previous day's events. Parviz recounted what had taken place after the three British operatives had left for the hospital.

"I managed to dispose of the body before the police arrived. I told them that the beggar had vanished down a side street."

"Who was he?" asked Peter.

"Well. He was a *Yezidi* from the Sinjar Highlands situated to the north west of Mosul and a dedicated communist sympathiser. I found a badge with the hammer and sickle on it in his coat pocket. The *Yezidis* are an esoteric sect whose beliefs are drawn from paganism, Zoroastrianism, Christianity and Islam. They are shunned by Muslims because their chief divine figure is Malah Taus, a peacock angel, who is reputed by them to rule the universe with other angels."

Peter and Asya had never heard of this sect before and looked at Parviz, expecting further information.

"Yes," continued Parviz. "They believe that the devil repented of his sin of pride, was pardoned by Allah and was reinstated as the chief of all angels. This persecuted beggar had nothing to lose by attempting to kill Jalal. Despised by many Moslems, no wonder he sought the help of communists in Iraq to get rid of a British spy. Jalal was a British agent, wasn't he, Peter?" Peter remained silent at this point, but Parviz refused to be diverted by his silence and continued his story about the poor *Yezidi* beggar.

"Peter. Did you notice the necklace he was wearing-the image of a black snake? This snake is an important sign for the *Yezidis* as well as the bird icon of Anzal. This sect has some strange customs. For example, they will not wear blue clothing or eat lettuce."
"Well. It is a pity you killed him," retorted Peter "We might have obtained more information about the spread of communism in the northern regions of Iraq."

Asya appeared somewhat bored by her brother's account of *Yezidi* customs and interrupted him.
"Peter. Today I received a telephone call from my father who is living in Tehran. Do you know that riots have been taking place in Hungary since October the 19th. He says that the Hungarians, mainly students, are demanding the withdrawal of Soviet troops from the country. They also want all elections to take place involving secret ballot and for all political prisoners to be released."
Peter's response was immediate. "Thank you, Asya. I know that Soviet troops entered Budapest on October the 24th because people wanted the popular Nagy to become prime minister again since he advocated a

type of national communism. Do you know that Mongolian troops had to be recruited to put down unrest in Hungary?"

Suddenly Peter regretted having mentioned this last point. He wondered whether his two friends had guessed that this information came from British SIGINT operations around the southern borders of the Soviet Union.

"How did you come by this information?" asked Parviz. "What you do not know, however, is that General Serov of the KGB has been sent to Hungary and that it was he who requested that Mongolian troops to be sent from the eastern front to deal with the situation there."

Late into the evening the two Soviet agents and Peter talked about the events which were unfolding in Hungary and the rights and wrongs of Soviet occupation of the country. When Asya and Parviz finally left Hotel Kadimiya, Peter, tired, but to a certain extent elated, contacted ODAT and asked if there was any news about the attempts on the lives of the two British operatives, that is to say on himself and *Aswad*. He was told that investigations were in progress and that he would be informed of the outcome in due course. Peter also mentioned the conversation he had with Asya and Parviz about the Hungarian crisis. ODAT's response was to remind him that he should keep a low profile in Baghdad, but at the same time retain his friendship with the Amampours, brother and sister.

Apart from his attendance at the language school and his meetings with Asya and Parviz, Peter heeded ODAT's advice and avoided visits to the bazaars and other places of interest in the capital of Iraq. Tensions were high over the actions of the British, French and Israeli forces in Egypt and anger was building up. A westerner was a 'persona non grata', so it came as a great surprise to Peter when two of the students at the language school, Pierre Leclerc and Georg Schulz, invited him to accompany them to a well-known museum.

"What are a blond-haired German and a light brown-haired Frenchman thinking about? It is obvious from their appearance that they are from Europe. There is going to be trouble," he said, but he agreed to go with them.

For him his dark skin, black hair and shabby western clothes allowed him to mingle with the Arabs of Baghdad with apparent ease. Only his blue eyes caused occasional suspicion.

It was the last week in November and the three of them had only reached Fallujah Bridge when they were snatched by a group of Shia Moslems who declared they were members of the IKP or Iraqi Communist Party. They were all blindfolded and taken to a large building in a district of Baghdad called Sadr City. Peter and Georg kept insisting they were not British, French or Israeli, but Pierre could not keep his mouth shut and said proudly,

"I am an important Frenchman and the son of a diplomat who knows Nuri es Said personally."

Unfortunately, he said this in Arabic and at the same time protested strongly at being captured by a group of what he called 'dirty rogues'.

His protestations became so loud that one of the Shi'ites guarding the victims became extremely agitated, pushed a rifle into Pierre's chest and pulled the trigger. When his blood stained body lay on the floor, all hell broke loose. His body was dragged outside and the Shi'ites started to scream and shout at Peter and Georg inside. Obviously the mention of Iraq's prime minister had somehow incensed the kidnappers. They began to threaten Peter and Georg. Peter had to react quickly. In desperation he shouted in Russian,

"My name is Piotr Ivanovich Kuznetsov and my friend here is Georg Schulz from Magdeburg in East Germany."

The sound of Peter's voice in Russian seemed to have a soothing effect on the kidnappers who lowered their rifles and withdrew. A thickset Arab approached Peter and said in broken Russian, "Where do you live in the Soviet Union and what are you doing in Baghdad? We have no knowledge of your presence here."

"I am a Muscovite," said Peter, and then with a flash

of inspiration calmly said, "Please telephone my friends, Asya and Parviz Amampour. They are Soviet agents like myself and will confirm what I am telling you. Here is Parviz's telephone number."

He then handed to the Russian speaking Arab a slip of paper with Parviz's telephone number on it. Without replying the leader of the kidnappers left the room and Peter realised that he was already in contact with Parviz and Asya because he left the slip of paper on the table in the room.

Within an hour Parviz and Asya appeared. Asya was wearing a black *hijab*, even though it appeared that she was uncomfortable wearing it. When the Shi'ites saw Asya they began to mutter among themselves. Some of them even raised their rifles and kept shouting that Peter and Georg were British spies because their Arabic had a British lilt. Their commanding officer, the thick set Arab who spoke Russian, managed to calm them down to a certain extent and then engaged Parviz and Asya in conversation, partly in Russian and partly in Arabic. The other men in the room were annoyed and there were shouts of 'execute them'. One kidnapper approached Asya and called her a *fâhisha* or whore and another said quite rudely,

"Why are you, a woman, so bold and confident and interfering in male concerns?"

Asya looked at him but did not answer.

Suddenly a small group of the Shi'ites came up to

Peter and Georg and some of them pulled back the bolts of their rifles ready to shoot both of them.

"No"….they shouted in unison and dived under the table. With some difficulty these kidnappers were hustled out of the room, whilst Parviz and Asya kept pleading with the commander to spare their friends' lives. After what seemed to Peter and Georg an eternity, they were both released and Pierre's body was dragged away. Nobody had questioned why Pierre was with the two make believe Soviet agents. However, there was relief all around. Obviously Parviz and Asya had convinced the Shi'ites that Peter and Georg worked for the Soviet Union.

Later the two men thanked the Amampours for saving their lives.

"What did you say to them eventually?" asked Peter.

"Well," said Asya. "We managed to persuade the leader of this IKP faction that you, Peter, lived in the same block of flats as ourselves in Moscow and that you were also a Soviet agent. For Georg we had to make up a story that he was a communist and a member of the *Abteilung* or secret service in East Germany. Now, I advise both of you to keep a low profile from now on and travel to and from the language school by taxi. Peter, you can pass as an Arab in appearance, but, when you speak Arabic, you employ too many English expressions. In any case both of you may be marked men. So, be careful."

This advice was difficult for Peter to stomach and, when towards the end of the year Aziz invited his four best students, including Parviz, but excluded Asya, to partake of a meal at a small restaurant just off Haifa Street, Peter jumped at the offer. Because he had important business to deal with, Aziz declared that he would join them later, but for them to start the meal without him. The four men sat round a large wooden table in the corner of this crowded restaurant. There was plenty on the menu to choose from: *mezza-tabouleh,* chicken, peas, yogurt, aubergines as well as other meat dishes and of course cold drinks. Peter ordered his favourite dish of s*emek masgûf,* a fish from the River Tigris, split open and roasted on a stake around a fire.

They were part way through their meal when Aziz appeared with a message to say that Asya urgently required her brother's assistance later on in the evening. When their tutor, Aziz, joined the group, the students realised that it was his usual custom to improve their knowledge of Arabic, especially the script, whether it was in the language school or even in a restaurant. Sipping a glass of lemon juice he said in a mixture of English and Arabic,

"For you all the most important part of learning Arabic is writing the script and getting the grammar right. Take for example the *hemza* or glottal stop. It is not a letter of the alphabet, but an orthographic sign."

Peter's head was reeling for he had been drinking *arak,* a potent alcoholic beverage in the Muslim world, which was probably condemned by religious leaders, but was drunk by some Arabs. This combined with the large amount of food he had consumed, and the stuffiness of the restaurant added to his discomfort. Meanwhile Aziz continued with his explanation of the *hemza.*

"When a short vowel sound occurs initially in a word or syllable, a slight consonant is detected by the slight contraction of the throat. This is indicated by a sign called a *hemza.*" His voice grew louder and louder above the chatter and hubbub in the restaurant. As he spoke Peter tried to follow his complicated explanation, especially the part in Arabic when he began to write down examples on a piece of paper.

Peter's attention suddenly wandered to a group of Arabs in traditional costumes who were sitting at an adjoining table. Some of them started to bang crockery and cutlery on their table, either in a heated argument, or more likely in a noisy friendly manner. The banging stopped abruptly, only to be replaced by the clink of a single spoon on a glass tumbler. Peter was startled by the sound. Yes. It was definitely Morse code-short, long, long, short (a P), then a pause followed by a short (an E), and then another pause followed by a long (a T)....

One of the Arabs was tapping out the word PETRUSHKA and then in Morse 'Please acknowledge this message'. Only Stefan would call him Petrushka. What was he doing here?

Aziz, meanwhile, began an analysis of a *sekun..*
"When a consonant has no vowel of its own following it, a mark called a *sekun* is placed over the consonant. Likewise a *sekun* is placed over a *waw,* or *ya* which go to form a diphthong."
Again, he showed his students an example on paper, but Peter was not paying attention. Instead, he began to tap out a message in return, using his pen and an ashtray. He transmitted the following,
"I have received your transmission, *Abdul*. Why are you here?"
The Arab who was trying to contact Peter got up, moved towards the door of the restaurant and as he passed Peter, he bumped into him and surreptitiously handed him a crumpled piece of paper.

Everything happened so quickly. Stefan alias *Abdul* left the restaurant without looking back at Peter who rushed after him.
"What is Stefan doing here in Baghdad?" said Peter to himself. "It must be important. He is stationed at Shenlan on the hills overlooking Beirut. What brings him here?"
By the time Peter had stepped outside the restaurant Stefan had disappeared. For a brief moment, he thought he saw him avoiding whining beggars and women with babies asking for *backsheesh,* but it was

somebody else. He then looked at the piece of paper handed to him and read in Russian,

"We must meet at nine o'clock this evening in Hotel Kadimiya. Important news. *Abdul.*"

Feigning a severe headache Peter left the restaurant followed by Parviz who seemed rather worried over his friend's behaviour during the meal. "You've dropped this piece of paper, Peter." declared Parviz and handed him the crumpled and partly torn remains of Stefan's message.

It took Peter almost two hours before he arrived at his hotel where he was approached by the receptionist who had been working there all day. In a weary and tired voice, the Arab said,

"Sahib. A certain Abdul Shenlan telephoned this morning and said he would contact you sometime today. I have written his name down on this card."

Peter took the white card, but instead of reading it he hurried to his room. As he opened the door, he realised that something was wrong. What he saw left him virtually paralysed for a moment. His friend, Stefan, lay slumped across the bed.

He was still alive, but only just, and was groaning in agony. He scarcely stuttered the following words, "Moscow, Ferdowsi, spy, As...."

The last word trailed off as Stefan's lips moved more slowly until only a hoarse whisper emanated from his mouth.

"Spy, Asy…."

Peter took the bedside lamp closer to his friend's face and noticed there was a discolouring around his mouth. There were also grey and white burn marks around his chin. Peter looked down on the floor at a glass which appeared to have dropped from Stefan's hands. He picked it up gingerly and examined the contents. Then he looked into his friend's mouth.

"He has swallowed or been forced to swallow a small quantity of poison, probably hydrochloric acid," he said quietly to himself.

Without panicking Peter went to the bathroom cabinet and took out a bottle of olive oil and some carbonate of soda. He bent over Stefan and tried to pour some of the olive oil into his friend's mouth.

"Asya is….," croaked Stefan and with a violent heave rose up on the bed and then crumpled to the floor. Peter felt his pulse. He was definitely dead. Perplexed and mystified Peter could only surmise what Stefan was trying to tell him.

"Was Asya really a spy? She came from Moscow, lived in Tehran and Ferdowsi was a famous Persian poet."

It only took him a minute to work out that Asya was a Soviet spy bearing the code name *Ferdowsi*.

Peter knew that he could not be implicated in Stefan's death. He glanced out of the window, which was partly open, and noticed there were three pairs of dirty footprints on the sill, two pair coming in and one pair going out. It was apparent to him that an assassin had entered his bedroom through the window, spiked a drink of lemonade on the bedside table and then hid in the bathroom. Stefan had obviously also climbed through the window and drank what he thought was a refreshing drink. The deed was done. Or had the drink been forced down his throat?

Suddenly there was a rustling sound at the window.
"*Menu...?*" shouted Peter in Arabic but did not finish the sentence. He then opened the window wide.
A dark figure slammed one of the shutters against Peter's hands, climbed over the *shenashil* and disappeared down the back alley. Peter returned to the body of his lifeless friend and noticed a stain near the bed where the acid had spilt onto one of the rugs. As if in a dream Peter pulled up the rug and took it to the garbage bin downstairs and then returned to his room to make an important call to ODAT headquarters in Iraq. Dialling the operational emergency number, Peter literally screamed down the line,
"Please come to Hotel Kadimiya, Room 8, and dispose of a dead body. I will lock the door and come back tomorrow You will find the key under the mat outside. I shall contact you tomorrow."

He then left the hotel, telling the receptionist not to go into his room and that he would be back tomorrow morning. Although the late evening was quite warm,

Peter felt a terrifying chill in his bones as he walked along the banks of the River Tigris. All the time he kept repeating,

"Asya cannot be a Soviet agent. Perhaps she is in danger. I must find out."

However, he could not reject the information that Stefan had imparted to him before he died. At the same time, he kept denying that she was a spy. Surely a kindhearted and beautiful woman like Asya could not be involved in such intrigue.

Early the following morning Peter was determined to make a call on both Asya and Parviz. So, he hailed a taxi from the small hotel where he had been sleeping that night and arrived first of all at the hostel where Asya was living.

"Asya left early this morning for Tehran," declared the warden. "and she has also taken her few belongings with her."

"Has she left an address or telephone number with you in Tehran?" asked Peter, but he could see from the warden's shrug of the shoulders and the look on her face that the answer was no.

He then rushed round to the house which Parviz shared with a friend in Sadr City but was told that he had also left for Tehran with his sister that very morning.

Peter returned to his hotel at eleven o'clock and was relieved to find that Stefan's body had been removed. He sat down at the pine table and opened his diary.

He had been writing down everyday events in Welsh without describing classified material. He put down that his best friend, Stefan, had died.

"Mae fy ffrind, Steffan, wedi marw. Fe oedd fy nghyfaill gorau."

Peter was sad. This was certainly the end of Operation *Shenlan* for Stefan and probably the end of Operation *Babylon* for him.

As he was writing the phone rang and his thoughts were interrupted.

"Abyadh." said the voice on the other end. "Your cover is blown and Operation *Babylon* for you is postponed. Please contact your operatives in Kirkuk, Mosul and Basra. For the time being *Akhdhar* will take over from you and we shall send somebody to replace you. Take your necessary belongings from the hotel and make sure you have your passport with you. You will notice that there is a visa stamped on one of the pages allowing you to study in Iran. Although the visa is out of date, you can renew it at Tehran Airport. Provide a report of your activities in Iraq and deliver what you have written either by post or by hand to the British Embassy. You have been booked on a plane for Tehran. It leaves Baghdad Airport at midday tomorrow. The last contact with us will be via your two-way radio tomorrow. Leave it in Hotel Kadimiya. All the best!"

Peter did what he was ordered to do, although he felt

that writing a report on all the activities in Iraq was rather asking too much within the course of one night. He then contacted the operatives to inform them that he was being replaced as their commander in the field. Towards midnight he was again contacted by ODAT.

"Peter," said the person who had spoken to him earlier. "Your mission in Tehran is to try and locate the two Soviet agents who were with you on the Arabic course in Baghdad. We know that their code names are *Rumi* and *Ferdowsi*. Be careful because we know that both alerted the killer of Agent *Abdul*, your friend, who had intercepted conversations in Russian when he was in the Lebanon, regarding a nest of Soviet agents involved in an operation called *Azady*. This is our last conversation by landline. Leave everything as it is in your hotel We will sort things out."

As he lay on his bed Peter's mind was again in turmoil. How could the kind, gentle and beautiful Asya be a Soviet agent? How could her helpful and considerate brother, Parviz, be an agent as well? As he began to doze off he became conscious of the fan in his room humming slightly and on occasions spluttering as it twirled around. He closed his eyes and the figure of Parviz appeared, adjusting the fan because it was making a loud spitting noise.

"That's it!" declared Peter instantly." The person who came once to repair the fan in my billet at Camp

Ddibben when I was there was none other than Parviz."

He climbed out of bed, went over to a photograph of Asya and Parviz on the dressing table, took a pencil out of the drawer and drew a moustache and beard on the face of his 'friend'. Then, as if talking to the ceiling he said,

"Yes it was definitely the same man who repaired my fan. Then he wore a beard and moustache."

Without doubt Parviz and his sister had set him up. They were definitely Soviet agents. Also, it was a coincidence that Parviz was the one person who had been around during the nefarious events in Baghdad, apart from the incident when Ibrahim and himself were wounded. Or, perhaps he was directly responsible for *Azrak*'s death as well, because he knew that Peter would have been in the crowd that afternoon. The night was spent writing the report required by ODAT and it was only when morning broke that he finally completed this arduous task.

The compilation of this report was a real headache for Peter. Somehow, he had to combine three elements: a comment on the general situation in Iraq as viewed by the four British operators, a reference to the dangers facing the Kingdom from anti-western forces and an analysis of the damage inflicted by the activities of Soviet agents in the country.

Peter's final contact with ODAT before leaving hotel

Kadimiya was via the two-way radio which had, until now, remained undisturbed under his bed. This short-range walkie-talkie must have picked up the voice of an ODAT operator somewhere nearby with links to the British Embassy. After a short conversation with him Peter was given further instructions with regards to his role in Tehran and his duty to uphold the principles of truth and justice. So, with a cheery *'vitam impendere vero'* and a 'goodbye' Peter evoked the motto of ODAT and left by taxi to deliver his report by hand to the British Embassy.

Whilst waiting in the airport lounge for the plane to Tehran, Peter reflected on what he had achieved in Iraq. Certainly he had gained access to two Soviet agents in a gradual and secretive manner. Or, had they infiltrated the defences of British intelligence? At the same time, however, the plotting and intrigue had resulted in a sort of illegality and harm to both British and Soviet agents and others caught up in the murky world of espionage.

Nevertheless, as he boarded the aircraft for Tehran Peter's main concern was not about espionage or what he had achieved, but about the fear that he might not see Asya again. During the flight he asked himself many questions regarding a future relationship with her, if he could ever find her. How was he going to locate her in any case and would her feelings towards him have changed? Only one thing was clear. He would make every effort to track her down, persuade her to give up spying for the Soviet Union and even return with him to Britain.

Chapter Four

Retribution and Punishment

Peter_White saw the reflection of a curved knife in a large coffee pot next to a carpet he was examining near a shop window. In a flash he turned round, but it was too late. The person who held the knife lunged forward towards Peter's head. At the same time another person with a beard threw himself in a rugby type tackle between Peter and his assailant. The knife, slightly grazing him on the shoulder, clattered to the floor. The miscreant then ran quickly out of the shop situated close to Jomhouri Eslami Avenue and disappeared into a crowded street.

Breathing heavily and gasping with relief, Peter clutched his left shoulder with a handkerchief to stop the trickle of blood flowing from a small graze. After getting his breath back he said to his saviour,
"Kheili mammon. Sepaasgozaaram."
Indeed, Peter was extremely grateful that his life had been saved by a complete stranger who leaned forward and helped him to his feet. Then in a quiet voice this Iranian said in Russian,
"Nichevo, moi drug."

Peter recognised that voice and looked at the stranger more closely. Yes. He was not mistaken. It was his former friend from Iraq, Parviz, but now sporting a beard and a moustache.

"Most murders in Tehran are carried out with knives or similar weapons," exclaimed Parviz. "They are noticeably noiseless. A revolver shot tends to attract attention. By the way, Peter. Are you alright?"
Certain thoughts began to go through Peter's mind. Why was a Soviet agent helping a British spy? Something else must be going on. Before Peter could ask any questions Parviz said goodbye in Russian, thrust a note into his hand and hurriedly left the shop. Peter struggled to the window and saw Parviz nonchalantly strolling along the street, stopping to examine a piece of merchandise and then weaving in and out of the crowd at a quicker pace.

Before looking at the note Parviz had given him, Peter approached the shopkeeper, who had witnessed the chain of events which had taken place and attempted to bargain with him the price of the Persian carpet which he had seen in the shop window. According to the shopkeeper this carpet was made by the most famous weaver and carpet designer in Iran-Rassan Arabzadel. Speaking partly in Farsi and partly in Arabic, Peter said,
"I have seen the real carpet in a museum. It has the same pattern with dark reds and powerful blues which

predominate as well as bits of ivory woven into it to form a contrasting colour. But, it is a copy. Isn't it?"

The owner of the carpet shop found it difficult at times to work out Peter's mixture of Farsi and Arabic, but he kept on insisting that only two such carpets existed and this was one of them. However, the price was too high. Realising that Peter was probably from the west, the shopkeeper suddenly decided that he wanted to be paid in dollars or pounds and not toumans. Peter eventually extricated himself from the purchase by saying that he did not speak Farsi.

"Farsi balad nistam."

Not to be put off the Iranian shopkeeper reduced his price considerably, but Peter was adamant. He needed to explore the carpet shops in Tehran's Bazar-e Bozorg and Bazar-e Kaffashha before making up his mind. So. with a curt handshake and a bow Peter declared he would give the reduced offer some thought and perhaps return.

It was a cold *do shambeh* or Monday afternoon in late February 1957 and the weather was beginning to chill Peter's bones Avoiding the traffic which seemed at times to clog up the capital's streets and ignoring the shouts of the drivers in their orange-coloured taxis, Peter made his way to his favourite café. There he ordered a slice of cake and a glass of tea with lemon. Then he began to take stock of what had transpired since he left Baghdad in December the previous year. The plane which had carried him and a few Shi'ite pilgrims to Tehran had been a Hermes. When he arrived in the capital of Iran, he was met by two officials from the British Embassy, both ODAT agents, who took him to Hotel Arg just off Takhtemjamshid Square and told him that he would like Tehran better than Baghdad.

Only two weeks after his arrival in Iran, Peter was able to write in Welsh in his diary that after the dangers and stifling atmosphere of Baghdad, he found Tehran rather refreshing. To a certain extent he noticed that the Iranians seemed more relaxed than the Arabs in Iraq. However, after the horrible incident in the carpet shop and one or two other setbacks he wrote,
"I am concerned that there are some Iranians who have threatened me. All I want to do is to study the customs of this beautiful country, learn Farsi and show the people generally that Britain is only trying to help Iran achieve democracy". Then with an appeal to all Iranians he added that he was in the country to help, and he did not want to be threatened,
"Yma i'ch helpu ydw i nid i fod yn darged."

Within two months Peter had explored the Province of Tehran from the southern slopes of the Alborz to the Dasht-e Karaj desert. He had also enrolled on a German and Farsi course at a community school which had been started by American Presbyterian missionaries in 1935. Obeying instructions from

ODAT, however, he was advised to become a student at the more prestigious *Daneshghah* or University of Tehran. Due to his almost fluent German Peter soon found that he was able to obtain a teaching post in this language at the university and to carry out research on Goethe's '*Dichtung und Wahrheit*' and his poems.

Peter was amazed to find that, although French was the dominant foreign language studied in schools and universities in Iran, German was growing in popularity. Many courses in this language were available at the Universities of Isfahan, Shiraz and Kermala, as well as in Tehran. Peter was also aware of the development of a small German community in the capital and the existence of Iranian doctors and engineers who had studied in Germany in the early1950s. Even though he was enjoying life and gaining many new experiences, one person was missing, namely Asya.

Throughout the months of January and February Peter could not forget his Asya. Her face dominated his thoughts and he often wondered what she was doing with her life. Peter's favourite poem was Heidenröslein. Franz Schubert's musical rendering of it was exquisite and Peter used to sing it to himself on numerous occasions. In the poem a wild young boy attempts to pluck a beautiful red rose without realising the consequences of being pricked by this enchanting flower. Peter compared himself to the wild boy who had been in such a hurry to capture his

Asya, a delightful red flower, as fresh as the morning dew.

"Is my red rose, Asya, an innocent illusion or is she an agent flourishing under the red banner of communism?" muttered Peter and became quite melancholy by the thought.

As he was drinking his tea and eating his cake, Peter remembered the note Parviz had pressed into his hand after he had saved him from certain death. How did Parviz know he was in the carpet shop in any case and who was trying to kill him? He opened the crumpled piece of paper and read in Russian,

"*Dorogoi Pyotr!*

I have a confession to make. Both Parviz and I were sent to Baghdad to make contact with a British spy called *Abyadh* and to find out what the British intended to do in Iraq and in the Middle East generally. Indeed, we are sorry. You have probably guessed that we were recruited as Soviet agents, but you must believe us now. We have given up spying. We intend to remain good Muslims and from now on lead blameless lives. Forgive us please.

Tvoya podruga. Asya

P.S. We will contact you soon in Hotel Arg."

Hotel Arg was pleasant enough and Peter enjoyed an excellent view of the capital from his bedroom. Situated on the higher ground around Shemiran, he was surrounded by residential buildings and the business quarter of Tehran. It was chosen specifically by officials from the British Embassy for security reasons. In fact, an Iranian guard was paid by ODAT to keep an eye on who entered and left the hotel in case Peter was contacted by Soviet agents.

Imagine the guard's surprise when one early morning in March three women in traditional Iranian clothes and a man dressed in a smart European suit entered Hotel Arg and asked at the reception desk to see Peter White. The guard, who had been sitting in the hotel lobby, was quickly on to his superiors.
"Three women and one man have asked to see *Abyadh* in the foyer. The women are wearing *hijabs* and the man a smart European suit. As far as I can ascertain all four seem to be Iranian, but they are the first visitors to the hotel to contact *Abyadh*. I shall try to follow them and report back later."

"Haale shomaa chetoore?" shouted Asya as Peter descended the staircase leading to the foyer.
Peter was 'over the moon' when he saw his visitors, especially Asya, and was pleased to notice that she seemed genuinely happy to see him.
"Khooban merci," replied Peter and his heart gave a leap. At last, he had found Asya, or she had found him. Shaking Parviz by the hand, Peter thanked him many times for saving his life, whilst at the same time bowing in the direction of Asya and her cousins, Mahnaz and Shanaz.

Peter ordered coffee for all of them and then began a long and often tearful conversation in Russian, interspersed occasionally by some Farsi so as not to exclude the two cousins who smiled and giggled continuously.

"Who tried to kill me, Parviz?" asked Peter after a while.

"We are genuinely sorry, Peter," replied Parviz, showing obvious concern. "The person who tried to kill you was a Soviet agent from Isfahan called Koorosh. His code name was *Khayyam*. He was told not to harm you, but he wanted to prove to the Soviet authorities that he was capable of ridding the world of a British spy. I had my sights on him straight away when you arrived in Iran. I have reported the incident and he has been recalled to Moscow for disobeying orders."

With tears streaming down her face Asya cut into her brother's account,

"We did not want you to be killed and therefore we have been guarding you from other Soviet agents. Well, Peter. We have all decided, that is to say the whole family has decided not to return to the Soviet Union. We feel our destiny lies with Allah from now on. In any case we have been unmasked by the British and we feel like 'mice being pursued by cats', both by British agents and the Shah's secret police, the SAVAK."

As she spoke, her hands were restless, and she kept pulling at an envelope which she eventually handed to Peter. "Everything is explained in this note, Peter. Read it later and please, once again, forgive us for all the distress we have caused you."

Listening to Asya's explanation, Peter then decided that from now on he would try and protect his friends from Tajikistan in return. In any case he began to feel quite angry with ODAT for having sent him to Iraq and Iran on what seemed to him to be a mission impossible. What had he achieved? He also had the feeling that he was 'a mouse caught in a trap' and there seemed to be no escape.

Parviz interrupted his thoughts. "We, that is to say, myself and my family, intend to remain in Iran for a while and perhaps act as double agents. We can inform our controllers at KPOK headquarters that you are giving us important information about British activities in the Middle East, and we can inform you of Soviet intentions here. What do you think, Peter?"

"I need time to reflect on what you say, Parviz," said Peter, bewildered by the recent chain of events. "I must also consider my future here in Iran as well."

Peter then looked at Asya and said that now that he had found her and Parviz, or rather that they had found him, they must keep in contact.

"This is true, Peter. We will telephone you very soon and arrange something." Then, as if remembering suddenly something important, added, "There is a mole somewhere in Britain who is sending a vast amount of information to the Soviet Union. Even before the Suez Canal region was invaded, we were obtaining details of an Operation called 'Omelette'. You need to inform British intelligence about this spy."

Peter thanked Parviz and stated that he anticipated further revelations such as this. He did not tell Parviz, however, that it would perhaps allow him to remain in Iran for a while until he had thought of a plan to lure Asya to Great Britain.

Throughout the meeting in Hotel Arg Peter was concerned about Asya. Apart from her initial reaction of joy when she saw him for the first time in Tehran, he noticed that she did not look well. Her face was pale, which was accentuated by a lack of make-up. It was obvious that she had been crying because there were traces of tears in her eyes and her cheeks were wet. Her lovely black hair was hidden by a blue scarf over her head and shoulders and not a single piece of jewellery adorned her arms or neck. He wanted to go over to her and give her a big hug, but he knew that men towards women or vice versa in a Muslim country must not display open affection in public.

Peter was surprised that Parviz had even brought his sister and two female cousins to the hotel to speak to him. Whilst Peter was thinking about Asya, Parviz broke the silence which had ensued.

"Peter. We would like you to visit us soon. You will then be able to meet our father and mother as well. Here is our address," and he handed over a card with an address printed both in Farsi and English. "Now it is time for us to leave."

So, with a *'Khodaa haafeez'* they said goodbye to Peter. He also wished them farewell, shook Parviz by the hand and made a slight bow in the direction of Asya and the two cousins, but in a dignified and solemn manner.

When they left Peter opened the envelope which Asya had given him and read the note. Well, it was more a letter than a note. It explained in great detail why he was such a good friend to her and her family. She also mentioned that Parviz and herself always looked forward to their meetings in Hotel Kadimiya in Baghdad. Finally, she ended with the hope that no harm would come to him and that he would consider giving up spying as she had done. Peter did not know what to believe. His only consolation was that now he had found 'his' Asya.

A week later Peter received a telephone call from Parviz who invited him to visit the whole family in the Abbas Abad area of Tehran. So, one evening he arrived at the Amampours's house situated in a smart *kucheh* or side street. He tried to remember what he knew about Iranian customs when visiting a family.

"I must avoid such vulgarity as extending my thumb or pointing the soles of my feet in the direction of another person, if I am sitting on a cushion on the floor and partaking of a meal."

He was also aware that Asya would be watching him very carefully. She was always quick to criticise him and he desperately needed her approval for everything he did.

He rang the bell, and the door was opened by Ali and Anastasia whom he had never met.

"Haale shomaa chetoore, aaghaaya Amampour va khaanome Amamapour," he said, and shook Ali's right hand and slightly bowed towards his wife. At least he had started to employ *'tarof'* or ceremonial politeness towards them both. He was sure Asya would be pleased. Soon the three of them were joined by Asya and Parviz and much to Peter's relief the conversation was carried out in Russian. Making one more effort to use his knowledge of Farsi, Peter turned to Ali and Anastasia and said,

"Bebakhsheen Engleesee meefahmeen?"

He then repeated this in Russian and when they both said *'nyet'* or no, he knew that he could communicate things to Asya and Parviz without their parents' knowledge, which of course he did not intend to do under any circumstances.

When Peter entered the living room Asya was concerned that he was continuously admiring the

Persian rug in front of the mantelpiece. Before he could say anything Asya said in English,

"Do not use the words 'I like this rug', because, if you over-compliment an object in a person's household, custom has it here in Iran that your host will feel obliged to give it to you."

At first Peter was amazed, stared at Asya and said,

"I shall not say anything about the rug in Russian or Farsi, even though it is beautiful. However, I intend to buy a carpet or rug for myself in the near future, because Iran is famous for its production of such objects."

Before the evening meal Ali took Peter into an adjoining room in order to explain to him that he was preparing a report for a Soviet organisation called KPOK.

"I shall not bore you with the details, but I have come to the conclusion that Iran is ready for revolution to overthrow the Shah without the help of Soviet agents here. You know that many Iranians are angered by the imprisonment of Dr. Mohammed Mossadeq. He was not anti-western, but an advocate of complete sovereignty for Iran. When he nationalised the oil industry and tried to take over the army from the Shah he was supported by the people generally."

Peter looked at Ali and realised from his tone of voice that here was a Soviet agent who had already summed up the situation in Iran. Then Ali continued with what seemed to be a set piece.

"Mossadeq's mistake was to rule by decree with the help of the communists and the Tudeh Party or Party of the Masses of Iran. Since he was overthrown in a pro-monarchist coup in 1953 there has been unrest in the army and amongst civilians who feel that the Shah is too pro-western."

Ali went on to say that there had been two assassination attempts on the Shah's life orchestrated by the Soviet Union and the Tudeh Party was blamed, persecuted and banned.

However, Peter knew that the Shah's reign had not been completely wasted. His 'White Revolution' included both economic and social reforms in an attempt to transform Iran into a global power. The nation was gradually being modernised and its natural resources utilised. Moreover, women were given the right to vote. Unfortunately, all this resulted in the traditional power of the Shia clergy being reduced. Modernisation and secularisation led to clashes and conflict with the Imams and the traditional class of merchants known as the *Bazaari*. What antagonised the Muslims in the country most was the Shah's recognition of Israel as a legitimate state and the suppression of political dissent by his secret police, the SAVAK.

Peter felt some sympathy for Ali's problems and said, "So, you feel your mission here is impossible and perhaps a waste of time. To me it seems that you wish to find a way out of your predicament and extricate your family from Operation…., what's its name? I remember now-*Azady*. Yes, Parviz has already told me about this organisation."

"Well, Peter." said Ali. "This is my dilemma. The whole family is 'fed up to the teeth' acting as stooges for the communist regime in the Soviet Union. Although we dislike the Shah and all he stands for, we are beginning to also hate the anti-God, atheist stance of communism. My biggest fear now is that, if KPOK finds out that we are trying to end our mission in Iran and defecting, then we are all dead. Your friendship with us may cost you dear, Peter. Somehow our destinies from now on are linked and you could be a marked man."

Peter looked at Ali, but was not convinced, especially by his last remark. Here was a Soviet agent, who was weary of working for his communist masters, but there seemed to be more to it than that. At that very moment Parviz walked into the room and had heard what his father had been saying to Peter. He also had something to say which he felt was important.

"Peter. You go on about democracy and freedom, but you do not understand the minds of Muslims in the Middle East. Only last week I attended a conference held by Islamists in Ibadan in the south of Iran. We were told that freedom for all Muslims is not just freedom to live in certain countries, but freedom from imperialism which exists, as we can see, in Iraq and

Iran."

Then, like his father, as if reading from a script, he added,

"The three principles of western civilization: secularism, nationalism and democracy cannot be imported into countries in the Middle East and are definitely not a solution to problems that exist there. These three principles are according to Islamic groups corrupt to the core and the source of all evil. There will always be resistance to elections and so-called majority rule, because democracy imposed by the west is apostasy. Sovereignty cannot rest in people, but only in Allah, and laws given by him must be *Sharia* laws which are divine, timeless and immutable."

Parviz's account was interrupted by his sister who came to let the three men know that the evening meal was being prepared.

"Peter," she said, "Do not let my brother and father confuse you with Islamic ideology. Even I am bewildered by it all."

During the meal the Amampours informed Peter once again of the fear they had for their own safety and that they had decided for the time being to remain in Iran where they had relatives. They were sure that, if they returned to the Soviet Union, worse would befall them. Parviz especially had been thinking long and hard about their situation and was ready to tell Peter about their feelings.

"To be honest, Peter. We cannot return to the country of our birth once we inform KPOK about our decision to remain in Iran. The Kremlin will have no use for us since we will not be able to do our job properly. We cannot go to Iraq because the British have found out that we were implicated indirectly in one murder and several assassination attempts. Also, even here in Iran we are not completely safe, because SAVAK agents are watching our every move. However, what is most upsetting is that we are afraid that Allah will punish us for being Soviet agents."

Ali kept nodding in agreement with his son's analysis of the situation and said,

"What grieves us most is that we have let Allah down for not completing our *jihad* here and not getting rid of the Shah. We all accept that we shall face some form of retribution for what we have done or not done. It is important, therefore, before it is too late to ask Allah for forgiveness and to promise to lead a pure and unblemished life from now on. We will all stand before him at the Day of Judgement, but we know that he is all-forgiving."

Asya kept shaking her head whilst her father and brother were speaking. Her concern was for her mother.

"*Matushka,* has most to lose in all of this. Once again, she has to cope with a different country, different customs and a different language."

Then turning to Peter she said,

"You, Peter, are also in danger here in Tehran and the fault lies with us. Do you not understand that there are Soviet agents here who will definitely try and kill you? Look what happened recently in the carpet shop. May I make a suggestion on behalf of the whole family? Come and lodge with us in a different location in Tehran. It can be arranged, because we have relatives here. It will be beneficial if we all disappeared for a while."

On hearing this Peter's heart jumped for joy. So, he decided forthwith to take up the Amampours' offer. In any case he would be nearer Asya and this would be a bonus. A few days later, collecting most of his belongings, he moved secretly on a Friday night from Hotel Arg, thus avoiding the Iranian guard whose duty it was to keep an eye on his movements at all times. The following day the poor guard realised what had happened.

"I've lost *Abyadh,* he screamed down the telephone to his superiors. "He must have moved somewhere during the night. I shall investigate and call you back later."

When Peter was installed in another establishment occupied by the Amampours, he wrote in his diary,

"This move gives me great pleasure, because it allows me to see Asya daily. I know I shall have to be circumspect in my dealings with her, because we shall be living under the same roof and we are of different faiths."

Well, Peter had no faith at all, but he was beginning to warm to Islam, probably on account of his love for Asya. He stopped going to Tehran University by declaring that he needed a sabbatical and would return later, but he did not leave a forwarding address, nor did he contact ODAT for a while.

By the middle of March, it was Asya's birthday just when preparations were due to take place to celebrate the Iranian New Year or *Nowruz*. Arrangements for this festival had really begun in *Esfand* or the last month of winter according to the Muslim calendar. Since they were in Iran all the members of the family started to prepare for *Nowruz* even earlier, because it was also Asya's birthday. It involved cleaning their house and, when they moved to their new home, also cleaning that as well. They bought clothes to wear and purchased many flowers.

When Peter entered the dining room on Asya's birthday, he was astonished to see the whole family in traditional outfits gathered around a beautifully laid-out *Haft Sin* table. They were joined by a few relatives to celebrate both Asya's birthday and the New Year. Asya explained to Peter in Russian,

"The *Haft Sin* table includes at least seven items beginning with the letter 'S' or *'Sin'* in Farsi. They correspond symbolically to the seven creations and the holy immortals protecting them."

Peter listened intently to Asya's commentary, and he could see the joy and happiness on her face as her father extended his daughter's explanation, pointing to some of the items on the table.

"All these items are significant. For example, *sabzeh,* a mixture of wheat, barley and lentil sprouts, is a symbol of rebirth; *samanu* or sweet pudding is a symbol of affluence; *sir* or garlic symbolizes medicine; *somaq* or berries symbolize the colour of sunrise and *serkeh* or vinegar represents age."

Determined not to be left out Parviz pointed to two other items, making seven in all.

"Especially for my lovely sister I can say without doubt that these two items refer to her: *Sib* or apples which symbolise beauty and health and *senjed* or the dried fruit of the oleander tree which symbolizes love."

Asya started to blush and looked at Peter whose heart missed several beats.

There were other items on the table as well, such as a hyacinth plant, *aajeel* or dried nuts, berries and raisons. There were also gold coins called *sehkeh* which represented health. Furthermore, a second table in the room contained lighted candles-a sign of happiness, a mirror reflecting cleanliness and honesty and decorated eggs which during the course of the evening were given out as signs of fertility to each person, including Peter. There was even a bowl of water with a gold fish in it. However, it was the Holy Qur'an which took pride of place above all other items.

In a mixture of Russian, English and Farsi, Parviz toasted Asya's birthday and Ali held up the Qur'an and said with reverence in his voice,
"Praise be to Allah for the joy he has given me; the gift of a lovely wife, a devoted son, a beautiful daughter, wonderful relatives and last, but not least, a special friend, Peter."
As a final treat Peter gave those gathered in the dining room a rendering of 'Happy Birthday' in Welsh- *'Pen blwydd hapus i ti,'* whereupon everybody clapped and Asya chuckled to hear this ancient Celtic language. Peter was conscious of the proud look she gave him when he sang this song, but it was spoilt by a conversation he had with her before going to bed.
In a meek manner she confessed to spying on him when they were in Baghdad.
"There is something I need to 'get off my chest', Peter. When you were out of your room in Hotel Kadimya I used a miniature camera supplied to me by KPOK to photograph some of what you had written in your diary. I could not understand what you had written, so I sent everything that I had photographed to Moscow."
At this point she shook her head in a vexed manner as

if chastising herself.

"Later, I received a message from the Professor of Celtic Studies at Moscow University stating that the language was Welsh, but that it did not contain anything significant except that you felt you were falling in love with me. I am sorry for what I have done. Please forgive me."

Of course Peter forgave her and promised to teach her some words in Welsh. Then, tongue in cheek, he taught her two unusual phrases, one to understand and the other to repeat, namely *'bore da, cariad'*,-,'good morning, dear' and *'bore da, bachgen digywilydd'*-'good morning, cheeky boy'. Within an hour Asya was able to understand the first phrase and to repeat the second. On returning to his bedroom Peter wrote in his diary that he was sure Asya was falling in love with him as well.

"Heddiw yw'r diwrnod gorau yn fy mywyd. Mae Asya wedi syrthio mewn cariad â fi"

The weeks seemed to fly by. Peter was living in the same house as the woman he loved and at the same time feeding irrelevant material about the Amampour family to ODAT. However, he did not divulge his new address, for security reasons, he said. On the other hand, there was trouble brewing. Asya told him that her father was becoming rather disorientated and kept repeating that he was going to be punished for allowing his family to be caught up in the dangerous 'game' of espionage.

"Retribution is round the corner," he kept saying on numerous occasions and then he would hug his wife and daughter. He also made arrangements with his son to approach Peter and see if there was a way of leaving Iran and taking up residence in Britain.

In July Ali told his family that he was going to contact the Soviet agents in Iran in order to tell them that he was going to abort Operation *Azady* and to persuade them to give up spying for the Soviet Union. In July he agreed to meet one of them in Tabriz- Behrooz, or to give him his code name, *Saddi*. He also persuaded Peter and Parviz to go with him. The road link from Tehran to Tabriz was a reasonable one. The three men decided to travel there by coach, mainly because Peter possessed a false passport and nobody checked documents when such transport was used. Tabriz, or the Dome of Islam, was a rendezvous for artists and intellectuals and boasted a great university founded in 1934. Like the other universities in the city-Sahand, Tarbiat Moalem and Azad, this main one offered various courses which attracted many scholars of repute. Within three days, Ali, Parviz and Peter hoped to make sure they contacted *Saddi* and to explore the city.

They booked in at the Siena Hotel on Bagh Golestan Square. Peter wanted to buy his dream carpet, whereas Ali and Parviz tried to look for *Saddi* and to call on a person called Shahryar who was being compared to one of Iran's greatest poets-Hafiz. Ali who loved Persian poetry said,

"Shahryar is writing a series of poems about the loss of simplicity, innocence and manhood because of the urbanization and migration of villagers to the cities. We must meet this wonderful man." Indeed, in 1957 Tabriz was a city which was beginning to make rapid progress, even though it was often called the 'Place of Revenge'. It was located in a mountainous area of Iran and was ideal for mystic scholars. It still possessed its long narrow streets which were hurdles for urban development. Yet, the various factories, workshops and handicraft centres gave this city a charm of its own.

Peter went alone to the large roofed Bazaar of Tabriz with its long passageways, inn yards, mosques and gates in order to buy a Persian carpet. After a successful purchase he met up with Parviz to visit the magnificent town hall which had been built in 1933 and constructed by the then mayor, Haj Arfa Almolk Jalili. Parviz explained the design of the building to Peter, because he had visited Tabriz before.

"This building is constructed in the form of an eagle with its wings outspread. On the top of the bird is a clock with four faces and every hour the clock bell is rung."

Tired, exhausted and hungry, Peter and Parviz returned to their hotel where they were joined by Ali who admired Peter's carpet.

"Now you can use it as your prayer mat, but not until we have had something to eat," he said rather sarcastically and led his son and friend to the restaurant.

That first night Peter could only dream of himself eating nuts and sweetmeats for which Tabriz was well known and sitting on the Persian carpet he had acquired. The three men had retired to adjoining bedrooms in the hotel after Ali and Parviz had told Peter about their meeting with Shahryar. No mention was made of an encounter with *Saddi*. Part way through the night Peter had an admonition. He woke up on a number of occasions, feeling that something was wrong and that danger was lurking nearby. At the same time, he could hear sounds of gasping and what seemed like scraping coming from Ali's bedroom. Looking at his watch, he noticed it was two o'clock in the morning. From that moment onwards he began almost to count the seconds on the large clock on the wall above his bed and, disturbed by the noises next door, he could not catch his sleep.

Suddenly he heard a groan which grew louder and louder and then shouts of pain. Peter rushed to Ali's bedroom, only to meet Parviz in the corridor who had also heard his father's cries of distress. They both entered Ali's bedroom and saw him sitting on the bed holding his stomach in agony and looking quite pale and ghastly and his face distorted in pain. Then he began to cough and vomited a mixture of food, phlegm and blood.

"Ring for the doctor," shouted Peter to Parviz. "I'll give your father some bicarbonate of soda."

Like a medic Peter fussed around Ali until a doctor arrived and carried out an examination Then in a grim voice the doctor said,

"You have eaten something which disagrees with you. I must send for an ambulance."

"Allah is punishing me for the sins I have committed," retorted Ali and seemed somewhat resigned to the fact that he was going to die.

"Have you eaten anything apart from the kebabs and fruit we all had for the evening meal?" asked Parviz.

In between gasps of discomfort Ali suddenly remembered.

"Yes. Before you and Peter returned to the hotel this afternoon, I received a parcel from *Saddi* which was delivered to my room. He wrote on a postcard in the parcel that, since he missed seeing me at *Nowruz*, then I should accept his present of pastry and nuts called *Ajil-e Moshkel Ghosha*. I ate one small piece of the pastry and put the remainder in my bedside locker over there." And he pointed feebly to the left of his bed.

The doctor took the present out of the locker drawer and handed it to the ambulance crew who had arrived to take Ali to the main hospital. Peter and Parviz followed in a taxi, and they had to wait two hours before a senior doctor approached them both. In an abrupt and official manner, he said,

"There is no cause for alarm, Parviz Amampour. Your father is very lucky. He only ate a small portion of the pastry which was poisoned. We have examined the present and what he has regurgitated, and we can ascertain that he has been slightly poisoned by a small amount of arsenic. If he had eaten any more, he would have died."

Saddi could not be found to explain this dastardly deed, so after a few days, when Ali had recovered, the three men returned to Tehran.

For the following two months the Amampours kept out of sight, all saying that they were obsessed by the fear of retribution and punishment for causing harm, injury and even death to others as a result of their spying activities.

This of course was highlighted by the assassination attempt on Ali. He declared one day to Peter that he wished to atone for his sins.

"For the death of your friend, Stefan, and the wounding of your tutor, Ibrahim, in Baghdad, retribution is required in the eyes of Allah because we have been associated with these events. The Qur'an says, 'O you who believe, retribution is prescribed for you in the case of murder' and 'There is retribution in wounds.' Islam allows the victims or their families to pardon us for the crimes we have committed. This is considered their right. What shall we do, Peter?"

Peter looked nonplussed and just shook his head, not knowing what to say. Ali did not wait for an answer and continued his lamentation.

"To be pardoned we must make either a payment of blood money to the victims' families, that is to say a fixed monetary payment, or the families can pardon us. Punishment can be waived on the grounds of repentance, and we are truly repentant. Indeed, pardon is encouraged and preferred. The Qur'an states 'To forgive is closer to piety'. Yet, one of the victims, Stefan, was not a Muslim. Is that true?"

Peter did his best to follow the intricacies and logic of this part of the Qur'an and Islamic law and answered Ali's question.

"Yes. I knew Stefan very well. His mother was a Christian Arab, but she does not know that her son is dead, I can write to her, if you wish. Ibrahim is a Sunni Muslim, and he will understand what you say about forgiveness. I can also write to him and explain that what happened in Baghdad to him was an accident. In any case you, Parviz and Asya were only indirectly responsible for the actions taken against the two victims, so I am sure this will be taken into consideration by Allah."

Ali was pleased with Peter's remarks and agreed that he should contact Ibrahim and Stefan's parents.

As time went by Peter became more curious about the religious rules and practices which governed this

Shi'ite family. This resulted in him showing greater respect towards Muslims generally and the Shi'ite interpretation of the Qur'an in particular. Although the stance taken by some men towards women in Iran was quite liberal, Peter could not understand why Asya educated in the west rarely went out and, when she did, was always accompanied by her father or brother or both. Although the wearing of the *hijab* or Islamic dress in Iran was not compulsory, most women decided that it was both proper and respectful for it to be worn in public places, especially during Ramadan and Moharram. Peter had noticed a few posters, mainly in the poorer areas of Tehran which stated that the veiling of women was a protection against lewd and derisory glances from men. These posters proclaimed such warnings as 'My sister, guard your veil' and 'My brother close your eyes'.

Asya, who had been brought up in a somewhat relaxed atmosphere for women in Moscow, found at first the restrictions for women in Tehran rather overpowering in spite of the relaxation of rules against them.

"I find it impossible to go around Tehran without my brother, father or a male relative. If I am on my own, I have to wear an Islamic dress, or at least a scarf to cover my head and neck. If we women go by bus, we are in some areas of the city segregated and can only enter by the rear door. This causes me terrible distress."

Peter could not let Asya get away with what she was saying.

"Asya. I have seen Iranian women enjoying the company of men on the streets and at the university. I have also heard that some of them have even joined the police force."

"Yes, Peter," retorted Asya." That may be true, but they are the daughters of the rich and upper middle classes, many of whom have been educated in European schools here in Tehran or even in Europe itself. Indeed, I am sometimes disgusted when they flaunt their freedom and in the process lose some of the respect for their religion."

Peter did not argue with Asya. He realised the dichotomy which existed. She wanted independence for Muslim women, but at the same time she realised that they should honour the perhaps rather old fashioned Muslim customs which had existed for generations.

Discussions often ensued in the Amampour household over the role of women in society and it was Asya who often dictated the arguments which ensued.

"Do you know, Peter," said Asya one day when they were all sat down after the evening meal, "that in Iran the birth of a baby boy for many families is a cause for celebration, because his parents know that he will grow up, remain at home and help with the running of the household? A baby girl, however, is considered a liability for she will leave home, and a dowry has to be paid when she is married. That is why I shall never marry. I do not want to be a burden to the rest of my family."

Peter was flabbergasted. Asya, the former feminist and women of independence, seemed to feel trapped in Iranian society. Once again, she was finding it difficult to relate the desire for her as a woman to be liberated in a Muslim country with the normal practices of the Muslim religion with regards females. In Moscow she was faced with a different dilemma, namely, how to exist as a Muslim in an atheist country. Peter tried to comfort her, but at the same time he could not understand why Islam could sometimes denigrate females in this manner. On the other hand, the other members of Asya's family were to a certain extent pleased that at last she was trying to conform to Muslim practices. Or was she still hoping after all this time to eventually become a successful ballerina?

However, Asya was stubborn and remained so. She was not going to accept all Muslim customs without question. She had inherited an enquiring mind, and this was put to test in Tehran where she saw contradictions regarding women's rights and responsibilities all around her. With her father's permission she joined one of the women's groups called *hay'ats,* which were mainly for religious instruction. But Asya was Asya, and she was not shy in questioning members of the *Ulama* or elders who preached and assisted her in the study of the Qur'an. One problem which beset her was the attitude of the elders to *sigha* or temporary marriage. Asya's response to this was instantaneous.

"I cannot understand how Shia Muslims can accept marriage for a certain length of time, even for hours. When you marry it is because you love somebody and that should be for life."

Most members of the group grew somewhat tired of Asya's attempts to stir up trouble and one of the *Ulama* rebuked her.

"When you are older, Asya, you will realise that *sigha* is necessary, in some cases to secure financial deals. We, Shi'ites, are pragmatic." This 'put down' did not satisfy Asya who continued attending the *hay'ats,* but questioned certain practices, especially those which affected women in a detrimental way. In the end, however, she was asked not to attend the meetings because she was too argumentative. Asya was glad that she had escaped what she considered to be a stifling atmosphere where women were ignored most of the time.

Towards October it seemed that Ali's prediction of punishment was going to come true. Not only was he ignoring his promise to KPOK to sow discord in Iran, but also his promise to Allah to carry out a *jihad*. On every corner of every street Ali could sense danger to his person and to the rest of his family He tried even to analyse what would happen now he had abandoned Operation *Azady*. Agent *Khayyam* from Isfahan had been sent back to the Soviet Union for disobeying orders and trying to eliminate the British spy, *Abyadh*. Agent *Saddi* from Tabriz had disappeared from view. After the abortive attempt on Ali's life and his appearance in another Middle Eastern country, it was blatantly obvious that he was working for Great Britain. This left only *Hafiz* from Mashad, who had not contacted Ali for some time.

Gathering Peter and his family around him, Ali announced to them that Operation *Azady* was dead on its feet.

"We now need to plan our survival and find out what is happening since I informed KPOK that I wished to suspend all operations here in Iran. *Hafiz* still needs to be contacted. He will know what is taking place and I can trust him because he is extremely religious. He will sympathise with our predicament and make positive suggestions on what to do next."

Peter wondered whether it was safe to contact *Hafiz* since he was still carrying out the wishes of KPOK. Ali, however, was adamant.

"Apart from you, Peter, we will have to go to Mashad and try and meet *Hafiz.*"

So, arrangements were made for the Amampours to meet *Hafiz* on the last Friday of October at a bookstall near the Grand Mosque of Gowharshad. Dressed as pilgrims the whole family set off by coach for Mashad, the men wearing Iranian robes and the women in black *burqas*. Ali reminded his wife and daughter that it was necessary for them to wear these garments because Mashad was a strict holy city. Asya did not feel comfortable wearing such a garment but agreed with her father that it would be sensible to go to a holy place in such attire. Before she left Asya explained to Peter that a *burqa* was an outer garment designed to cloak the whole body.

"I shall wear it to cover my long dress underneath. However, the *burqa* I am going to put on possesses a veil revealing only my eyes and my forehead. This is known as a half *niqab*. I understand that it is unusual for women in Iran to wear this item of clothing, but my mother and I must dress extremely modestly, if we are going to Mashad," she said.

Peter did not fully understand the significance of the *burqa,* so Asya added,

"Many Muslims believe that in the Qur'an and the collected traditions of the life of our prophet, Mohammed, men and women are required to dress and behave modestly in public. That is why my mother and I are going to wear *burqas* because they cover the whole body."

Although not too happy with the garment, Asya told Peter it could be worse. Some of the women she knew wore the full Afghan *chador* which was a *burqa* with a net or grill for the eyes and known as a 'shuttlecock' *burqa.*

Peter was told that a few women from other Muslim countries going on the pilgrimage to Mashad would be wearing this blue garment made of light material with a sort of cap fitted and decorated with embroidery.

"The rich go on a pilgrimage to Mecca and the poor to Mashad," said Asya after explaining about the *burqa.* "Pilgrims who go to Mecca receive the title of *Haji,* whereas those going to Mashad are given the title *Mashtee.* So, Peter, when we return in a weeks time you will be looking at four *Mashtees,* all being well."

Peter was relieved to see that both Asya and Anastasia were wearing black *burqas* and not the full *chador* which covered the entire face.

It took the Amampours three days by coach to reach Mashad, the largest city in Iran after Tehran and one of the holiest places in the Shi'ite world. It was situated in the valley of the Kashan River between two mountain ranges, Binalood and Hezar-e Masjed. Located on the borders of Afghanistan and Turkmenistan it contained a large university named after the poet, Ferdowsi. It was also the centre for religious learning and favoured by the T*aliban* or students. When the family arrived, it was quite cold. Apparent were the large number of pilgrims in the city, wandering through the large, beautiful parks and visiting the numerous shrines.

"Do you know that over twenty million pilgrims visit Mashad every year," said Ali, always willing to impart statistical facts.

Yet, his wife, son and daughter were fascinated by the well laid out and regular rows of trees along the roads with their brown autumnal leaves What was more interesting, however, was the sight of the golden cupolas and minarets within the city and the Kooh Sangi and Mellat Parks for young children to play in, whilst their parents devoted most of the day to prayer and supplication.

Asya was excited that the family was going to Gowharshad Mosque. Before setting out for Mashad she had read about this holy city and as a keen feminist she was eager to impart to the others her knowledge of this wonderful building constructed on the orders of a woman.

"This mosque is a testament to the genius of Gowharshad, the wife of Tamberlane's eldest son, Shahrock," she said with pride in her voice. "She alone supervised its building in the early fifteenth century. If you look carefully at it, I am sure you can see what a remarkable artist and architect she was. Here she has created one of the wonders of the world which I believe surpasses many architectural delights of that century." The whole family gazed in awe at the mosque with its fifty metre high domes and cavernous golden portals. Situated to the south of the Holy

Shrine of Imam Reza, it was on that day visited by many pilgrims.

The Amampours mingled with the pilgrims leaving the mosque after Friday prayers and made their way towards the bookstall where they hoped to meet *Hafiz,* Ali and Parviz in the front and Asya and Anastasia a few steps behind, as was the custom. Asya had met *Hafiz* only twice, once at KPOK headquarters and then in Camp Badkube. In fact, she was the only one who could remember his real name-Amir. What struck her at the time was that he was very tall.
"Not a good height for a KPOK agent," she told her father. "He will 'stick out like a sore thumb' in a crowd."
However, today all the men looked the same with their dark beards and Asya strained her eyes to locate a tall man with a long beard and possibly wearing the clothes of a pilgrim.

Suddenly such a man appeared, approached Ali and without any hesitation, muttered in his ear that he deserved to die.
"Marg bar kafaran," he shouted.
At the same time, he slashed with a dagger at Ali's arms and legs. Parviz was right- a dagger or a similar weapon with a blade was a sure silent device to kill somebody. Always on the lookout to defend his father, especially after the attempt to poison him in Tabriz, Parviz acted spontaneously. He set about the

tall stranger, wrenched the weapon from his hand and held him in a firm grip. Asya looked at the assailant and shouted to her brother,

"It's definitely *Hafiz.*" and then rushed to assist her father who had slumped to the ground.

Meanwhile Parviz had pushed *Hafiz* behind the bookstall, whilst various questions ran through his head. Why was *Hafiz* trying to kill his father who after all was his KPOK commander and in charge of Operation *Azady?* Did he know that the Amampours had renounced spying and did not wish to return to the Soviet Union? Had he been given orders by SMERSH to eliminate traitors who had changed sides? But then, why had he slashed with a dagger only at his father's arms and legs and not at his heart?

By this time groans were coming both from Ali and his assailant. Blood was seeping through the sleeve of Ali's coat and Anastasia was trying to quell the flow. Her husband kept muttering between the groans that he was suffering punishment for all his misdeeds.

"Oh, Allah. Please forgive me my sins. My fate is in your hands. Let me enter paradise."

In the meantime, Parviz did not relax his grip on *Hafiz* for one moment but increased the pressure until the tall man's face began to show signs of agonising distortion.

"Have I killed the unbeliever?" he kept repeating, spluttering and groaning at the same time.

Parviz did not answer, but he soon realised that the incident which had taken place over the past few minutes had attracted a larger crowd than usual near the bookstall.

"There are SAVAK agents in the crowd dressed as pilgrims," murmured the owner of the bookstall, looking warily at the dagger now in Parviz's hand and which was still being directed towards the neck of *Hafiz* who was looking extremely frightened. Dragging him away from the crowd which had gathered, Parviz shouted to his sister that he would meet her and his mother later once they had arranged to take Ali to the hospital.

So, it was left for Anastasia and Asya as well as a few helpful pilgrims to support Ali and hail a taxi to take him to the hospital. Luckily, he had suffered only a few superficial cuts which were bandaged, and he was allowed, accompanied by his wife and daughter, to return to their hotel. Whilst this was going on, Parviz was questioning *Hafiz* about his intention to kill his father.

"You know my father is a devout Shia Muslim and is by no means an infidel," he declared, pressing the dagger slightly into this poor Soviet agent's neck and drawing blood.

"Yes. He is an infidel," answered *Hafiz*. "*I* have been told by KPOK command that he has given up on Operation *Azady* and, also, the *jihad* here in Iran. He has at the same time disobeyed orders from Moscow. Moreover, he is harbouring a British spy in his house. Is this true?"

Parviz shook his head and breathing heavily said, "You have it all wrong. My father has come to the conclusion that the *jihad* against the Shah is misplaced, and, in any case, he is concerned that he is helping an atheist country, the Soviet Union, and this would not be Allah's will. Surely as a devout Shi'ite yourself you will understand this. My father also has the support of the whole family in supporting a British agent who is also fed up with spying for his country."

Hafiz seemed taken aback by what Parviz said.
"I did not intend to kill your father in any case, only to frighten him. That is why I slashed at his arms and legs. If what you say is true, then I am sorry. Kill me if you wish. I have sinned."
After some consideration Parviz decided that *Hafiz* was truly repentant and immediately released the dagger from his throat.
"Seek repentance from Allah," he said shaking his father's would-be assassin. "Now you must decide what you are going to do from now on. I cannot help you. If you do not give up spying, then you are going against the wishes of your maker."
With that warning he pushed *Hafiz* away and threw the dagger into the bushes at the side of the road. *Hafiz* looked relieved, came up to Parviz and kissed

his hands before disappearing into the crowd in front of the mosque.

That very evening the Amampours decided to leave Mashad and the following morning they were on their way back to Tehran. Asya, however, was a little disappointed because she wanted to visit the Bazaar-e Bozorg and buy a souvenir, perhaps turquoise prayer beads or a payer mat. Parviz himself had set his heart on calling in on the Ayatolla Al-Khoei Madrassa which was a centre for religious learning frequented by the *Taliban.* All that had to be put on hold, and the family had to forego some of the delights of this city. Anastasia particularly was worried about her husband who was still convinced that he was being punished for his sins.

Peter was rather upset when he was told what had happened in Mashad. So. on the spur of the moment and without consulting anybody he advised the whole family to seek asylum in Britain Typically, he had not checked to ascertain whether he had the right to do this or whether it was possible.

"You know you are not safe here in Tehran or in any part of Iran," he said. "I will contact the British Embassy and try and arrange a safe passage to my homeland for you all."

He hoped that what he was suggesting would take place without too much difficulty. So, he said to convince them, that they were in a unique position to divulge to the British all they knew about Soviet intentions in Iran, Iraq and the rest of the Middle East.

Ali and Anastasia were reluctant at first to accept Peter's kind offer, mainly because Ali wanted to return to Tajikistan to end his days there, whilst Anastasia felt that another move to a different country would be too much for her. Parviz was in two minds. On the one hand he longed to complete further studies at Moscow University, but on the other hand he knew that a return to the Soviet Union would probably result in his death. What mattered most to Peter were Asya's thoughts about going to Britain and he was surprised to learn that she was the only one who warmed to his proposals.

"My life has been transformed over the past two years," she declared. "I really intended to become a famous ballerina, but I now realise that I have outgrown this desire. My father is right. Such a career is not for a women who embraces Islam as I do. However, we must be pragmatic. I support Peter's offer of asylum. In any case it is better to live in a country like Britain which is secular and allows all faiths to flourish than in a Muslim country like Iran where espionage and danger exist. I can understand the reasons why my brother and my parents are reluctant to move to another country, but we cannot live here in permanent fear or return to the country of our birth."

It was obvious that Ali, Anastasia, Parviz and Asya were worried about remaining in Iran. All of them missed to a certain extent the lives they led in the Soviet Union. Ali, especially, was still proud of 'his' country's success in the development of science and technology. With a glint of pride in his eyes he said to his family on the 4th of October,

"Last month my country fired the first inter-continental ballistic missile and today it has launched the world's first artificial satellite called *sputnik*. Travelling at a speed of 29,000 kilometres an hour it is capable of circling the earth a number of times."

Peter was impressed but could not imagine that the Soviet Union would be the first country to launch a satellite into space. He was sure that the USA would do this, but he knew there was a race taking place between the two countries to be the first in this field. Ali saw that Peter was dubious about this claim.

"If you don't believe me, Peter, then you and the rest of my family can watch the satellite passing overhead tonight, when we all sit on the roof."

So, Peter and the Amampours stayed up all night on the flat roof in order to witness *Sputnik* passing overhead. Peter did not have the courage to tell Ali that the Soviet satellite looked suspiciously like a plane flying over Tehran. That would have broken Ali's heart, so he kept silent. Only a few days later did members of QDAT still in Camp Ddibben inform

Peter that the *Sputnik* could be seen quite clearly in the sky over that part of Iraq.

"I am sure you are amazed by Soviet technology," remarked Ali.

Peter did not answer, but he was mystified. If the former Soviet agents were so proud of the achievements of the Soviet Union, why then were they so reluctant to return home. But, at the same time he realised their predicament. To return to their homeland would result in retribution and punishment which could ultimately lead to death. However, to remain in Iran would probably result in the same fate. For Peter the only answer was for them to seek a safe haven in Britain.

From this point onwards Peter discussed with them the possibility of going with or without him to Britain. He told them that there was the possibility that they might be interrogated by the British authorities and that they might not fit in with the system of government there, but that was a risk they had to take. He promised them, however, that they would not suffer any punishment for their espionage activities in the past. In November he informed officials at the British Embassy in Tehran of his offer to the Amampours which was gladly accepted both by ODAT and other intelligence organisations and arrangements were made to secretly extricate the family from the capital of Iran.

Meanwhile, Peter continued to lodge with his friends

who slowly but surely began to inform him more about Shia Muslim beliefs and the difference between Sunnis and Shi'ites. Ali as usual explained.

"When our prophet, Mohammed (peace be upon him), died in the early seventh century, one group of Muslims, the Sunnis, elected Abu Bakr, a close friend of the prophet, to be the next caliph. However, a smaller group, the Shi'ites, believed that the prophets' son-in-law, Ali, should be the caliph."

"Don't bore Peter with a long-winded history, father," said Parviz impatiently.

Peter was intrigued and asked what the main differences in practice were between Sunni and Shia Muslims.

"Mainly through the interpretation of the Qur'an and the *Hadith*," said Parviz taking up the explanation. "The Sunnis consider the *Hadith*, or sayings of Mohammed, are those narrated by any one of the twelve thousand companions of the prophet. The Shi'ites give preference to the *Hadith* as narrated by Fatima and Ali and their close associates. In practice Sunnis pray five times a day, whereas the Shi'ites pray three times. Surely you have noticed that we pray as a family in the morning, the afternoon and at night? You have also seen that we place a small tablet of clay from a holy place on our forehead whilst prostrate in prayer. During ablutions we pour water from the palm of our hands to the elbow and not the other way around like the Sunnis."

Peter still wanted to know more about Shia Muslim beliefs and questioned the family even more.

"How could you live in an atheist country like the Soviet Union and follow their laws and how do you reconcile this atheism which exists there with your beliefs?"

"Well," replied Ali. "When we were in the Soviet Union, we had to be pragmatic and hope that the Shia Muslim doctrine of *taqiyya* would allow us to conceal our true beliefs as a form of protection in the face of persecution."

At this juncture he broke down because, as he confessed, he should have avoided the practice of *taqiyya* more often.

Although he was learning more about Islam, Peter waited anxiously for the Amampours to come to a definite decision with regards political asylum in Britain. After long discussions all the members of the family eventually agreed to take a chance and follow Peter's recommendations. Visas were issued, medical checks were carried out and Ali and Anastasia started to learn English with the help of their son and daughter so that the transfer to yet another country would not be too devastating. It was impossible for the British and Iranian governments to neutralise the effectiveness of KPOK's operations at Camp Badkube and this left Peter and his 'friends' in a perilous position. Ali, for example, could not give up complaining about retribution and punishment and in many ways, he was justified in doing so.

Two events took place in November which were to cause great consternation to Peter and the Amampours. Unable to purchase one of the new or second-hand American cars beginning to flood the Iranian market in the 1950s, Parviz had decided to buy an old and rather rusty German Opel Kapitän. Each day he would spend hours carrying out repairs on his new 'toy', painting the exterior and driving through Tehran. His favourite pastime was to drive to Karaj, some forty kilometres from the capital, park his car near the facilities which provided water sports for the residents of Tehran and relax whilst reading English and American literature often provided by Peter.

One day he was at this delightful spot reading an American comic book called T-Man. Peter had managed to get hold of a number of back copies of this comic produced between 1951 and 1956 which provided a snapshot of Iran's attempts to nationalise the oil industry. They also highlighted the espionage and intrigue between the Soviet Union and the United States of America in Iran. Parviz was eagerly looking at the pictures and speech bubbles of the American agent, Traske, or was it a Soviet agent, throwing a pig at an Iranian nationalist, when he suddenly noticed a large car in his rear mirror. Well, the car seemed to resemble an American jeep, and it looked as though it was about to bump into his precious 'banger'.

Trying to remember his evasive driving skills Parviz also thought about his own survival and so he said to himself,

"If a car driven by myself is under attack, my response should be to get out of it as quickly as possible."

However, not wishing to lose his car, he ignored this advice, turned on the ignition key and the engine roared into life. Then he moved his car forward, did a reverse spin and tried to ram the 'jeep'.

Unfortunately, the gears on his rusty 'banger' crunched and made a terrible noise. Turning off the ignition, the steering wheel locked, and the car came to a halt. Parviz then realised he was caught.

Three men emerged from the jeep and made their presence felt by speaking in Farsi and dragging Parviz out of his car.

"We are British agents. Come with us."

"What is happening?" thought Parviz as he was pushed into the back of the jeep. "I know Peter has informed the British authorities that we are going to give up spying for the Soviet Union and are being taken to Britain. But, why, therefore, am I being kidnapped by British agents?"

As Parviz was being driven back to Tehran, leaving his Opel Kapitän at Karaj, he was comforted by the one thought that Peter had told him that the British never used torture methods.

How wrong he was. Both in English and Farsi the three men in the jeep kept saying,

"Are you *Rumi,* a Soviet agent, and what do you know about Operation *Azady?"*

Parviz denied he was *Rumi.*

"You have the wrong man. What is this Operation *Azady?* I am confused."

This annoyed his captors who took him to a large building somewhere near Tehran University and began to subject him to twelve hours of continuous torture until he was only released when Peter found out what was happening.

"I am so sorry, Parviz," said Peter, showing definite relief that his friend bore no visible marks of being tortured.

Exhausted, but obviously pleased to see Peter, Parviz mentioned what had happened to him.

"At first, I was kicked and slapped by my abductors whilst I was blindfolded and sitting on a chair. When I did not answer the questions to their satisfaction, they told me they were rubbing pages of the Qur'an against my face. What sacrilege!"

Peter was incensed by this account and asked Parviz whether they used any other form of torture on him.

"Yes," he said. "Later they removed the blindfold and began to attack my cultural sensitivity, especially that which involved issues of gender and sexual identity. They made me stand naked in front of a female interrogator who accused me of being a homosexual.

What was really degrading, however, was that women's underwear was placed over parts of my body."

Peter was adamant that the British did not use methods of torture in any form.

"You have been kidnapped by rogue elements of the British secret service or the SAVAK. I shall find out which in due course."

"That may be so, Peter, but there was more to come," declared Parviz, scarcely believing what Peter had said. "I was taken to another room where I was again blindfolded. I was then placed in a bath which seemed to be full of water. Somehow, I was tied to the bottom of this bath with my head held just above the water level. Then jets of water were poured over my nose and down my mouth until I felt like I was drowning. The torturers kept saying that they would leave me to drown if I did not tell them about Soviet operations in Iran. But I kept my nerve and said nothing. I do not know how long the torture lasted, but it was terrible."

By this time Peter was furious and indicated once again that he would try and get to the bottom of what had happened and would inform the British Embassy of what had taken place.

"I am sure there has been a mistake somewhere along the line Your captors must have been members of SAVAK. Anyway, I hope this incident will not deter you and your family coming to Britain."

Initially Parviz did not say a word, but then a wan

smile appeared on his face.

"If you say, Peter, that rogue elements were to blame, then I believe you and I hope they will be punished. However, to help me get over my sorrow please drive me to Karaj so that I can retrieve my car."

Peter agreed at once and towards late evening he drove Parviz to Karaj in order for him to pick up his beloved car.

After months of playing 'cat and mouse' with the Amampours SAVAK agents decided it was time to act and pick up at least some members of the family, if they could, and interrogate them before the British intervened. The SAVAK, a contraction of the Farsi words for security and information organisation, was hated and feared by thousands of the Shah's opponents. Dissidents were often captured, tortured and killed for speaking out against the Shah and his regime. Therefore, the Amampours were quite right to be wary of this organisation and to try and look as inconspicuous as possible at all times.

Towards the end of December Parviz and his mother took a different route to the British Embassy than Asya and her father. Walking along Shech Faziellah and Nood Highways between Nasr and Pardisan Parks, Ali and his daughter hailed a taxi to take them to meet Peter at ten o'clock outside the British Embassy. Peter had stated that this was an opportune time for them to be smuggled into the embassy without arousing suspicion. As the taxi, a black saloon car, stopped at the side of the road, Ali slid into the front seat and Asya in the rear. Before it could pull away from the kerb a man with short, cropped hair and wearing a black leather jacket ran towards the taxi, opened the rear door and grabbed Asya, pushing her to the floor. Ali shouted at the taxi driver,

"What are you doing? Who is this man? Are we being kidnapped or what?"

The driver did not answer but drove quickly away. At the same time Ali turned and glanced out of the rear window. He saw a similar, but larger black car, containing two men also in black jackets, following them.

"The Shah's secret police are on to us, "shouted Ali to Asya in Russian, but she did not respond because she was struggling with the man in the rear seat.

"Leave her alone," roared Ali in Farsi, now extremely agitated as he tried to stop the taxi by pulling on the steering wheel. It slowed down and drove into a side street followed by the pursuing car.

"*Ist va garn tir mizanam*," screamed the man in the rear seat, grappling with Asya and trying to extricate a revolver from his jacket in order to threaten Ali and Asya.

"Yes. You have been kidnapped by the Shah and the British government" and he aimed a Smith-Wesson at Ali who promptly let go of the steering wheel and remained still with his hands in the air.

The taxi stopped abruptly and the man holding Asya motioned with his revolver for them to climb out of the car. One of the SAVAK agents in the car behind, also holding a gun, came towards them, jerked open both front and rear doors and ordered Ali and Asya to follow him to the back seat of the other car.

"*Manra bebar be edareh markazi*," he said to his companion in the front seat so he could be driven to SAVAK headquarters. At the same time, he sat between Ali and Asya, waving his pistol at both of them in turn. Slowly the two cars moved off and stopped at a building somewhere near the British Embassy.

"Be brave," whispered Ali to his daughter in Russian. Then turning to his captor he said in Farsi, "Where are we going?"

"To hell and back," came the answer.

Asya tried to say something and to move her hand, but this movement annoyed her captor who suddenly slapped her face and kicked her to the floor of the car. He then placed a chloroform cloth over her face. She struggled but soon lost consciousness. Ali went to help, but the SAVAK agent caught him a blow on the jaw which sent him flying backwards on the rear seat. By this time the car was moving slowly along a path to the side of the dark concrete building and stopped in front of a side door. The driver came round to the rear door of the car and opened it. He grabbed Asya by her hair and dragged her outside, where she lay motionless, obviously recovering from the effects of the chloroform. As she lay on the ground the driver of the car said to both Ali and Asya,

"Leave what you are carrying in the car. You won't need anything where you are going."

An Iranian policeman in uniform then appeared with what looked like a sub-machine gun, but the two prisoners were in no condition to notice exactly what type of weapon it was. On the orders of the two rather brutal SAVAK plain-clothed agents the policeman led father and daughter along a dark and dismal corridor and kept demanding that they should follow him.

"Don balam bia in taraf."

At the end of the corridor, he opened one cell for Ali and a similar one for Asya, pushing them both inside.

"Take off your clothes down to your underwear and wait until I return," he snapped.

The policeman slammed the gates shut and the prisoners could hear the bolts being driven home. It was too cold to take off their outer garments, so they sat shivering in the corners of their respective dimly lit cells.

Asya, who had slightly recovered, took the opportunity to smooth down her hair and to study the prison cell into which she had been thrown. There was no real furniture or heating. In one corner there was a sort of gimlet hole in the wall with a bung in it. Asya removed the bung and a trickle of water dripped out, allowing her to at least quench her thirst and wet her face. A dim light overhead revealed a waste hole which existed below a spigot as well as a toilet with a curtain which was pulled back. A dirty mattress in another corner was meant to serve as a bed. The light flickered on and off until eventually it was completely extinguished.

The next day nobody came to the cells and the only conversation Asya had was with her father who tried to keep her spirits up. He was complaining that his cheeks were swollen as a result of the SAVAK agent's blow to his jaw.

"Have faith in Allah," he said to his daughter. "Do not despair."

On the morning of the third day the cell doors were unlocked, and track suits, trainers and socks were handed to the two prisoners followed by an unappetising gruel which father and daughter ate avidly. A few hours later the doors swung open and two policemen shouted in unison,

"Come on. It is time to go."

Both prisoners walked in front of their guards, Ali having to support Asya who was so weak that she stumbled at every step. Meanwhile Ali's mouth continued to cause him pain as well.

They were taken to a small room which contained only a long table behind which sat three SAVAK agents. On the wall was a picture of the Shah and the

Iranian flag. Before they could say anything the agent in the middle spoke quite slowly and gravely.

"Ali and Asya Amampour, or should I say Amampourov. You have been sentenced to death by this special tribunal for spying for an organisation called KPOK from the Soviet Union. There is no appeal. However, you can escape this ultimate punishment if you tell us all about Operation *Azady*. Otherwise, you will be executed by firing squad within a week."

Both prisoners shivered at the thought of dying, especially in a foreign land, so Ali said that they would both return within a few hours and decide what they would reveal about their spying operations in Iran. With that the SAVAK agents indicated to the two policemen that they should return the prisoners to their cells.

Meanwhile Parviz and Anastasia were going frantic. They were supposed to meet Ali and Asya at ten o'clock outside the British Embassy. At noon they saw Peter coming out of the embassy together with an official. Peter informed them that there had been a mix-up and that Ali and Asya had been kidnapped by SAVAK agents with the connivance of the British secret service which included ODAT. He stated that without his knowledge the movements of the Amampours had been monitored for some time. Patting Parviz on the shoulder, Peter said sympathetically,

"Leave everything to me, Parviz, I will rescue your father and sister."

Parviz, however, could not be comforted and both he and his mother began to weep uncontrollably. Peter again tried to reassure them both and advised Parviz to take his mother into the British Embassy. At the same time, he promised that his father and sister would come to no harm.

Nevertheless, Peter was worried. Promises by the embassy staff that the Amampour family would come to no harm were sacrosanct in his eyes.

"Why the difficulty now?" Peter said to himself. "Why have two members of the family been picked up by SAVAK agents? Not only have the Amampours given up spying for the Soviet Union, but their safety will benefit British intelligence, if they can be transferred to the United Kingdom."

Help for Ali and Asya was at hand, however, and after two days Peter arrived with British Embassy staff at the SAVAK prison where his two friends were held and their release was negotiated. Imagine the relief on the faces of Ali and Asya when they saw Peter.

"I hope this is the last of our punishments," gasped Ali. "We hope we will be safe in your hands, Peter, from now on."

Only when the four members of the family were in the British Embassy did Peter feel sure that his mission in Tehran was complete.

Although Peter was convinced that he had found a

'safe haven' for the Amampours, he was still beset with problems. Somehow, he needed a way out of spying for his country, but this was impossible whilst he was in the RAF. Moreover, the so-called mystical sword of truth as put forward to him by ODAT no longer appealed to him. This also applied to the Amampours who were sceptical of KPOK's claim to advocate the truth. In reality these swords of truth had brought disappointment, doubts and heartache to all of them. The romanticism inherent in espionage and the appeal made to support British democracy and Soviet communism had resulted in their swords of truth becoming blunt and it seemed unlikely that anything could sharpen their blades. At least for Asya and her family truth and justice now lay with the Islamic Sword of Truth. But where did that leave Peter? Above all he needed to look elsewhere for real truth and justice.

Indeed, Peter's mission was complete, because the following day he was flown from Mehrabad, Tehran's main airport, to London via Rome in a Hermes aircraft. Prior to his departure he wished the Amampours all the best and said that he would see them very soon in Britain. On arrival in London, he was summoned to GCHQ in Cheltenham and asked to make a report on the situation in Iran. Only being there for one year his report was brief. He stated that the main obstacle to democracy in the country was the controversial and disliked figure, the Shah. He also mentioned his secret police had imprisoned and killed a large number of people who opposed his rule. He also stated that religious fundamentalists, the KGB and other groups were preparing to depose the Shah. He also felt that the defection of Russian agents, his 'friends', who belonged to an organisation called KPOK, was his main success in Iran.

Peter then began to reflect on his accomplishments in Iraq and Iran and whether Britain's attempts to support democratic groups there had been successful. He could not blame millions of people in the Muslim world for their disenchantment with western democracy. In the early 1950s many believed that the British and American way would empower the masses and help them build societies based on liberty and justice and eventually economic prosperity. Yet, after the events in Egypt, Muslims began to find out what democracy looked like in reality. To them the so-called truth of this western ideology was a lie, and they realised they had been deceived.

Nor was democracy advocated by the Soviet Union any better. The policy of western and Soviet ideologies to seek and support the growth of democratic movements in the Muslim world and to end tyranny really meant a violation of human rights and the creation of a network of spies. It was obvious that freedom fighters who wanted to resist their tormentors and be free would be classified as terrorists. Peter had seen at first-hand how the people of Iraq and Iran had despised not only their pro-western governments, but also the attempts by foreign governments to become involved in what to them was a domestic issue.

Had Peter been one of those whose spying activities in the two countries added to the suppression of freedom? He was not sure. He was only a cog in a vast machine of espionage. Now, all he wanted to do was to ensure that his beloved Asya would soon arrive in Britain with the rest of her family. Moreover, he hoped that in a 'democratic' country like Great Britain, where he still thought that on the whole truth and justice prevailed, the Amampours would witness an end to their fear of retribution and punishment.

Chapter Five

Secret Operations and a Conversion

One Wednesday morning in July 1960 Flying Officer, Peter Smith, arrived in Cambridge after a long journey from a joint army and air force base in West Berlin. His intention was to be accepted on a course leading to a degree in Russian at the great university there, starting in October 1961. Resplendent and self-assured in his RAF uniform, Peter felt both relaxed and confident that he would do well in the forthcoming interview. Never a shrinking violet he had learnt that in this materialistic and capitalist world it was not a good idea 'to hide one's light under a bushel'. His motto was 'if you got it, flaunt it', which was the reason why he often boasted about his qualifications in languages and wore his officer's uniform as often as he could.

In any case Peter possessed sufficient GCEs at 'O' and 'A' level to matriculate. He also had service and civilian certificates in Russian, German, Arabic and Farsi, including the ability to speak Polish fluently. To him it seemed that the interview would be simply a rubber stamp for entry onto the Russian degree course. All week he had been adopting a sort of self-congratulatory pose.

"Haven't I done well over the past five years. If my father were alive today, he would have been proud to see that his son has become an officer in the RAF and soon to become a Cambridge undergraduate."

He also remembered his promise to his mother that he would gain entry into a prestigious university and added,

"I have not let my mother down either."

He glanced at the clock on Great St. Mary's Church and realised he had four hours to spare before the interview at three.

"Perhaps a visit to the University Library to see what selection of books it has would be advantageous. In any case it will pass the time of day."

So, instead of going to the Slavonic Faculty Library where the interview was going to be held. Peter entered the hallowed portals of the magnificent University Library and wandered rather aimlessly to one of the sections where he picked up a few books relating to philosophy and read some introductory remarks about the authors on the inside covers. After an hour, however, he became somewhat bored and began to make his way to the main entrance with the intention of viewing some of the university's inspiring architecture. As he moved to avoid a trolley of books being pushed by a petite librarian, he happened to look at her face.

"Goodness gracious", he said to himself. "It's Asya.

At last, I have found her."
He then darted behind another trolley of books in order to look at her more intently.

She was dressed like a prim and proper librarian should be in a black skirt and white blouse. The only thing that looked incongruous was the head scarf she was wearing which covered her beautiful black hair, her neck and shoulders. He watched how carefully and methodically she went about her business and the way in which she helped students find certain books. She seemed more attractive than ever as well as being cool and efficient. From time to time jealousy pierced his heart whenever he saw a number of male students looking intently at her ravishing beauty.
"Where has my Asya been since I saw her last in December 1957 in the British Embassy in Tehran? At least she has managed to get to Britain and now to Cambridge," he said to himself.

As he looked at Asya, Peter's thoughts turned towards what had happened to him since he left Tehran. When he arrived at his new posting at GCHQ in Cheltenham, he was able to wear for the first time the coveted uniform of a Flying Officer and was granted a vast amount of backpay. Moreover, he was given the option to sign on for a further three years, which meant five years in the colours backdated to 1956 and a further four years on the reserve. He was also given the chance to transfer to West Berlin and become involved in SIGINT and espionage activities there, which had been his original wish back in 1956.

Secret operations in Berlin were quite different from those in Iraq and Iran. The city itself symbolised the clash of ideologies between the communists, the so-called democrats of eastern Europe, and the capitalists, the so-called democrats of western Europe. From 1945 Berlin was a divided city. Following the defeat of the Nazi regime at the end of World War II, the Allied powers, that is to say, the USA, Britain, France and the Soviet Union, divided Germany up into four zones, each occupied by one of the Allied powers. Berlin was similarly divided into four separate sectors, even though it was in the Soviet zone.

In 1949 the Soviet sector, East Berlin, became the capital of the German Democratic Republic or East Germany and in the same year Bonn became the capital of the Federal Republic of Germany or West Germany. It meant that West Berlin, which still contained the American, French and British sectors, remained an island surrounded by communist East Germany. Thus the city became a focal point of the Cold War and subsequent secret operations. The lines of battle in Berlin were clearly drawn. British, American and French spies wore black, and the East German and Soviet spies wore grey. Peter knew the following off by heart,

"Don't shoot at possible KGB men. They don't shoot

at us, so we don't shoot at them. This is the silent war."

Peter witnessed occasional feeble mock gun battles between the East Germans in uniforms and the armed forces from the west, all of which came to nothing.

The SIGINT centre to which Peter was posted lay in the Spandau area of the former British sector and was nicknamed *Artur-Axmann-Kazerne*. He was told that this joint army and air force base had been the last defence by the *Hitlerjugend* or Hitler Youth who had been incorporated into the *Volksturm* or Home Guard during the last week of the second World War. Their leader then was Artur Axmann who had replaced Baldar von Schirach in 1940 as the head of this organisation. The plush barracks of *Artur-Axmann-Kazerne* had by the 1950s become the living quarters for the British military. When Peter, whose code name was now *Schmidtlein,* arrived, it also housed a Scots' infantry regiment whose members earned the name of *'Giftzwerge'* or 'poisoned dwarfs' due to their ability to 'rub West Berliners up the wrong way' with their drunken antics.

Peter found a few members of ODAT amongst the operatives in *Artur-Axmann-Kazerne,* all of whom worked extremely hard- eight hours on duty and eight hours off, followed by two days leave. Peter was relieved when he was transferred to more exciting secretive operations. This meant, travelling disguised as an East German or Polish citizen on the underground or overhead railway systems in order to locate weak spots in certain areas of East Berlin. Peter also spent time as a Flying Officer trying to persuade young air force personnel not to be attracted by well-groomed Fräuleins who tried to lure them into East Berlin or East Germany and to their fate.

However, here in Cambridge Peter had now at last found Asya, who had been in his thoughts continuously for over two and a half years, and this time he was not going to let her disappear. Quietly he approached her as she was trying to locate a book for a female student. She half-turned towards him, looked somewhat surprised and then turned her back on him until he said in Welsh,

"Bore da, cariad."

On hearing Peter's voice, Asya dropped the book she was holding and almost fainted. Then in a faint and rather strange voice she gasped,

"Bore da, bachgen disgywilydd."

Asya still could not believe it was Peter who stood in front of her.

"Where have you been all this time? I thought you had forgotten me forever," she said, picking up the book she had dropped and handing it to the young student.

Then she turned around completely to face Peter and began to look with horror at his uniform.

"Asya. I am coming to Cambridge next year to study

Russian and…..." he said, but could not finish his sentence.

His words were rushed and he felt embarrassed by Asya's disapproving inspection of his officer's uniform. He tried to finish what he had to say, but Asya met his gaze and gave him one of her stern rebukes, interrupting him.

"Why are you wearing that ridiculous uniform? Have you no shame?"

Peter answered that he hoped to impress the members of the interviewing panel by wearing the uniform of an officer and a gentleman.

"You were never good at being modest," grunted Asya and she continued to stare at him, whether with joy or sadness, he could not tell.

Then he noticed tears in her eyes and for the first time since they met, he felt guilty that he was wearing this 'ridiculous' uniform. He also remembered that, when they were both in Tehran, he promised Asya on occasions that he would abandon a military career and give up spying. Indeed, he did not intend to upset his precious Asya for the whole world.

"Can we talk later?" said Peter, trying to defuse the awkward tension between them. "I have an interview this afternoon, but I am free this evening."

"Alright," replied Asya with some relief and, looking at Peter, she realised that he was upset as well. "Parviz and I can meet you in the foyer of the Gonville Hotel at seven o'clock. My duties here end at six. But please do not wear your uniform because it reminds me of our espionage activities both in Iraq and Iran."

Peter was right. The interview was a mere formality, and he was accepted on the Russian course to start in a year's time

With time to spare Peter walked through the centre of Cambridge, the city of crocuses and daffodils, crisscrossed the river Cam several times and admired the breathtaking view of King's College Chapel and the rich intricacies of other buildings. Cambridge University was founded in the thirteenth century by monks wishing to escape the hurly burly of Oxford. Although the semi-independent colleges were virtually closed after the examinations had finished in June, there were still a few students about, some even in their gowns, walking and cycling and punting on the River Cam.

Peter sat on a bench near the river next to a rather young man, who said that he was a post-graduate student, and watched the intriguing method of punting. He was amazed by the number of boats which passed by and the attractive way in which the men dug their poles into the river bed and how the women seemed to be relaxing at the other end of the boats.

"Why are the men doing all the hard work, whilst the women are just sitting in comfort?" asked Peter. The post-graduate then produced a description of punting in a precise and orderly manner.

"Punting is a stereotype activity at Cambridge. It involves propelling yourself, or better with a girlfriend sitting on a seat, in a long wooden boat and pushing, as you can see, a pole against the shallow bottom of the River Cam. For full effect you need to take strawberries and champagne to eat and drink as you and your girlfriend glide effortlessly downstream."

At this point Peter began to dream of Asya sitting in such a boat, whilst both glided gently downstream. He knew that she would never drink champagne, but perhaps she would eat the strawberries.

On his way to meeting Asya and her brother at the Gonville Hotel, Peter wondered what had happened to the Amampours since he last saw them in the British Embassy. Wearing a smart suit, he entered the hotel at a quarter to seven. Asya and Parviz were already sitting in the lounge with soft drinks in front of them. They greeted him with great enthusiasm.

"Where have you been for the past two and a half years, Peter?" asked Parviz instantly.

Peter explained as best he could that he was now a flying officer in the RAF and that he was stationed in West Berlin.

"How did you and your parents get from Tehran to Britain," enquired Peter.

Parviz looked at him and turned to his sister who, stumbling over her words, gave Peter a short account of the events leading up to their arrival in Britain.

"Under the circumstances it was not an easy task," she said in a mournful voice. "We knew that SAVAK agents were lurking outside the British Embassy. I am sure they intended to kill us all and...."
Parviz helped his sister continue the account.
"There were also Soviet agents and Islamists who were both annoyed that we had given up on our *jihad* to rid Iran of the Shah. We were all extremely frightened. Remember, Peter, that Asya and my father had been kidnapped by members of the SAVAK, only escaping death by a narrow margin and I was tortured by so-called rogue elements which turned out to be a combination of the Shah's secret police and British agents. But everything has turned out well, mainly thanks to you."

Peter was then told that the Amampour family was smuggled out of the British Embassy and taken to the main station in Tehran, Ali and Anastasia separately followed by Parviz and Asya later. There they boarded a train which took them to Ibadan and crossed the Iran/Iraq border to Basra from where they were moved to various locations along the Shatt- al Arab River.
"All I could do at the time," explained Asya, "was to admire the beautiful Arab boats entering and leaving Basra. Do you know, Peter, that the native boats of Basra especially are a wonderful creation?"

Parviz seemed annoyed and agitated at his sister's attempt to romanticise about Arab boats.

"Asya. You are far too romantic at times," he said. "This is a definite lapse in your make-up."

For a moment Asya was taken aback and gave her brother a withering look.

It transpired, however, that the four members of the Amampour family went by rail to Baghdad and then, helped by the British authorities, flew from the capital of Iraq via Rome to Heathrow Airport. "Why are you in Cambridge and what are your parents doing now?" enquired Peter.

"We will tell you sometime later, Peter," answered Parviz. "I can say that we are worried about our father. He keeps apologising to us for being alive and he is still talking about penitence for his sins. He is also receiving notes from somewhere and they are all in Russian. They hint that KPOK has 'tabs' on him and that he will eventually meet an untimely death."

"He keeps talking about returning to the Soviet Union to explain everything and live his final days in Tajikistan," said Asya. Everyday we try and persuade him that his and our future is now in Great Britain. Parviz is studying mathematics at Trinity College, and I take small groups for conversation practice in Russian as well as acting as a librarian."

Peter was pleased that Parviz and Asya had found a niche in Cambridge, but he felt some sympathy for Ali and Anastasia, especially Anastasia, who apparently found it rather difficult learning English and adjusting to the British way of life. Moving so quickly from the Soviet Union to Iran and then to Great Britain was perhaps too much for them both, but at least they were safe.

Later Ali and Anastasia embraced Peter when he, Parviz and Asya arrived at a neat, terraced house in the centre of the city. Ali was keen to tell Peter about the events which unfolded after they had left Iran.

"When we arrived in London," he said, "we were all taken to a building to be interviewed by MI5 and MI6 and a secret organization you belonged to, Peter, called ODAT. Really, I was the target of their investigations because I had been a colonel in charge of a number of spying agencies in the Soviet Union. Indeed, my espionage work stretched as far back as 1918 when I first came to Moscow from Dushanbe and joined the Extraordinary Committee for Combating Counter-Revolution. or CHEKA."

This was true and Ali was able to inform the three British intelligence services about the activities of the State Political Directorate which had been placed under the control of the People's Committee for Internal Affairs or the NKVD, later to become the KGB. Ali continued with his story.

"Of course they wanted to know more details about my spying activities, especially about the success and failure of Operation *Azady* in Iran and why I had decided to defect."

Peter emphasised that he had already informed ODAT of the knowledge he had received from this family about the KGB's PR line which dealt with political, economic and military intelligence from Iran and Iraq, but that was all.

"But the British authorities wanted to know about the other KGB lines which dealt with counter-intelligence as well as operations dealing with illegal support and émigrés living abroad in the Middle East. All I could offer them were rough details about the KGB's X line, that is to say about scientific and technological support, as well as the RP line which involved SIGINT operations."

So, after his discussion with Ali, Peter and the Amampours talked well into late evening, not only about their respective experiences and their attitude to different ideologies, but also about Asya and the growing affection she seemed to be cultivating towards Peter and how much she had missed him since his departure from Tehran.

Peter booked into a small hotel in Cambridge and visited the Amampour family before setting out for the long journey to West Berlin. Prior to his departure Asya approached him and reminded him of his promise that he would give up espionage activities, leave the military and for her sake look carefully at the benefits of becoming a Muslim, if he truly loved her. This was the first time she had used the word love.

"*Ya vas lyublyu tak iskrenno*," whispered Peter in Russian. He could sense the joy in her face when he mentioned that he really loved her, but at the same time he could see the unhappiness in her eyes when he did not reply to her request to him to consider converting to Islam. In fact, his response was then rather non-committal.

"I have to serve one more year in the RAF and then I shall give up espionage work and for your sake think about any submission to Islam."

Asya did not mess around with niceties. In both a concerned and consoling manner, she said directly,

"Listen, Peter. In order to love me you must become a Muslim. I cannot have any true feeling towards you, if you do not embrace Islam and surrender to Allah's will."

"But this is a form of coercion," replied Peter. "You need to love me as I am, whether an atheist, agnostic or a Muslim," but he could see the hurt in her eyes and so he shut his mouth.

She tried to change the subject and asked Peter about his work in West Berlin. In the end, however, she said sadly,

"Peter. Remember, everything is in the hands of Allah. May he keep your path straight and true, wherever you are."

During his long journey to West Berlin, both by road

and rail, Peter thought carefully about possible conversion to Islam. It was obvious to him that Asya loved him, but this love came at a price: it was love her and convert or lose her completely. As he climbed into his car Asya stated that she did not want to pressurise him, but she made it clear what she thought.

"Love between us requires peace and contentment associated with surrender to the will of Allah. You will soon learn, if you convert to Islam, that your submission will far outweigh so-called secular advantages inherent in any creeds or religions."

As the night train from Helmstedt thundered through the rail corridor linking West Germany and West Berlin Peter again began to think about Asya and about truth.

"Is there any absolute or real truth in this complex and uncertain world? I don't believe there is one truth in any one religion. Does truth lie in Islam? There are so many different people and so many different ways you can look at things. Asya says there is only one truth- Islam. Perhaps she is right."

Soon, however, Peter felt tired and tried to sleep in the dark carriage in which he was travelling. He tried to peep under the blind, but could see nothing apart from occasional lights, whether on stations or buildings, he could not tell.

This military train, which ran once a night, was the

only rail connection allowed in this direction by the Soviet authorities, and all blinds had to be drawn to prevent western military personnel from seeing anything in the eastern part of Germany. Peter was unable to sleep and made several attempts to visit the toilet at the end of the corridor in order to splash his face, but the sign on the door always displayed *'besetzt'*. Several times he made the same journey to the same toilet only to be confronted with the message that it was engaged.

"There is an RTDF Op 1A operator with a knowledge of German who is always in that toilet," said a friendly sergeant Peter met in the corridor. "He is trying to pick up Russian and German military traffic as the train travels to West Berlin."

Peter then had to virtually walk the whole length of the train in order to find a toilet that was free. However, he saw the humorous side of the situation and said to himself,

"Even some spying in the Cold War is confined to a toilet in a military train. What a life for the operator." Peter was reminded not to volunteer for such a mission. In any case his talents would be needed elsewhere, and he was looking forward to the next part of secret operations in Berlin. Before he left Cambridge Asya had given him copies of the Qur'an, both in English and Arabic, and made him promise that he would read a section each day, if possible. She also handed over to him a list of rules which Shia Muslims needed to obey in their everyday life.

Peter had no idea that, when he reached West Berlin in the middle of July that he would be back in the United Kingdom by September. The moment he arrived at *Artur-Axmann-Kazerne* his squadron leader, Alex Jones, informed him that a special assignment in East Berlin had been arranged for him and that he was to meet an ODAT commander called Jacobson that very day. Yes, it was the same Samuel Jacobson whom he had met at ODAT headquarters in London in 1956.

"*Schmidtlein,*" said Jacobson when they met. "There is talk that the East Germans are going to fortify the borders between the western and eastern sectors of Berlin and along the East German zone around West Berlin, but we do know when, why and exactly where. Tomorrow, I want you to meet Berndt Vogel, a special double agent, who is working for ODAT and the *Abteilung* in East Berlin. He has a vital rendezvous with the *Stasi* or secret state police in Lichtenberg and then a further meeting somewhere in the district of Marzahn."

After imparting this information to Peter, Jacobson then handed him two sheets of paper which explained the arrangements with Berndt Vogel.

Peter had expected to spend the first two weeks doing SIGINT work at *Artur-Axmann-Kazerne* and devote his spare time exploring the western sectors of Berlin. Up to now his leisure activities had been confined to mainly the British sector which included the districts of Spandau, Charlottenburg, Wilmersdorf and the Tiergarten. He had also managed to visit French military clubs in Reinickendorf and Wedding whenever he wanted to enjoy superb cuisine. On those occasions he tried to remember Asya's warning about drinking alcohol and eating non-*halal* meat. He also tended to avoid the Bratwurst stalls and the Biergarten whenever he could. His knowledge of the American sector was limited, although he had visited Tempelhof Airport and Neuköln where he heard that the Americans had dug a tunnel into East Berlin.

This time on the orders of his ODAT commander he was destined to become involved in his first real secret operation.

"Berndt will take you by car to Marzahn once you have met him near *Stasi* headquarters," said Jacobson. "Take your bogus Polish and East German identifications papers with you. Berndt's second meeting in Marzahn is extremely important because the East German government is going to explain about the fortification of the borders and you need to be there."

Before now Peter's visits to the Soviet sector of Berlin had only been slightly risky and involved mainly incursions from the French sector into the districts of Pankow and Prenzelberg. On one occasion he had slipped from the American sector into Treptov, but to go much further was even for him highly dangerous.

Marzahn, which was the district the Soviets hoped would become a rival to districts in the western sectors, was heavily guarded and difficult for westerners to penetrate. Jacobson realised the mission he had sent Peter on was a difficult one.

"I must admit, Peter, that this is perhaps the most dangerous mission you will ever have to undertake," said Jacobson, puffing with his cigarette into Peter's face. "However, we can trust in you. I was pleased with your espionage techniques in Iraq and Iran and the way in which you persuaded some Soviet agents to defect. Your excellent knowledge of German and Polish has been of great value here in Berlin. Nevertheless, be careful. Only last month three American soldiers somehow managed to stray into the district of Köpenik, got drunk and were arrested. We had difficulty in arranging their release. Stick close to Berndt who will meet you at three o'clock tomorrow. The exact spot is in the instructions I have given you. Good luck!"

At exactly three o'clock the following day Peter stood near the approaches to the headquarters of the *Stasi* and was met by Berndt Vogel in an old pre-war Volkswagen which still had the grill instead of the window in the rear.

"Guten Tag, Schmidtlein. Ich freue mich, Sie *kennen zu lernen"* said the red-faced stocky German who opened the door for him.

Berndt then slipped easily into an informal mode of

speech after Peter had climbed aboard. They drove quite quickly to Marzahn, even though the Volkswagen bounced and bumped along the cobbled roads. They passed the occasional East German car, the Trabant, and Peter gazed in amazement at the areas which had been devastated by allied bombing and the fierce house-to-house fighting when the Soviet troops captured Berlin in 1945.

Marzahn had become the show piece of Soviet reconstruction in East Berlin and contained a number of prefabricated high-rise apartment blocks. In the central area of the district there were shops and playgrounds as well as institutes and schools for the workers and their children.

"The important meeting is being held in the school over there at four o'clock," declared Berndt, pointing to a large building and driving his car through the gates. "Do not say a word. Stay close to me at all times. You are my assistant and secretary, and you need to make notes."

In the car park they were joined by men in grey mackintoshes and trilby hats. Peter noticed East German policemen and Soviet military men in uniform. Over the main façade of the school hung the East German flag under which were the words *'Proletarier aller Länder vereinigt Euch'*.

When everybody was assembled in the school hall an important looking official accompanied by a Soviet officer stepped forward. With some indignation in his voice the former announced why the meeting was taking place.

"The British, Americans and the French are determined to make West Berlin a showcase for the benefit of capitalism and, also, to the detriment of communism. They wish to ensure that West Berlin is equal to any modern city in the western world."

Peter's hands were beginning to shake as he wrote down in a mixture of shorthand and longhand what was being said and then listened intently to what was to come.

"For economic and political reasons, we have decided to build a wall where the borders exist at the moment. Too many scientists and intellectuals educated at our expense are moving from east to west. Also, Berliners are living comfortably here because it is cheaper and working in West Berlin to enrich the economy there."

As the official spoke Peter glanced at a placard strung across the stage on which he read the motto of the German Democratic Republic *'Auferstanden aus Ruinen'*. Meanwhile the speaker continued with his diatribe.

"Furthermore, the western allies are interfering in the districts of East Berlin and sending spies into certain areas. This must stop."

A lump appeared in Peter's throat, and he felt a blush spreading over his face. However, he kept calm and scribbled furiously away.

Then followed a number of statistics from the speaker's mouth.

"Between 1954 and 1960 East Germany has suffered a brain drain. Almost 37,000 citizens with academic and professional qualifications, plus over 12,000 students have moved to the west. As I have said before, they have been educated at our expense. All this has to stop."

In spite of everything Peter could see why the building of a wall was necessary for East Germany.

"We must also put a stop to the activities of the eighty odd spy centres and similar organisations working against East Berlin. A wall will eliminate some of the ninety checkpoints on the borders and stop our citizens leaving. We also need to control the flow of buses and trains travelling from east to west and vice versa."

With his hands shaking somewhat Peter momentarily looked at the ornate ceiling and began to feel embarrassed that he was a British spy, but he could not give any reason why he felt so. When the announcement was made that the wall would be started sometime in August 1961, Peter wrote down this important piece of information in shorthand. Before he could finish, however, several East Berlin policemen burst into the hall and started to shout, *"Herr Vogel. Wo sind Sie?"*

Berndt grabbed Peter by the arm and pushed his car keys into his assistant's pocket and said quietly,

"*Bleib nicht hier, Schmidtlein.* Here are my car keys. Take my Volkswagen and leave it at one of the underground stations. Return swiftly to West Berlin."

With his head in a whirl Peter slipped quickly away, thrusting his notes into his jacket pocket He looked back and saw a group of policemen surrounding Berndt who was led away. Driving the Volkswagen slowly and carefully, Peter went as far as the underground station at Friedrichsfelde where he left the car and then took the tube via Stalinallee and Alex to the border. Only when the train passed Stadtmitte and entered West Berlin did he feel safe. All the time he was in a sweat because he assumed that somebody must have noticed that he was with Berndt and that he would have been reported to the authorities.

Reporting to his wing commander at *Artur-Axmann-Kazerne,* Peter related the chain of events which had taken place and asked to see Jacobson.
"Samuel Jacobson, your ODAT commander, has returned to Britain." said Wing Commander Cox. " You need to pass the information you have to me and I will contact him. Meanwhile, you must keep a low profile. No more incursions into East Berlin or East Germany for your own sake and ours. You may now be a marked man, and we cannot risk losing you."

In a way Peter was pleased with this news. Now at last he had the opportunity to explore West Berlin in more detail and perhaps visit some of the interesting spots along the River Havel. He then asked the wing commander what would happen to Berndt.

"Well, Peter, he will be handed over to the *Stasi*, probably interrogated for crimes against the German Democratic Republic, sentenced to death and then shot."

Peter shuddered at the thought that he could have been arrested with Berndt and suffered the same fate. He was also put out by his superior officer's matter-of-fact explanation of Berndt's fate.

Peter had no alternative but to settle down to routine SIGINT work and in his spare time to explore West Berlin, this oasis in the heart of enemy territory. Until the first week in August Peter enjoyed a rest from secret operations in East Berlin, but then a thought came into his head.

"I have marks, pounds and dollars in my pocket. How can I spend some of this money, especially the marks?"

This was his main worry on a certain hot day, so he decided to cross the border into East Berlin, thus breaking his promise to Wing Commander Cox, but it was a way of getting rid of some of his marks and other currencies. Always looking for risky adventures and against strict orders, he was tempted to wander once again into enemy territory.

Once inside East Berlin he intended to spend most of

the marks on cigarettes for his friends, newspapers and a few postcards. But he already had numerous postcards, so he decided to buy a few souvenirs, which ensured that his marks began to dwindle. Then, he bought a few items of clothing with his dollars and joined the foot traffic back to West Berlin through the Brandenburg Gate. On the spur of the moment, he took a taxi to one of his favourite spots, a sandy beach on one of the bays where stretches of water were separated by metal wire dividing the western sectors from the eastern. Since 1945 West Berliners and the western allies had chosen to take seriously their leisure bathing activities, either along parts of the river Havel or the Wansee. For the West Berliners it was an alternative to the Baltic Coast, which would have been the custom before the outbreak of World War II. In any case the Baltic Coast was now in East Germany.

Peter changed quickly into his new swimming trunks, which he had bought in East Berlin, and placed his pile of clothing and purchases near one of the bathing huts. He was about to run into the water, when he realised that his clothes, identity cards and money would perhaps be stolen. Returning to the beach he met Flying Officer Dean Crouch sunbathing with his wife and two children.

"Hi, Peter!" shouted Dean with a chuckle and a smile on his face. "I would have thought you would be swimming with the nudes at a *Freikörperkultur* beach, a young unmarried man like yourself."

Peter ignored his jibe but asked if he would keep an eye on his possessions.

"Certainly, old chap," was the answer, "but don't swim beyond the cable or thick rope of wire separating east and west."

Peter ignored his friend's advice because he was already in the water swimming towards the cable. He looked back and saw Dean picking up his clothes and other possessions and placing them in a bathing hut. As he swam in the cool water Peter was conscious of the presence of a few swimmers who appeared to be following him and, also, swimming towards the centre of the bay.

"Don't swim beyond the cable." Dean's words echoed in his ears.

"Why not. I have nothing to fear," he said to himself and throwing caution to the wind, began to swim rapidly onwards and forwards. Changing from the crawl to the breast stroke, he decided to take a chance and swim into enemy waters.

Then Peter noticed that one of the swimmers following him, a young man probably in his early twenties, had outpaced the rest and had also ducked under the cable. Suddenly he seemed to jump up and down in the water, waving his hands furiously in Peter's direction.

"Is he trying to tell me not to swim any further?"

thought Peter.

Not so. A sound like pebbles being struck violently on a rock, followed by a whoosh as they entered the water, woke Peter up from his dream-like trance. He then realised the pebbles were in fact machine gun bullets. The lone swimmer seemed to be indicating the exact spot where Peter's head appeared.

"Oh blast! How am I going to get back?" gasped Peter and as he spoke he dived into the clear water and remained there a few seconds before coming up for air.

Unfortunately the machine gunner had spotted him again and released another round of bullets. Peter realised he was moving closer to the opposite shore, so he dived once again into the water, swimming back the way he had come until he felt the wire rope hitting the top of his head. He then resurfaced and without looking back hastened his pace by employing the crawl.

Trembling, ashen-faced and shivering, he reached the friendly beach where by now a crowd had witnessed what had happened.

"I told you not to go beyond the cable," shouted Dean as he helped Peter dry his body and gave him a swig of whiskey from a flask which he had with him.

Peter took a deep breath and drank some of the whiskey, but then he remembered Asya's warning about drinking alcohol or spirits of any kind, so he pushed the flask away.

"The person who was swimming close to you and who also went beyond the cable has gone over to the opposite shore. He must have known who you were and was intent on getting you killed," said Dean, fussing around his friend.

"I don't know, and I don't care," replied Peter visibly shaken by the event and only now realising just how near death he had been.

Nevertheless, he composed himself, thanked Dean for his assistance and for looking after his belongings, got dressed and hurried back to *Artur-Axmann-Kazerne,* determined not to mention the incident to anybody.

That evening there was a knock on the door of the apartment where Peter lived. It was Wing Commander Cox, who was obviously angry, and snapped at him in a venomous manner.

"*Schmidtlein.* I am disappointed in you. I considered you to be one of my best agents with your knowledge of Russian, German and Polish. You were an ideal person for our secret operations here in Berlin. Now you have blown it all after today's debacle. I told you not to enter East Berlin or East Germany. Now I have no option but to order you to return to England Your talents are of no use here now."

Peter's jaw dropped. Who had informed on him? Was it Dean? However, he was unable to change anything, and he had to pack his bags and leave West Berlin.

His only consolation was that now he would be able

to be nearer to Asya and to see her more often. The following morning, he reported to headquarters and was told that he would be posted to GCHQ in Cheltenham. Gathering his few belongings in two kitbags, he said farewell to the SIGINT team in *Artur-Axmann- Kazerne* and caught the night train from West Berlin to Helmstedt and then travelled to Cheltenham by car. Ringing in his ears was the recommendation from Squadron Leader Jones who said,

"We shall all miss you, Peter. Your information about the intention of the East Germans to build a wall was invaluable. Good luck for the future!"

As soon as he reached Cheltenham Peter telephoned Asya and informed her that he was now back in England.

"Have you been true to me?" she asked. "I hope you have not been spying too often or drinking or even doing things which my religion forbids. And have you been thinking about converting to Islam?"

Peter tried to reassure her that he had tried to make a brave attempt to comply with her wishes, but that it was difficult at times. He also reminded her that he had avoided strong drink and that he had read most of the Qur'an. He then explained to her in detail how he had avoided death on two occasions, but he did not mention that he had swallowed some whiskey. That would have been too much for Asya to take in.

Cheltenham GCHQ was established as the post Second World War successor of the government's code and cipher school which had been the central SIGINT organisation since 1919. Peter was destined to work at one of the two GCHQ sites on the outskirts of the town, and he was soon extremely busy, but not too busy to lose contact with Asya completely. He kept declaring his dying love for her and promised that now was perhaps the time to seriously consider conversion to Islam. He mentioned marriage to her, but she said,

"Marriage is out of the question unless you can show me by word and deed that you have converted. We must meet here in Cambridge more often so that we can talk everything over with my parents and brother. In any case you must stop espionage activities."

To stop spying completely was out of the question. At GCHQ Peter was engaged in monitoring and deciphering a variety of communications and other signals coming mainly from the southern republics of the Soviet Union and the Warsaw Pact countries in Eastern Europe. He also had to provide advice and assistance to government departments and the armed forces on the security of communication networks. After a few weeks of this type of work he was called by the head of his department to work on a special assignment which at least was different.

"Peter. We know that you are an expert in decrypting Russian, Polish and German messages. The American

Investigation Authority or CIA has been working on a mass of material obtained from the Berlin 'tap'."

Peter knew about the tunnel when he was stationed in West Berlin and that the Soviet Union had begun to shift from wireless communication to encryptical land lines for military traffic around about 1953. "Yes", continued Peter's head of department. "A mass of data was obtained between 1953 and 1956, in fact 40,000 hours of telephone conversation, mostly in Russian and six million hours of teletype traffic from the one 'tap'. The information dealt with orders for battle readiness and the disposition of forces. The CIA has stated that everything has been analysed, but we now need to decide what is valuable for us. In any case, have the Americans missed anything?"

During this briefing all Peter could think about was how he could disassociate himself from being involved in his work as a spy. He tried to think what Asya would have done under the circumstances. But she was not a member of the British armed forces. What could he do? Shaking his head and putting her out of his mind for a moment, he succumbed to reality and accepted his head of department's request to start analysing the 'tap'. Under him were ten deciphers who would be working steadfastly and continuously on the mass of material. In fact, there were certain areas amongst the telephone and teletype traffic which affected British forces in West Berlin and which had been overlooked by the CIA.

After working at GCHQ for a month Peter went to visit the Amampours in Cambridge. He drove from Cheltenham in a new Mini Cooper and made sure he did not wear his officer's uniform. In any case he did not wish to seek the wrath of Asya again. His visit required the presence of all the members of the family because it concerned Asya and her relationship with him. Falling in love and getting married for Shi'ites from Tajikistan or, for that matter for all Muslims throughout the world, demanded certain modes and customs. Moreover, Peter was still in the eyes of Muslims a *kuffar* or non-believer.

"Have you read the book I gave you entitled 'How to convert to Islam?'" were the first words spoken to him by Asya. Peter's reply was in the affirmative. Indeed, he had made a determined effort to understand what it meant to convert. All he could say was that he was bewildered by the large number of rules.

Peter questioned also the inhumanity of *Sharia* law, which in strict Muslim countries sometimes meant beheading, stoning to death and the amputation of limbs. Even forty lashes by hand, sandals or pieces of cloth appeared to be the punishment for drinking alcohol. The Amampours tried to reassure him that in civilised societies this did not happen. In any case they referred to the USA which they said had barbaric methods of putting people to death. They tried to explain the benefits of *Sharia* law. Ali explained to Peter that under *Sharia* law there was virtually no crime, no homeless people, no rapes and no illegitimate children. Moreover, he claimed that this law had to be confined within the laws of a country and in the case of Great Britain barbaric punishments would be illegal.

Asya looked at Peter and realised that he had made an effort to digest some of the complicated aspects of conversion to Islam. Giving him one of her disarming smiles she said,

"Peter. You know that conversion can be done in private. However, it is better done in the presence of others. All you have to do is to submit to the will of Allah and pronounce the *'Shahàda'* or 'testimony of faith' which is the first and foremost of the Five Pillars of Islam. But it must be done with sincerity and conviction."

Peter's response was immediate. "When I was in Cheltenham, I met an Imam who said that, once I had entered the fold of Islam, all my previous sins would be forgiven. That's a blessing because my life has not been entirely blameless. He said that repentance of the ways and beliefs of my previous life would be granted, in other words 'the slate would be wiped clean.'"

It was Ali who decided to come to the crux of the matter with regards his daughter and Peter.

"Let us get down to serious business, Peter. Asya has told me that you love her and that you wish to marry her, but I am worried. Let me quote from the Qur'an: 'Do not marry your girls to unbelievers unless they become believers' and 'It is better to marry a slave who believes than to marry an unbeliever.' So, Peter, you can see my problem, can't you?"

Peter could understand Ali and the rest of the family's predicament. What should he do? For perhaps the first time in his life he acted decisively and decided to accept the Muslim faith as the only one for him.

Then with the help of the Amampours he pronounced the *Shahàda* and said in Arabic and English,

"*La ilàh illa Allàh wa Muhammad rasùlu Allàh-* There is no god but Allah, and Muhammad is the messenger or prophet of God."

The whole family was excited, and Peter was embraced by all of them, including Asya.

"Now, there is only one worry that I have," stated Ali after the celebrations had ended. "Have you, Peter, accepted Islam only because you wish to marry Asya? That is not the best reason for changing to our faith."

Peter told him honestly that it was only one reason, but he was now convinced that Islam was the true faith for him.

"Asya has been the main reason why I became interested in the Muslim religion in the first place and she has shown me that my happiness with her is submission to the will of Allah."

Peter told the Amampours that his service with the RAF would finish within less than a year and that would mean an end to all forms of espionage. Ali and Anastasia were happy both for their daughter and Peter and gave their blessing to a marriage which could possibly take place within a year once Peter had shown by word and deed that he had become a devout Muslim and a suitable husband to be. Although Anastasia had been quite reserved whilst events were taking place, she was the one in the household who had experienced conversion to Islam. She took Peter to one side and said,

"Let me tell you what the Qur'an says, Peter, namely that 'believing men and women are associated and helpers of each other'. This helped me when I converted and married Ali, for I knew that we would make decisions together."

Anastasia then announced that she was really concerned about her daughter and needed to confide in Peter. "I have noticed that here in Cambridge morals are occasionally lax. Some female students sleep with their boyfriends before marriage and this worries me. We know that you are an upright man, but we cannot leave you alone with Asya. You understand that, don't you? She will remain with us until you are married. You can continue to see her of course. Islam accepts that the proper mixing of the sexes is appropriate, if one maintains Islamic behaviour. Men and women of our faith, your faith now as well, should talk together in a decent and chaste language and with good intent. What I am trying to say is that, when you and Asya are alone together, temptation can emerge. Do you understand what I am trying to tell you?"

Peter assured Anastasia that his intentions towards her daughter were honourable and that he understood her concerns.

Peter was surprised that Anastasia could tell him about her fears in broken English and he wondered how she and Ali, who knew no English at all in Tehran, were now able to converse reasonably logically in a new language in such a short space of time. As they were speaking, they were joined by the whole family and Peter decided to change the subject from himself and Asya to asking how the Amampours generally were coping with living in England. Had they made the right decision to leave Iran or not? As usual Ali spoke for all of them.

"There are advantages and disadvantages in living here. We appreciate the apparent freedom and so far, apart from occasional distant menaces from Soviet agents, we do not feel threatened. However, we are conscious that real truth and justice do not exist here in their true form. Capitalism seems to emphasise ownership, profit and gain. As Muslims we believe that all this is against morality and contrary to the interests of the majority."

At first Peter thought that Ali was being rather ungrateful for all the efforts he had made to bring his family to Britain, but then he realised that as a new convert to Islam he needed to explore the raison d'être of a pure Muslim society. In fact, Ali tried to explain. "We believe as Muslims that all people are created equal by Allah and this provides a proper base in which equality and justice can be enforced. The communists are right to enforce equality, but it becomes a baseless ideal, because for them there is no God and the survival of the fittest and the strongest is for them the reality of life. This is sometimes the case in capitalist Britain where money and status in society replace equality."

Peter interjected.

"Are you saying that Allah believes in equality and that he grants equality of worth to all humans regardless of race, sex and age and this works outwardly to equality of opportunity for all?"

"Just so," said Ali with delight. "You are learning fast," but he could see that Peter was shaking his head, obviously perplexed and subject to mixed emotions.

Over the next few months Peter was torn between his desire to become a good Muslim and to continue with his work involving secret operations in Cheltenham. Apart from declaring his conversion at a mosque in London he found that it was only the Amampour family who gave him any support. Although satisfied with Islam on an intellectual and theological level, he found the practical aspect of being a Muslim rather difficult. Only one Imam came to visit him in Cheltenham, and he only took him once again to London to reaffirm his faith and to try and help him resolve his problems. The advice he received was that it was his duty to search for knowledge in the Qur'an and the *Hadith*.

"But where is the real support?" he asked on one of his regular visits to Cambridge. "I have been to a Shi'ite mosque on two occasions and there seems to be no systematic induction there for converts to Islam. I know that both the Anglican and Roman Catholic churches have excellent programmes for converts to Christianity and courses which teach them about the Christian faith."

"Peter," said Ali on one occasion "You are lucky because you have us to help you and you will not be left in isolation. I will come with you to the Shi'ite mosque in London and transmit your worries to the Imam there."

Peter told Asya that he felt that some Muslims resented converts to Islam. She tried her best to reassure him to always submit to the will of Allah and all would turn out well in the end.

"Do not be despondent and do not be harsh on those who do not help you. Allah is mild and fond of mildness and he gives to the mild what he does not give to the harsh."

Peter tried to work out what Asya was getting at. Did she mean that there were Muslims who resented new members of the Muslim faith?

Parviz confirmed his worst fears.

"Yes. I have read in the papers that there are a few British converts to Islam who are sometimes picked upon by Muslims who are hardliners-absolutists. After Friday prayers some of them act as though they are Imams and they push a radical agenda."

Peter had also heard that there were radical Muslims who considered it was their duty to harass and even kill unbelievers and he conveyed this information to the Amampours. Ali had to admit that there were some Muslims, both Sunnis and Shi'ites, who had been known to distribute the so-called keys to the gates of heaven to those who wished to kill non-believers and become martyrs for Allah's cause, but he told Peter that they were few and far between.

"It is a sin to neglect the peaceful spiritual core of Islam," said Ali, aware that he had to give this new convert hope. "Peace and good relations between peoples of all races and creeds are often as important as giving to charity or fasting, or prayer. Peter. Do not be diverted from the path of Islam by radical Muslims and stick to the practices of Shia."

As he travelled back to Cheltenham Peter knew that he had to try and adhere to these practices which consisted of prayer, fasting, charity, love of the family of Mohammed, avoidance of evil and submission to Allah. His commitment to a *jihad* and a pilgrimage had to be postponed until verification had been established. How could he do all that when he had to concentrate on his work at GCHQ? In fact, his work at this establishment began to alter from a concentration on the Berlin tunnel 'tap' to analysing data obtained when the Cold War entered a new phase. Feedback from the trial and imprisonment of Francis Powers, the pilot of an American U2 spy plane, had to be analysed, even though he had been shot down over the Soviet Union as far back in May 1960. Furthermore, the USSR and Communist China had broken off relations as a result of Khrushchev's revisionism. This resulted in Albania and Cambodia allying with China. The backlash of this split in the communist world occupied analysts, including Peter, in even more work as a result of vital material emanating from SIGINT operations, mainly in Hong Kong.

Then on April 12th 1961, Moscow announced putting the first man, Major Yuri Gagarin, into orbit around the earth. This meant that even more data had to poured over and of course analysed. Peter's promises to Asya were beginning to fade as more and more work occupied his time. He was often unable to visit Cambridge, and she continually reminded him by telephone of his commitment to her that he would give up his career in the RAF and devote his life to her and Allah. So, it was a relief for both of them when he was finally demobbed in August 1961. This meant that, not only was he able to avoid the fall-out of information when the East Germans began to build the Berlin Wall, but he was now in a position to devote his time to the forthcoming wedding.

Between August and October, when he was due to become an undergraduate at the University of Cambridge, Peter tried with the help of the Amampours to live the pure life of a Shia Muslim. At the same time, it was his aim to obtain after three years a good Honours degree in Russian within the Slavonic Studies part of the modern and medieval Tripos. In spite of many temptations and with the help of his future wife he was more able to relate to the practices of his new faith. Asya often reminded him of the problems she had to face when she lived in Moscow.

"I had to become virtually a vegetarian because we did not have access to *halal* meat there. Moreover, the clash of ideologies between communism and Islam almost tore our family apart. Temptations and tensions existed for us, both within and without our household. I was often to blame for insisting that I should become a successful ballerina. I know now that such a career was unsuitable for a Muslim female, but then I was young and stubborn."

To compensate Peter for not going to London

University at the end of the Russian course at Blue Mountain, even though he had obtained the requisite marks, the RAF agreed to pay for his tuition and subsistence at Cambridge whilst he was on the reserve. When he started in October he found the cultural ethos of the course was geared towards the spirit of Russia, that is to say towards its classics and literature. Although he had to adhere to the structure and content of the agreed syllabus, there was room for elements of the old service school course which had been wound up in 1959. In this respect he was gratified that some of the lessons were taught mainly in Russian and that there was a mixture of old and young tutors consisting of Russian émigrés as well as a sprinkling of English lecturers.

How he enjoyed conversation classes, especially when the students were introduced to a popular teacher, namely Asya. A good answer from a student in her group would receive the cry of '*molodyets*' or 'excellent'. Yet, she would chastise, but at the same time joyfully help, any student who could not find the correct word or expression in Russian. But there was always a twinkle in her eyes. During the earlier part of the course, she helped Peter by handing him a *voprosnik* or questionnaire on some of the books he had to read. This became a valuable building block in his study of Russian literature especially.

In spite of his advantage over many of the other

students on the course Peter had to work hard at his studies in Cambridge. He especially appreciated the work of the English teachers who filled in many of the gaps in Russian grammar and thus provided him with a basis for both oral work and the study of literature. As a result, he was making progress towards Part 1 of the Cambridge University Tripos. It was the stress on certain words which caused him problems, and he was extremely grateful to a former female Russian lecturer who had cause to print copies of 'Crime and Punishment' by Dostoyevsky with the stress over every single word.

By December 1961 Asya decided to leave her post at the university so that she could concentrate on her marriage to Peter and to avoid a conflict of interest with him being her favourite student. Meanwhile Peter was making great strides and his knowledge of the Suez crisis and ethnic problems in the Soviet Union, so often talked about in Baghdad, helped him considerably. To his obvious relief Peter's name never appeared on the noticeboard below any fail line. On occasions he wanted to question the views of the lecturers, but he soon realised it was tantamount to disaster to do so in an aggressive form.

As 1961 drew to a close, Peter was conscious of the fact that he had only visited his mother on two occasions since returning from the Middle East and had definitely not told her about his conversion to

Islam. Anastasia's recollection of the time she had to tell her parents about her conversion, and their negative reaction helped him eventually to face up to the fact that he needed to inform his mother as soon as possible. But he kept putting off the dreaded day. Should he phone or perhaps write a letter? He knew that the perception of most westerners was that Islam was for strange, backward and frightening foreigners. It was alright for Arabs and Asians, but not for the British.

So, one day in December Peter plucked up courage and drove to Rhyl, determined to confront his mother with the good news, or perhaps for her, the bad news, about his conversion. Asya gave him a few words of advice.

"The Qur'an says 'Be kind to parents. Do not say a word of contempt or repel them but address them in terms of honour and kindness."

Parviz supported his sister in this respect.

"Our prophet, Mohammed, well your prophet now, Peter, commanded that a believer should care for his non-Muslim parents instead of taking part in a Holy War."

Peter's reaction was that it was alright for them to quote the Qur'an, but he had to 'grasp the nettle'.

Entering his mother's bungalow Peter embraced her and kissed her with affection. After a short conversation he noticed that she was about to prepare the evening meal- a roast pork joint. He felt this was the best time to break the news about his conversion to Islam. He did not insult her by telling her that pigs to Muslims were filthy animals and that they had more fat on them than muscle. Nor did he mention that their meat was more liable to transmit diseases such as trichinosis. Instead, he said,

"Mother. Please do not be angry. I cannot eat the meat you have prepared because I must confess that I have changed my faith. Well, I am no longer an atheist. You know that when I was young, I was a practising Catholic. Then I became an agnostic and finally an atheist. Now I have converted to Islam and believe in the oneness of Allah, and I accept Mohammed as the main prophet of God. My new religion does not allow me to eat pork or any non-*halal* meat. However, in my new religion I have found an intellectual satisfaction that I have never known before."

At first Peter's mother began to weep, but, later drying her tears, she started to ask questions. "Islam is a violent religion, isn't it? What about its treatment of women? What will the neighbours think when they see you in Muslim dress? Doesn't Islam teach retribution, whereas Christianity teaches forgiveness?"

Peter tried to answer his mother's questions with patience and understanding, showing her at the same time both love and kindness.

"Mother. Islam is a peaceful religion. Do you know I am now leading a moral life? There is also discipline and stability for me in my new faith."

He then tried to explain that women were treated with respect and the stories she had heard about a Muslim having four wives was symptomatic of orthodox, rural and traditional Muslim countries and in any case, this was not going to happen in Britain. He then went on to say that the neighbours could think what they like about his conversion, but he was not going to change his mind.

"I shall keep the same name, wear the same western clothes and eat normal food, apart from the fact that the meat must not be *haram* or harmful. Nor will I drink alcohol."

This seemed to placate his mother to a certain extent. "I know, Peter," she said, sighing deeply and suggesting why her son had converted. "It's that girl you are hoping to marry, isn't it? She has bewitched you."

At that point Peter produced a photograph of Asya and showed it to his mother so that she could see what a beautiful daughter-in-law she was going to have.

"Yes, mother. It is true that I love Asya and she loves me, but it is only one reason why I have converted. The difference between Islam and Christianity is not great. Jesus is considered by Muslims to be an important prophet, but they do not believe that he is the son of God or that the Virgin birth took place."

Although visibly shaken by the news brought by her

son, Agata seemed to calm down and said in a broken voice,

"Well. I am pleased that you are no longer an atheist and that you have turned to God for salvation, even though to me he is an alien God. Do you think that you will ever wear Muslim dress or have a Muslim name?"

"No, mother," declared Peter. "Although I respect the simple modest dress code of Islam, I shall continue to wear western clothes. Some pressure was brought to bear on me to change my name to Ashraf Mohammed Haddad, *haddàd* meaning smith or blacksmith in Arabic, but I chose to keep my own name- Peter Smith."

In the end Peter's mother was understanding over his apparent redemption.

"Well, Peter," she said, "At least you can eat the vegetables I have prepared and the pudding. Please do not persuade me to give up the pleasure of enjoying this Sunday joint."

Peter had no intention of persuading her to do anything she did not wish to do. He embraced her again and told her that he was grateful that she finally understood what he had done.

Although he lodged in a hall of residence at the university, Peter saw the Amampours every weekend and lively discussions would follow over his observance of Muslim rules and customs. His main worry amongst others was confined initially to the duty of fasting. He was aware that in Iraq and Iran visits to restaurants were mainly confined to the hours after sunset, particularly during the first month of the Muslim calendar- *Muharram,* the seventh month-*Rajab,* the eighth month- *Sha'aba* and the ninth month-*Ramadan.* It was apparent that Peter found difficulty in equating the Islamic months to the western calendar. Ali explained that really it was the ninth month- *Ramadan* which was crucial for Muslims to fast. The other members of the family also stated that, when they were in Moscow, it was difficult to follow the rules of fasting.

"Nevertheless, we all made a determined effort to fast during the month of *Ramadan"* said Ali "because during this month the gates of heaven are opened and the gates of hell closed. So, with the devil chained up, we are not tempted to eat or drink between sunrise and sunset on those days."

Peter thought that was a fantastic way of teaching somebody to fast and he apologised for his laxity in the past for not observing the rules of *Ramadan,* but assured them that with their help he would be able to abide by the rules in the future.

"In any case I need to lose weight," he said jokingly. Indeed, he was not leading a healthy lifestyle and the pounds were mounting up. Fasting and exercise would be beneficial and would please Asya.

"Do not fast for my sake," said Asya rather annoyed.

"but for the sake of Allah. You can eat after sunset during *Ramadan* and eat normally during the three days which follow. Then we can visit friends and give to charity. The Arabs call this period of time *'Id al fitr'*."

In January 1962, a month and a half before Peter and Asya were due to be married in a Shia Muslim ceremony, tragedy struck the Amampour household. Ali's body was found one morning lying on one of the 'backs', that is to say the gardens behind the colleges, leading down to the river and not far from the Bridge of Sighs. He had been shot in the head and pinned to his jacket was the word for traitor in Russian- *predatel'*. He had become just one more victim of the Cold War. In his trouser pocket was a note also written in Russian which stated that he had been executed by members of the KPOK section of the KGB and the East German *Abteilung*. The note read as follows:

"You are a traitor, Ali Amampourov, because you failed in your Iranian venture called Operation *Azady*. Moreover, your connection with the British spy called *Abyadh*, and later *Schmidtlein*, was a threat to the security of the Soviet Union and East Germany. Worst of all the information you have given to the British secret services is inexcusable. Death to all spies."

Anastasia, Parviz and Asya were inconsolable in grief.

"Gunned down in England of all places and it is my fault," sobbed Peter. "How can you forgive me?".

Asya, supported by her mother and brother, and with tears rolling down her cheeks, answered Peter,

"It is not your fault, Peter. My father anticipated an untimely death because he could not justify sufficiently his behaviour during espionage activities. He also had a twinge of conscience when he came to Britain and gave information to MI5, MI6 and ODAT."

Parviz tried to cheer everybody up by announcing that at least his father was in heaven and that on the final day of judgement he would sit on the right hand of Allah.

Arrangements were made for Ali's funeral, not at a mosque, but in the family's house. No announcement was made in any newspaper. Instead, information about the funeral was scrawled in white and yellow paint on black banners, partly in Arabic and partly in Farsi, and hung outside the house and on a tree near where Ali was assassinated. Since there were no relatives, apart from the immediate family to help with the funeral arrangements, everything was left to Parviz and Peter. Anastasia and Asya spent hours painting in white letters on a banner the names of Ali's relatives in Tajikistan and Iran as well as the date and place where the funeral was going to take place. This was then placed outside the Amampour's house.

Ali's body was taken to Bagh-e Zahr cemetery to a Shia Muslim section of Brookwood Cemetery in Woking outside London where he was laid to rest.

Ali's wish to be buried in Tajikistan, or even in Gorno-Badakhstan, was not carried out for obvious reasons. Peter and Asya agreed to postpone their wedding, but Anastasia, embracing them both at this sad time and with tears in her eyes, said to Peter,

"My husband's wish would have been to see you and Asya become husband and wife on the day set, once Shia rules for mourning have ended."

The traditional cycle of mourning for Ali took place on the third, seventh and fortieth day after his death. This allowed the members of the family to keep Ali central stage in their thoughts.

Two days before their marriage in late February Peter and Asya accompanied by Parviz strolled down to the Bridge of Sighs, passing the spot where Ali was killed. Pausing in the middle of the bridge, Peter and Asya suddenly on the spur of the moment decided to ceremoniously give up once and for all times the only symbols they had which still reminded them of their lives based on spying and all the intrigues and deceptions associated with it. Peter led the way. He took his ODAT badge out of his briefcase and with a definite shout of relief, threw it into the waters of the River Cam. Made of hard metal it sank straight away to the bottom of the river. With a burst of unconstrained laughter and in a rather mocking voice he said,

"There goes this symbol of ODAT's so-called truth and justice which was always associated with spying."

Reaching into her handbag Asya produced her KPOK *znachok* and likewise threw it as hard as she could into the river. Made of inferior plastic it bobbed up and down on the surface until it slowly floated downstream and out of view.

"Chort voz'mi," she said in Russian and then in English, "May the devil take it. This is the end of the deceit inherent in communism."

Parviz held his sister's hand and shouted, "An end to all spying and death to all agents of tyranny."

He then plunged into a story about how he had destroyed his KPOK badge a long time ago in Iran. As they left the bridge Asya linked arms with Peter and her brother and said,

"For me and I hope for you there is only one symbol of truth- Islam's Sword of Truth which can now replace what we have thrown away. Praise be to Allah!"

Two days later Peter and Asya were married in a Shia Muslim ceremony in Cambridge at the house owned by the Amampours. To a certain extent an air of sadness prevailed because Ali was not present in person and was sorely missed by the small number of guests which included Peter's mother.

"My husband would have been proud of his daughter this day marrying a convert to Islam," remarked Anastasia, kissing both her daughter and Peter on their cheeks before they were separated and went to different rooms. Asya wore a white robe and had placed cardamoms amongst her toes and fingers. She had also purified her feet with a pot of water which had been scented with sweet smelling leaves. One tray filled with sugar and another with saffron and cinnamon were brought into the wedding room where they were displayed in the hope that the married couple would enjoy a happy and full life.

The religious Shi'ite elder, sitting with Peter on one side of the partition separating them from Asya just before the ceremony, explained,
"This Shia Muslim ceremony is both a cultural and religious event. What is important, however, is that you and Asya devote yourselves to Allah."
Twelve times the couple had to repeat prayers in Arabic to Allah. Both had been practising them for weeks on end. Two of Asya's women friends, both Shi'ites, had been chosen to partake in the ceremony because they had found happiness in their marriages. The first sprinkled sugar on the bride's head, whilst the second lit a candle and stood with her so that her life would be full of brightness. Finally, the bride and groom went to an adjoining room to meet the registrar to receive civil recognition of the marriage.

Now Peter and Asya could say that they no longer found glory and glamour in the world of spying. That was all in the past. For them it had only led to denial, deceit and death. The only good thing that came out of espionage was that they were lucky to meet each other. By the time they were married, Great Britain and the USA were beginning to witness the results of a slight change in Soviet policies, often known as 'Khrushchev's thaw' or 'communism with a human face'. The Soviet Union's grip on socialist realism was loosened and underground literature emerged called *Samizdat*. Moreover, occasional student groups from the west were allowed to visit the country for cultural reasons. However, a tight grip was kept on 'illegal' activities under the chairman of the KGB, Alexander Shelepin.

Spies or mercenary agents were recruited for money and not ideological reasons, and they could be found in Britain in hotels with rolled-up copies of the Observer or Times. British and American agents employed similar activities in the Soviet Union. Stories were told via the press and radio in Britain about Marxist drunkenness and corruption. MI5 and MI6 peddled disinformation and employed numerous rent-a-gobs who tried to embarrass the Soviet Union. Soviet and British businessmen continued to be seduced by champagne dinners, chocolate éclairs and pretty women to reveal state secrets. Spin and propaganda had replaced deadly operations. Peter and Asya heard all about this and, as though reading each other's thoughts, said, "*Do svidanya* or goodbye to all of that espionage and deceit."

How had the Cold War affected the lives of the newly married couple and what had they achieved during the period of their spying activities? Well, in both cases, precious little. The various operations such as *Desert Sand, Babylon, Svoboda* and *Azady* were confined to the dustbin of history. *Abyadh, Schmidtlein, Akhdhar, Aswad, Azraq, Ferdowsi, Rudaki,* and *Rumi* as well as other code names in Iraq, Iran and Germany never made the headlines and were in some cases aborted or changed. ODAT and KPOK, the British and Soviet organisations to which Peter and Asya belonged, continued to exist in some form or another, but their agents had to regroup and react to the slight thaw in the Cold War. The only benefit which came out of it all was the unusual meeting of Peter, a British spy, and Asya, a Soviet agent, in Baghdad as well as his conversion to Islam and her complete submission to the same faith, not forgetting of course their subsequent marriage.

For Peter and Asya the symbol of truth, the sword of truth, was important to them as Muslims. What was this truth? Was it a terrible weapon of aggression? They knew that, as British and Soviet agents, it had been possible to lie, deceive and even commit murder for so-called truth. Not for them anymore. The Islamic Sword of Truth was what made people free. It was above all things great and mighty. They realised that Islam was spreading throughout the world through its Sword of Truth and through intellectual argument. This was the sword which conquered the hearts and minds of people. There was no sword of compulsion for Peter to convert. He chose Islam because he found peace and contentment in his new faith.

Truth was bound up with justice which meant giving people their proper dues. This was not a simple statement. All are faced with the complexities of life-temptations, conflicts and dilemmas. To guide them Allah had sent down the prophets with signs contained in the Book and the Balance. The Book, the Qur'an, contained the revelation, that is to say what is true and what is not. The Balance referred to people's ability to measure and calculate so that they might follow the path of the Book. Asya once pointed out to Peter a reference in the Qur'an which said, 'We sent aforetime our messengers to follow the path of the Book with clear signs. Both the Book and the Balance were sent down so that they may stand forth in justice'.

Before going on a journey many Arabs quote the first words from the Qur'an *'Bismillah ar rahmen ar rahîm'* which translated means 'In the name of Allah, the most Gracious, the most Merciful'. In February 1962, Peter and Asya, former spies of the Cold War, were together setting off on a journey into the future, Peter as a Muslim convert and Asya, his wife as a reformed Shi'ite. As Peter put it,

"For me the Sword of Islam is the sword of truth. So

penetrating is this sword, that it has pierced my heart. So sharp is its edge that it has caused both my soul and my body to yield automatically to Allah."

Both husband and wife felt safe and were sure that the Islamic Sword of Truth would never become blunt in spite of the efforts of persons with vested interests who wanted darkness to prevail over light. They stepped into the future with the same thoughts.

"The Sword of Islam has now struck even deeper into our hearts. It has not brought death, but a new life. It has delivered awareness as to who we are, what we are doing and why we are here."

However, they knew that as individuals they were responsible for their own actions, but they were firm in the belief that Allah's subsequent judgement of these actions would be in accordance with his truth and justice.

They had both lived for the most part in non-Muslim countries, Peter in a so-called Christian yet secular state, and Asya in an atheist one. They would often talk about the benefits of living in these countries, for example the freedom of expression and democracy in Britain and the stress on education and equal rights, especially for women, in the Soviet Union. Now the couple were likely to live in Britain for the remainder of the 1960s and beyond. How would they cope as Muslims in a country which, although accepting other religious groups, welcomed atheists as well? What about living in a country where community life was often centred around a public house which sold alcohol?

There were a number of questions which they felt they could only answer with the help of Allah and by referring to the Qur'an. How could they equate allegiance to Allah as well as allegiance to Britain? What if the laws of the land were directly opposed to the divine laws of Islam? Would the influence of westernisation result in the reformation or demise of Islam? Both Peter and Asya were grateful of the fact that they could live in a country which had greatness and potential, and on the face of it was tolerant to their faith. They were also grateful that they could continue to learn more about Islam without the introduction of certain norms which existed in Muslim countries.

Peter summed up the philosophy of both himself and his wife in their attempt to live in the country of their choice.

"As Muslims and British citizens, we will follow the laws of this country as best we can, pay our taxes and give to charity, not just to Muslims, but to all in need."

Asya, who wanted to train as a nurse, felt that she could care for the people of all faiths, whether they were Christians, Jews or Muslims and, as if appealing to the British public at large, said,

"If we have children, remember they may be your teachers, lawyers, doctors and even politicians. They will also be Muslims and as Muslims they will hopefully be tolerant towards you as you should be tolerant towards them."

Through the remainder of their life both Peter and Asya were sure of one thing, namely that the symbol of truth for them was the Sword of Islam. They were convinced that Allah would continue to sharpen it, if ever it became blunt, and that they would continue to live in the peace and simplicity of their faith.

Printed in Dunstable, United Kingdom